CW01214116

THE WYVERN

&

THE WITCHFINDER

By

Peter Turner

The Wyvern & The Witchfinder by Peter Turner

Copyright © 2022 Peter Turner

All rights reserved.

No part of this book may be reproduced, or transmitted in any form or by any means, mechanical, photocopying, recording, or otherwise, without express written permission of the author.

The locations used in this story are real, but the characters and situations are unreal, and any resemblance to persons living, dead, or not quite dead, is purely coincidental.

The author wishes to express his thanks and gratitude to Michael Murray and Tony Locke for their invaluable help.

Contents

1) THE WARNING	1
2) THE PILGRIMAGE	6
3) THE TIN CHURCH	12
4) SHOWDOWN ON SOLSBURY HILL	19
5) THE LURE OF TADWICK	27
6) UNEXPECTED REUNION	32
7) ABORTED MISSION	38
8) GREETINGS FROM TENNESSEE	42
9) THE GUEST HOUSE SIGHTING	47
10) THE TWO BLADUDS	53
11) THE AUGMENTED-FOURTHS	59
12) THE FEATHER-RUFFLING CLERGYMAN	64
13) MISHAP IN SYDNEY GARDENS	68
14) PHEROMONE-FUELLED ELEVENSES	77

15) PHEROMONE-FUELLED JOURNEY	83
16) SIX GOOD TURNS	89
17) STORE-ROOM SATANISTS	99
18) TEMPTATION OF THE TIN CHURCH	107
19) UNORTHODOX SERMON	116
20) BACKFIRING BLACKMAIL	122
21) TROUBLE DOWNSTAIRS	131
22) AN ALCOHOLIC'S ANGST	141
23) DOUBTFUL FOLLOWERS	147
24) DEMISE OF THE DISCIPLES	161
25) THE SHOOTING STICK	168
26) THE ANIMAL-LOATHING VET	174
27) GOING UNDERGROUND	182
28) ANYONE FOR TENNIS?	189
29) TEARS OF THE CLOWNS	199
30) THE NIGHT BEFORE THE STORM	205
31) NASTY CORRESPONDENCE	209
32) SAVE OUR SOULS	218

The Wyvern & The Witchfinder

1

THE WARNING

Barry Loadall sat back in his pattern faded armchair and took a deep inhalation from his intricately crafted bong. After a ten second coughing fit that threatened to relocate his internal organs, he returned the ornate apparatus to the coffee table and again submerged into the chair. The seat of the armchair sank deeper with the passing years, and now when sat, the wiry soft drug dealer's kneecaps were above his eyeline.

Loadall's fuzzy headed thoughts were interrupted by his front doorbell chiming the vibraphone melody of the Westminster Quarters. He wearily affixed his size six Zorro slippers and plodded toward the door. Loadall's feet were unusually small for such a tall man, and he seemed to defy the laws of physics by not toppling over when stood. His other notable physical characteristic was an unusually large and protruding chin.

Apprentice plumber Ally Lee, and trainee electrician Ronan Rhodes were stood on the doorstep.

"Come on in, young men. Tis a filthy night, and not at all one to be wandering about under the eye of the Devil."

The Wyvern & The Witchfinder

Barry Loadall spoke with a strong upper-class accent, the sole remaining clue to his aristocratic heritage.

Lee and Rhodes glanced at each other and exchanged nervous grins before stepping inside to escape the foul weather. Loadall ushered the teenagers toward the withered sofa that sagged in the middle.

"Make sure you sit either end, otherwise you'll end-up on your knees paying homage to the carpet."

The only light in Loadall's living room was provided by a large candle in each corner. He traipsed over to plug in the lava lamp to commence its evening vigil.

"Apologies for the subdued lighting, but one never knows who might be watching."

Loadall stared warily through the window before returning his gaze to the sofa.

"May I enquire if both of you live locally?"

"Yeah..." Ally Lee replied. "we're from Snow Hill."

"And is Snow Hill within the boundaries of Larkhall village?" asked Loadall as he retook the armchair and eyed his new clients suspiciously.

"Well, no..." Lee continued, "but it's less than a mile away."

"In that case you don't live locally, do you?"

Loadall glared at the boys as he fumbled for the battered biscuit tin beside his chair.

"...How did you come to hear about me?"

"We saw your ad in the newsagents." answered Rhodes.

"...The bloke we used to go to suddenly went all religious and chucked his gear in the river."

"I see. Well, I hope he finds peace and fulfilment in this new phase of his life."

A blinding flash of lightning, followed swiftly by a crash of thunder, illuminated the house and rocked its foundations.

Loadall turned his face upward and broke into a knowing half-smile.

"...The storm must be very close-by. I'd calculate that its epicentre is at present hovering over Solsbury Hill."

The host's half-smile morphed into a frown as he returned his attention to the youngsters.

> "From Larkhall to Tadwick He'll ride
> The souls of the locals at His side
> But one day He will
> Gallop o'er yon hill
> From Tadwick to Larkhall He'll ride"

The Warning

A minor aftershock of thunder endorsed Loadall's limerick before he again succumbed to a fit of coughing.

"Of course, it's all complete nonsense." added the bespectacled drug dealer when his lungs eventually granted permission.

"Watcher goin' on about, Baz?" asked a curious Ally Lee.

"Local superstition and legend. For several generations within Larkhall village, that limerick has been passed down from father to offspring."

Barry Loadall had a dour and serious demeanour, and he gave down to earth reasoning as to why the legend was flawed.

"According to the story, Solsbury Hill was the Devil's hideout, and there's no doubt that this is the hill referred to in the limerick. Now, if He were to gallop over the hill from the direction of Tadwick, He'd end up in Batheaston, which is about thirty degrees in a more easterly direction; and Batheaston is devoid of any mention within the legend."

Loadall paused to relight the bong, and after his latest round of coughing ceased, again continued.

"Having said that, you know that Graham Curnow fellow who lives beside Lam Brook?"

Lee and Rhodes shook their heads as Loadall passed the bong.

"Well..." continued Loadall regardless, "he says he encountered the ghost of the Larkhall Simpleton in a field at Tadwick."

The boys remained silent, and Loadall waited until both had helped themselves to his mind-altering offering.

"...And the ghost of the simpleton chased after him by performing a chain of cartwheels."

Lee and Rhodes collapsed into bong induced hysterics before a savage crack of thunder spooked them into returning straight faced.

"Mind you..." Loadall added, "Curnow was in a perpetual state of intoxication for the best part of a decade when he saw what he said he saw. That incident occurred thirteen months ago, and he hasn't touched a drop of alcohol since. Good thing too, because if Curnow walks through the doors of The Wyvern ever again, that'll be the end of him."

Another doorbell chime interrupted Loadall. He struggled to wriggle free of the armchair, stood-up to tower lankily over his new customers, and left them with another limerick concerning the Devil's alleged possession of Larkhall and the surrounding area,

> "The Witchfinder rode into town
> To plunder The Devil's crown
> The Devil said, 'It's my turn!'
> 'Summon-up me The Wyvern!'
> 'And foul it upon the damned crowd!'"

The boys again sniggered, and Loadall gave them another glare as he began his journey to the front door. He returned a moment later accompanied by the village florist, Lenny Yeo.

"Can't stop long Baz, I'm on me way to pick-up a Chinese and get back for the missus. Do us an 'Enry, will ya?"

As Loadall prepared the shadier half of Yeo's takeaways, Ally Lee asked the new arrival what he knew about the Larkhall legend.

"Utter bollocks, the lot of it..." retorted Yeo. "This isn't the middle-bloody-ages you know. Never heard such codswallop in me entire bleedin' life."

Yeo's dismissiveness turned to foreboding as he stared at the boys on the sofa.

"...Or at least that's what I reckoned 'til I heard about what happened near 'ere a few decades back."

Another peel of thunder shook the house as Loadall handed Yeo his order, while Lee and Rhodes stared up at Yeo with expressions willing him to continue.

"Two local blokes got found running away from Tadwick. They went right bloody doolally and spent the rest of their lives in a nuthouse. The man who found them returned to the field they ran from, and he ended up in the loony bin an' all."

The boys again descended into giggles before Loadall added his support to Yeo's story.

"This episode occurred over forty years ago, and it even took up column inches in the long defunct Larkhall Tromboner. The legend states that the original battle between the Devil and the Witchfinder for control of Larkhall occurred in the seventeenth century, and it appears credible that those men so sadly consigned to insanity may have witnessed a diabolical coupling between Witchfinder Thomas Crabbings and his greatest supporter, the Larkhall Simpleton."

More tittering emanated from the boys, but the laughter was cut short by their host.

"I'd gather from your childlike frivolity that neither of you have been confronted by an apparition of the Larkhall Simpleton?"

Lee and Rhodes again had the jollity wiped off their faces by Loadall's deadpan delivery.

"...I'm not sure what your idea of a good time is, but I doubt if it would include being visited by a backward, heavily built six-foot-seven-inch spectre with one eye and a shattered mess where his face used to be?"

The effects of the bong had now completely vacated Loadall's new customers, and both faces were drained of colour.

The Warning

"...I'm a sixty-year-old man, and I've seen a lot of strange things happen within the confines of Larkhall village; but surely medieval beliefs and hysteria have no place in this modern age of enlightenment and reason?"

Loadall didn't blink as he stared without emotion at the wide-eyed Lee and Rhodes.

"...The question is of course; just how enlightened and reasoned are we?"

After a moment of silence, Lenny Yeo added more of his thoughts.

"That's not to say any of it's true, mind. Graham Curnow's the one who knows more than we do, and you'll find out more from him than you will from us. All I'll say is that it takes a lot to drive someone from bein' a total piss head to bein' sober overnight. Course, we all keep an eye on him as we're his mates, and that Rensenbrink bloke who runs The Wyvern is under strict instructions never to serve him. The problem is that even if Curnow were drinkin' two bottles of vodka a day, nobody would know 'cos he'd still appear totally sober. He never slurred his words, and nobody's ever seen him puke or have a hangover."

Both Loadall and Yeo produced deadly serious stares, and just before leaving, Yeo gave the boys some brief advice with a stern expression and pointed finger.

"Lads, if you go up Solsbury Hill, just get yerselves back down before the light begins to fade."

The meatiest thunderclap of the evening followed, and as the teenagers jumped out of their skins, Loadall and Yeo raised their arms skyward and yelled *Oh my Lord!*

2

THE PILGRIMAGE

"Just a few minutes from now, and we shall be viewing Solsbury Hill from afar in all its majesty!"

The five passengers inside the hired minibus whooped with delight, while the driver made sure his wide smile was visible to all via the rear-view mirror. He switched the windscreen wipers to full blast to cope with the rain that had suddenly become heavier.

"Followers, just another few hundred yards and we shall wave goodbye to the A4 Londinium Road. Thence we shall climb the short hill to join the St Saviour's Road that brings us into Larkhall village. We must drink well from the unique atmosphere provided by this most strange and wonderful place."

Excited murmuring came from behind the driver, who in turn was excited for his followers. He was the only one to have previously viewed Solsbury Hill and its stone pillar from this vantage point, and enjoyed the thought of soon sharing the experience with his underlings.

To enhance their status as Devil worshippers, the group of six were to use aliases when going into cult mode the following morning, and its leader chose his own to reflect his expectation that the end times were fast approaching.

"...As soon as the short climb levels off, we shall have a clear view ahead despite the gloom. The Hill and the pillar will be seen looming in the distance to welcome us, with the pillar aligned perfectly above the centre of

The Pilgrimage

the road."

The group leader smiled with approval as he sensed the anticipation from his passengers.

"...Though I must advise you all to keep your gazes straight ahead. On the left of St Saviour's Road is the monstrosity of St Swithin's Church, a site where enemies of our own saviour plot his downfall to this day."

The left indicator was flicked, and all were united in an electric hush as the vehicle began the short climb into Larkhall.

The disciples cooed with awe as Solsbury Hill and its stone pillar suddenly stared them in the face. The group leader's eyes moistened in response to the wonder emanating from behind, and all looked forward to paying homage to the Hill the next morning.

"Are we all happy and proud?" asked the driver.

"We are happy and proud, dear leader!" chorused his five loyal followers.

"Today and tomorrow will be the biggest days of our lives thus far. On this day, we shall visit the inn where the ghastly Thomas Crabbings tried in vain to rid the village of our Lord's presence."

The disciples reacted to the mention of the Witchfinder's name with a mixture of curses, boos and theatrical raspberry blowing.

"...We shall park our vehicle a good distance from The Wyvern & The Witchfinder, and from there we shall make our way on foot to sample the glowing aura of this most sacred place."

"Once inside, I simply cannot emphasise enough that we must appear as ordinary visitors. No mention of our true intentions are to be let slip to the locals at any stage. Are we all agreed?"

"We are all agreed, dear leader!"

"That is good, my fine followers. Once we've departed the place where the Wyvern scared away Crabbings, we shall seek out our bed and breakfast establishment and gain ourselves a refreshing night's sleep in preparation for tomorrow's main event."

***

"You now have my blessings to go into cult mode. From this point on, we shall all be known by the devilish pseudonyms I've created on all our behalves!"

Sunday morning was grey and damp, and the followers signalled obedience to their leader as they left their overnight accommodation to begin the climb to Solsbury Hill.

"...And don't forget; should anybody ask, we're all cricketers preparing for an overseas tour by partaking in a rigorous bonding session."

The group leader knew his choice of footwear for himself and his disciples wasn't ideal for the task ahead, but the Devil would surely be pleased with them for making this bonus sacrifice. After glancing left and right to make sure eavesdroppers weren't in range, the troops were given a last piece of advice.

"We are now at the eastern boundary of Larkhall, my dear followers, and the gradients ahead are of varying degrees of severity. We must steel ourselves toward moving onward with cheer and good grace to pay tribute to the Dark One."

The group began to ascend Ferndale Road, one of the steepest sections of the journey. At the top of the short climb, they crossed the brief flatness of the old A46, a virtual ghost road since completion of the Batheaston Bypass. On the other side of the old highway was the foot of Bailbrook Lane.

"Dear followers, the Tin Church of Bailbrook Lane shall soon be in view!"

One of the cornerstone beliefs of the group was that the Devil was shut inside the church, and that after a stand-off lasting several hours, he burst without warning through the locked door to make an unstoppable ascent to the summit of Solsbury Hill.

Bailbrook Lane marked another sharp climb that only flattened out on approach to the tin church, and on arrival, the group marvelled at the sight of the dilapidated place of worship; its façade scarred with creepers, and the few steps leading up to its entrance wildly overgrown. The gate to the church was heavily padlocked and accompanied with a large *Keep Out!* notice.

"This church has been locked tight for over a century." claimed the group leader.

"Forty years ago, a group of local children attempted to enter this rusted dwelling, and the person they enlisted to force entry met with a violent end within seconds of fleeing the horror he encountered. Since that day, access to the building and its grounds has been completely sealed off."

The long-abandoned church was left behind as the group marched back the way they came; this time to take the right-hand fork in the lane that would lead them to the next trying instalment of the journey.

Before branching off, the group stopped at the old cottage that marked the triangular crotch of the fork. The group leader stood beside the left-hand gatepost, clenched a fist, and with its underside, banged against the tall and thick pillar of stone six times. He ordered his disciples to do the same, and they obeyed without question. Just as the third disciple prepared to bash the post, an old man rushed from the cottage.

The Pilgrimage

"What the bloody hell do you mad buggers think yer up to?"

The group leader smiled apologetically at the old man.

"Good morning, we're all cricketers preparing for an overseas tour by partaking in a rigorous bonding session."

"Yes, well I don't see how punchin' me bloody gatepost is gonna help. Now sod off before I give the bloody lot of you a thick ear!"

"Now, now my dear man. We are a peaceful gathering of clear and good thinking folk, and we wish nothing but fair fortune to all local residents we meet. Please don't be alarmed."

The old man picked up his garden shovel and pointed it threateningly at the group leader.

"If you don't bloody clear off right now, I'll whack you so 'ard and 'igh, yer'll come down with snow on yer bloody shoulders!"

The spade was thrust sporadically toward the rest of the group as its leader held aloft his hands in a gesture of acceptance.

"We shall abide by your wishes, sage villager."

The old man kept the shovel aimed at the group leader's head as they finally headed off toward Solsbury Hill.

"And if I see you lot 'angin' round 'ere again, yer'll get my bloody twelve bore up yer arses! It 'ain't true what they keep sayin' about this place."

The clan leader turned his head as the group ambled away from the cottage.

"Such action will be unnecessary, wise old man. As a parting gesture of sheer goodwill, may I compliment you on a beautifully manicured lawn; immaculate enough to host a Test Match, if I may be so bold."

"And if I may be so bloody bold..."

The old man showed surprising agility by chasing after the group while wielding the shovel high above his head.

The six visitors had to sprint to leave the old man behind, and when they were eventually out of sight, the group leader recommended they pause for a while to regain their breath.

"T'was a close shave, dear followers. We must now erase this brief skirmish from our memories and continue with our anointed quest."

The group soon joined onto an inhospitable and slippery mud track surrounded by tall bush. The path ran parallel to the border cutting of the bypass deep below, and its narrowness dictated they walk it in single file.

"Dearest followers, we must constantly remind ourselves of the great joy we'll experience once we've met with our destination, and that this difficult journey will meet with much approval from Him."

Following a bumpy and winding climb along the mud track, the group eventually reached Solsbury Lane. As they turned right, a brief interlude of flat, man-made terrain was enjoyed before the next arduous leg of the trek.

They reached a clearing in the hedge at the left-hand side of the lane and entered a long and steep field of tall foxtail grass. The northern hedge was a long way off and only just visible through the rain and low cloud.

"Steel thyselves, dearest and most dedicated followers. Rain and weariness cannot harm us, and we must push on with plentiful gladness."

The saturated grass ensured everybody became filthy from the waist down, while the slanting rain drenched the rest of their bodies. Bits of soggy sheaf from the grass tips clung to their lower halves to add more discomfort as they made painfully slow progress to a third of the way up the field.

The leader held up a hand and asked his disciples to stop. On the other side of the hedge to their right stood a rusty brown corrugated barn in a state of near collapse; its four sides and roof desperately clinging to each other at abstract angles.

"Followers; around the time of the tin church episode forty years ago, the Wyvern was seen flying into this barn. The man who saw the magnificent creature ran as fast as his legs would carry him back toward Larkhall village, and he returned that evening accompanied by about half a dozen local men, all eager to catch a glimpse of the entity they feared rather more than we do!"

The group smiled with pride at the thought of the Devil's lieutenant being inside the very ramshackle building they were viewing.

"...The men were in no doubt that the Wyvern was still inside, as every few seconds, the walls of the barn gave off strange whistling and buzzing acoustics, as if produced by the contented snoring of a huge creature not of this world.

"Each man was too frightened to attempt access to the barn, but kept vigil until the small hours of the following morning before giving up hope of a sighting. The men kept looking over their shoulders during their descent to the village, just in case the Wyvern decided to leave its hiding place and fly after them."

The weather was deteriorating steadily, and the group leader had to funnel his hands around his mouth and shout to be heard.

"...Their return home was made without incident, but when the man who'd originally viewed the Wyvern returned the following day, the barn had taken on its current near to collapse state. He ran back to the village in a state of terror, and the only word they could get out of him for several weeks was 'Aaaargh!' He refused to enter the field ever again, or even venture as far up the hill as Bailbrook Lane."

The disciples wore defiant grins in reaction to both their leader's story

The Pilgrimage

and the incessant battering from the weather.

"...Still, we have absolutely nothing to fear from the great Wyvern, as it is the close friend of our most-revered Lord and Master. They form, if you like, a kind of illicit version of the Holmes/Watson partnership."

The five followers cheered with delight at their leader's analogy before continuing their attempt to rendezvous with the summit of Solsbury Hill.

An energy sapping ten-minute trudge was required before they reached the field's northern border, with each upward step sinking deep into the waterlogged soil. As that segment of the journey was finally completed, they one by one threaded a narrow stile, beyond which was a badly rusted sign giving a lacklustre welcome to Solsbury Common. The underfoot conditions became noticeably more unpleasant and unforgiving from that point, with craggy rocks and lumps of irregular muddy knolls hampering their already difficult progress.

The joining of hands was required to negotiate the treacherous ground, and amid much slipping, sliding, and occasional collisions between bone and rock, they inched their way upward. All around were wild bushes with snaking brambles adding to the severity of the challenge, and the disciples began to wonder if the summit of the hill would ever come into view.

"Keep working dear disciples, for we are most-assuredly nearing the great mound."

After a journey of just over an hour, and with the time striking midday, they came to a clearing. The stone pillar of Solsbury Hill suddenly revealed itself to its newest pilgrims, and as if the group was being congratulated on passing its stiff examination, the Sun appeared from behind the clouds for the first time in several days.

3

THE TIN CHURCH

Earlier that morning, the landlord of The Wyvern & The Witchfinder stood in the centre of the local park and watched heavy and dirty clouds scamper over Solsbury Hill. During most Sunday mornings, matchstick figures would be visible moving slowly on top of the mound, but the dreadful weather ensured that nothing accompanied the proud stone pillar.

Dave Rensenbrink's daily exercise consisted of walking the two hundred yards to the park and back and using his ancient wooden tennis racquet to belt a bald tennis ball for his Doberman to chase. After three underarm forehands, the weather decided it was time to get back indoors. Still, a dry and sunny interlude was forecast for the afternoon, and that'd bring some relief from the constant drenchings of the past two months.

Once back and safely holed up in his free house, Rensenbrink unlatched Clive from his lead and pondered the various reasons behind his dwindling trade. The biggest reason of all was Graham Curnow suddenly kicking the bottle. Up until a year ago, Curnow parted with a small fortune every week in the endless pursuit of quenching his thirst, and although Rensenbrink was pleased for Curnow that he was no longer drinking himself to death, his sentiment wasn't shared by the pub balance sheet. The only times he'd bump into Curnow these days was when he was dressed in his rambling regalia, or when spotted in the greengrocer's stocking up on a wide array of unusual vegetables.

The other big reason profits were taking a dive was the horrendous spring weather, as attested to by the landlords of the other two pubs that catered for Larkhall.

"Even if they live just around the corner, people aren't going to put up with their umbrellas being blown inside-out to get here." was the resigned opinion Rensenbrink garnered from the landlord of The Bladud's Midriff; the pub that marked the south eastern boundary of Larkhall, and from where the land rises steeply toward Solsbury Hill.

Rensenbrink poured himself a well-earned pint as the clock struck midday, and within seconds of the afternoon, he'd emptied his jug. At the same moment, the pub became illuminated as the Sun appeared for the first time in several days. Ten minutes later, Rensenbrink took his final swallow from a more sedately supped second pint, and the scrawny figure of Dick Joy entered to become that day's first customer.

"Aft' noon David."

"Ow's 'ee goin' then Dick, me ol' babber?"

"Strugglin' with me bloody fuckin' back again."

"Oh dear. Whassit to be then, ya daft old sod?"

"I'll 'ave a Flamin' Witch Rogerer, I reckon, and you can throw in a dash o' black to make it a bit less fuckin' 'orrible."

"A fine choice, master Dick. A tipple to make the Devil sob as he looks down from the Hill."

Dick Joy was laid off from the local shoe factory fifteen years earlier, and since that time became the newspaper delivery boy for the parish.

"...Ow's the job goin', old mate?"

Joy took a generous swallow from his orangey-purple pint before answering.

"Well, I could do without the bastard soddin' hills. Got to do the whole fuckin' lot on foot these days – no way me Chopper can handle it. And o' course, it buggers me back right up."

"Well, a few pints of that, and yer back'll be the least of yer worries." advertised the landlord.

"...Just make sure it don't give you a ringpiece like the middle of the Japanese flag."

Next to enter the pub was Jeremy Bennett-Brewer, an old-fashioned music teacher in his early thirties. Bennett-Brewer fitted the teacher stereotype by wearing a corduroy jacket complete with elbow patches. He'd moved to the area a month earlier, and this was his second visit to his new local.

"Good lord, we're in the grip of the type of inclement weather that surely must've inspired Vaughan Williams' Pastoral Symphony; brooding, wild, and with a forebodingness all its own."

Rensenbrink and Joy gave the new customer a warm welcome.

hic... a few of us... went up to that old... tin church up... Bailbrook Lane. D'ya know it?"

Bennett-Brewer shook his head, but was intrigued enough to hope Joy would be able to finish the story before he was either too incoherent or slung out by the landlord.

"...The... church wasn't used for... donkeys' years... and was... locked-up to stop... the kids gettin' in... hic. Any...way, we couldn't... pick the lock to get... in... so we went up...to the house a...few doors...along...to call for...the bloke Chatterton to come along...and...do it for us."

"HEY DICK!"

Joy's staccato storytelling was interrupted by the appearance of the landlord from The Bladud's Midriff, who'd come in for a quick pint on his day off from bar duties.

"...I've been meaning to ask you this for years; which part of America are you from?"

"Hic...eh?"

"Well the thing is, I've never been sure 'cos I've seen you in so many states!"

The off-duty landlord followed his quip by ruffling Dick Joy's frizzy and almost spherical grey hair, saying his goodbyes and swiftly vanishing.

"Where...was I?" Joy asked Bennett-Brewer with a look of drunken bewilderment.

"You were at the tin church...you couldn't break the lock and called for that chap to do it for you, remember?"

"Aaaaah...that's...right! When I...was a kid...which is... going back donkeys' years now, a few of us went to the... tin church along... Bailbrook Lane...you know it?"

Bennett-Brewer shook his head with exasperation. Time was of the essence, underlined by the sudden appearance of a dark patch around Joy's groin.

"...The church... wasn't... used for... donkeys' years... so we knocked on the...door of that... one-eyed bloke... Chatterton, to...pick the padlock... an' get us in. D'ya know him?"

Bennett-Brewer shook his head again, this time with less disguised annoyance.

"...Not surprising really...as he's been...hic...dead and gone these last forty years...or more."

As if Joy had run out of batteries, his last few words faded before his head drooped forward to rest against his chest. His right hand was still clasped tightly around the bottom of a full pint.

After returning up the cellar steps behind the bar, Rensenbrink was now

The Tin Church

busy serving a round for the ramblers, who along with Joy and Bennett-Brewer, were now the pub's only customers.

The teacher resigned himself to the show being over and made a trip to the lavatory. When he returned, Joy hadn't moved a muscle. Bennett-Brewer planned on finishing his drink and waving goodbye to the landlord. As he drained his glass, Dick Joy suddenly returned to life, and didn't spill a drop as he lifted his arm to take a generous gulp from the full pint.

"Ah, splendid to have you back with us again!"

As if a hypnotist had clicked his fingers, Joy continued his story.

"This Chatterton bloke picked the lock, poked his head inside the church, and then ran off screaming. I never saw him move so bloody fast."

To Bennett-Brewer's delight, Joy appeared to have miraculously sobered up, and was now speaking fluently.

"...Chatterton was the village idiot-cum-petty thief. He was a bit of a cocky loudmouth for someone so simple, but he was a big bloke; six-foot-seven 'ee were, and that intimidated a lot of people. The look on his face as he ran from the church scared the lot of us, and even the bully of our group wasn't ashamed to admit it. The way Chatterton fucked off, no way any of us were gonna have a peek inside.

"It were just after 'alf nine in the evenin', but it was the longest day of the year, an' still some daylight left. Anyway, whether it was anything to do with him only havin' the one eye, I dunno, but he kept veerin' left and right along the lane until he was out of sight.

"He was running back toward Larkhall, where the lane starts to go sharp downhill. Just after where we lost sight of him, there's a fork in the lane; left to carry on down to the village, and right for the path going up to Solsbury Hill. We all had a feelin' something bad was about to happen, and the smallest kid of our group started to cry.

"A few seconds later we all heard what sounded like the crack of a rifle shot. What a fuckin' echo it made. We had to go after Chatterton, even though we were really shittin' ourselves by then. When we got round the corner, we saw what must've happened; 'ee ran straight into the left-hand gatepost of the old cottage. The 'rifle shot' was when he smashed his face full on and clean broke his neck. Killed 'imself outright, 'ee did."

Dick Joy went quiet for a few seconds and stared aimlessly ahead. He eventually stirred and returned to his original drunken state.

"Will you gennalmen...please ex...cuse me while I...go an' powder my cock?"

"Course, Dick...but after that I think it's time you were gettin' yerself home, there's a good lad."

Rensenbrink had just returned from polishing a few glasses at the other end of the bar, and observed Joy taking a long time to slide off the stool and zig-zag his way to the toilet. He turned his attention back to his other customer.

"You look a bit troubled, me ol' mate."

"You wouldn't be far from the truth, mine host. Did you hear about what happened to that one eyed chap all those years ago?"

"Oh, don't take no notice of Dick, he could fit Lansdown racecourse into that bloody mouth of his."

"Yes, but what was all that business about him running into that gate post and breaking..."

"HAVE ANY OF YOU TWO SEEN MY DICK?"

Both the landlord and teacher jumped in reaction to the loud interruption.

Rensenbrink looked over to see Jemima Joy standing in the doorway.

"No I haven't, Jemima love, is he supposed to be here?"

"WELL OF COURSE HE'S NOT SUPPOSED TO BLOODY WELL BE HERE, I WOULDN'T BE SHOUTING OTHERWISE, WOULD I?"

"Fair enough, love. Maybe he's popped down the Midriff for a swift half?"

"BOLLOCKS! NO SUCH THING AS A SWIFT HALF FOR THAT USELESS TWAT!"

"...If you do see him, tell him to get some aspirin for when I belt him one, and, you can tell him Chatterton's on his way."

4

SHOWDOWN ON SOLSBURY HILL

In the thirteen months since Graham Curnow booted the bottle into touch, he kept himself active by becoming a full-time pedestrian and cutting-out the consumption of anything that had addictive qualities. On top of the drink, caffeine and tobacco were also frogmarched out of his life. From the moment he became clean, he promised himself he'd never again be an embarrassment to the community.

Suitably invigorated by his long Sunday morning walk, Curnow looked forward to the final two-mile stretch from Lansdown to low-level Larkhall. The heavy rain gradually lessened the further he descended through the single-track country lane, and his already-healthy mood was boosted with each regimented stride. The foliage around the lane had become noticeably wilder and more colourful in recent weeks, and this reminder of nature's cycle from death to life buoyed him to the extent of humming the melody of *Sumer Is Icumen In*, which he repeated intermittently until arriving at Barry Loadall's doorstep some thirty minutes later. Curnow looked at his watch and wore a proud smile to see it display the time as just striking midday. A few seconds later, the Sun suddenly appeared for the first time in several days, and Curnow's sense of wellbeing was at full capacity.

"And the warmest of greetings to you, my good friend."

Loadall's eyes squinted in reaction to the sudden brightness as he invited Curnow into the mellower lighting of his lounge.

"...You'd better sit in the chair, I fear the sofa will soon be gathered-to-God."

Curnow removed his waterproofs and made himself as comfortable as the old armchair allowed.

Loadall wore a concerned look as he removed the planetary ephemeris from the well-stocked bookshelf. He spoke gravely as he found the relevant page.

"June will see a grand cross formed of Mars, Pluto, Saturn and Uranus. Mid-month will see a waxing moon form a conjunction with Mars. Both Saturn and Pluto will begin retrograde motion during that time, and Venus and Mercury will be performing a transit of the Sun. Granted, the modest sextile aspect between Saturn and Neptune in itself should provide respite, but any comfort drawn from that will be negligible in the grand scheme of things. It makes for a bleak outlook indeed."

Loadall returned the ephemeris to the bookshelf and sunk with resignation into the other armchair. He removed his round National Health spectacles and wearily pinched the top of his nose.

"Well, if we're all headed toward oblivion..." answered an unbothered Curnow, "a delicious cup of dandelion & liquorice tea certainly won't do any harm in the meantime."

The drug dealer struggled to wriggle free of the chair and made his way toward the kitchen to fix his friend's favourite tipple. A couple of minutes later, Loadall returned with a steaming mug displaying a bright green cannabis leaf and inscribed with the words, *I 'heart' GETTING CANED*; a gift from the retired postmistress of the village.

Curnow took a sip of his herbal medicine and smiled.

"Oh, the sheer joy of being freed from the bondage of addiction!"

"Your sheer mental strength and unbreakable discipline is something we must all aspire to." responded Loadall before he lit his pipe, widened his eyes, and coughed violently.

"I do so wish I could join you in your newfound puritanism." added the host before he dry retched a couple of times.

"...though I fear it's a little too late for that."

***

From the summit of Solsbury Hill, Trevor Expectorant aimed his binoculars toward The Wyvern & The Witchfinder public house. The view was poor, as the recent rain had combined with the angle of the Sun to dazzle the road that branched off the A4 and threaded Larkhall. Expectorant sighed, then clapped his hands to make an announcement.

"Gather round, most dear and dedicated apostles."

The five followers obediently lined up before their master. Each wore the Expectorant-provided worship attire of cream cricket sweater, cream cricket flannels, and cream, un-socked sandals. Each clothing item of every group member was filthy and sodden.

"We are here to offer our prayers and love to the darkest one of all, and after fitting retribution has taken place, we shall join hands to circle the remains of that most meddling and misguided enemy of the truest and purest; Witchfinder Thomas Crabbings."

The air was filled with boos and hisses as Expectorant retreated to the side of the stone pillar to allow his followers clear aim. Each was armed with a large onion net filled with decaying apples and tomatoes, and all stood ready to throw their overripe ammunition.

"Disciples, we have made the difficult journey, and as a result our clothes are filthy and saturated. But, because we've put ourselves through the pain and hardship of getting here, then the special pleasure we shall derive from what we are about to do will make the experience all the more rewarding!"

Before the ritual of the dance commenced, the stone monument was bombarded with rotting fruit, accompanied by furious expletives and obscene gestures.

***

"I've done further research, and a similar planetary alignment occurred in June 1651."

Barry Loadall stared blankly at his reformed guest before taking a swallow from his beaker of beetroot juice, his single concession to healthy living.

"Well, all I know is that I'm glad to be alive."

Curnow smiled and raised his mug toward Loadall as he spoke, which inspired a frown from the drug dealer.

"Being glad to be alive is all very well, but it'll count for little if what you experienced in Tadwick is a sign of things to come."

"To be fair Barry, when I woke up in that field, I'd drunk the west country dry over the previous forty-eight hours. I'm sure if I actually had seen the ghost of the Larkhall Simpleton, he'd have chased me off in a slightly less silly way than by doing lots of cartwheels.

"What I experienced in Tadwick was down to me being continuously tiddly, and now that I've knocked it all on the head, these weird visions seem to have set up shop in my dreams; and these dreams seem to be my penance for kicking the booze. I'm now sober and rational, and I won't give credence to some daft supernatural explanation."

Loadall nodded understandingly and pondered Curnow's words with a stroke of his lengthy chin.

"Graham, my good friend, I have no reason to doubt your integrity and sincerity. Even so, surely it must be more than coincidence that two healthy men returned from Tadwick as blubbering madmen, and that the journalist who reported the story in the Larkhall Tromboner was found soon after tied to the sycamore tree beside Lam Brook wailing like an abandoned infant?"

Curnow inwardly laughed at Loadall's extraordinary version of events, and politely dismissed the claims.

"Do you know this is already the wettest spring since records began?" continued an unperturbed Loadall.

"I am indeed aware of that, Barry."

"Of course, we only have official records going back a couple of centuries, but from what little information we have, 1651 round these parts was notorious for violent cloudbursts. People caught out in the open suffered fractured skulls from the force of the downpours, and a procession of drowned ducks bottlenecked the estuary of Lam Brook and River Avon."

***

After the ritual of the stone pillar bombardment and dance, Expectorant's followers tightly embraced one another.

The leader of the group glowed with pride as he witnessed the emotional depth his disciples so clearly felt. He raised his arms skyward in acceptance and obedience to the Devil.

"My fine, fine followers; we have done what we came to do, and it is now time to replenish ourselves with nothing but the finest fare."

Expectorant handed each disciple a lunchbox that contained a freshly prepared fruit salad, two asparagus spears, three crispy potato skins, *Curly Wurly*, two slats of Garibaldi biscuit, and a carton of cauliflower flavoured milk.

"We still have plenty of rotting fruit left, o chosen one, let us again pummel the disgusting Crabbings!" asked one of the disciples, before following his leader's orders by munching away on the wrong end of his asparagus.

"All in good time, my fine and proud warrior of much darkness; first we must give strength to our mortal bodies via hearty banqueting. Once our stomachs are full from feasting, we shall again bombard Mr Crabbings before returning to our guest house to re-clothe ourselves. Thenceforth we shall..."

"LOOK OUT!"

Expectorant's second in command raised the alarm as he viewed a group of sightseers emerge over the southern edge of the hill's summit.

"Leave it to me..." whispered Expectorant. "Everyone step up to shield the monument from prying eyes."

The leader and his disciples lined up side by side and with arms folded in front of the stone, before Expectorant raised an arm in a gesture of greeting.

When the group came to within thirty yards, he raised his voice to address them.

"Nice to have some sunshine at long last, though I suppose we needed a drop of rain. My guess is that those who lovingly tend their gardens will soon be confronted with a riot of blooming colour!"

The approaching group mirrored Expectorant and his followers by being composed of five men and one woman, although they were far more appropriately kitted out for the nasty conditions. They all smiled at Expectorant, and one of the men stepped forward to shake his hand.

"Wow, that sure is some real crazy but mighty fine bunch o' gear you folks are all wearin'!"

Trevor Expectorant was relieved to hear a broad American accent, and before he could continue his charm offensive designed to deter suspicion, a member of his group chimed-in.

"We're all cricketers preparing for an overseas tour by partaking in a rigorous bonding session."

Expectorant was delighted that one of his disciples had used the pre-planned excuse behind their attire, and showed his gratitude by aiming a secretive thumbs up in his direction.

"Well, we don't know nothin' about this cricket all you English people play, but I sure as hell didn't realise just how darned dirty ya had to get!"

"That's all part of the fun!"

"...and I've always said that unless we get truly dirty, then the game cannot be enjoyed, hence the reason behind how dirty our clothes are."

"Sir, is this cricket thing played by men and ladies together?" the lead tourist asked while staring at the female member stood at the end of Expectorant's group.

"Good Lord, no..." replied the slightly caught off guard group leader. "Denise here is in charge of laundry concerns."

The woman in question smiled and nodded back at the American contingent.

"Well, there's one lady who'll be real busy when y'all get back down the moun'ain!"

Expectorant gave a polite laugh in response, and encouraged his disciples to do the same.

"I do hope you're all enjoying your stay in our humble part of the world. We do pride ourselves on our hospitality, and you only have to ask if you need any help with..."

"We're NOT here to worship the Devil!"

Expectorant aimed a momentary glare at the interrupting disciple at his side. He quickly regained his smile as he readdressed the tourists.

"He's right, you know! We're just a group of ordinary Englishmen enjoying the veritable tranquillity offered by Solsbury Hill, whilst wearing the traditional attire of our cherished game of cricket; which, as I mentioned earlier, is the reason behind our clothes being so dirty."

"Now that sure is something...!" replied the female tourist member, who appeared awestruck as she surveyed the group and its leader. "I'm so glad to hear you guys want nothing to do with Satan. Why, we've come all the way from lil' ol' Tennessee to say hi to the awesome Thomas Crabbings!"

"Who's Thomas Crabbings?"

Expectorant shot another disapproving look at the disciple who again proved unhelpful.

"As my discip...FRIEND says, who is...sorry, what was the name again?"

"Thomas Crabbings. Why, he's the guy who bust Satan's ass right here!"

"Well in that case..." replied Expectorant. "Mr Cribbins is a friend to us all!"

Much to the delight of the tourists, the disciples were ordered by their leader to sing a hearty rendition of For He's a Jolly Good Fellow, followed by the mass tossing of their cream-coloured top hats high into the sky. Unfortunately for the group, and especially Expectorant, the top hats were blown away and became enmeshed in one of the several large bramble bushes that dotted the area just below the summit.

"Say, you guys sure do know how to give praise!"

"Oh, it's nothing..." offered Expectorant with a dismissive wave of the arm, as his comb-over hairstyle was savagely exposed by the high-altitude gale-force wind. "We're always happy to do what we can to support those who do such marvellous work in the Lord's name, and this Tony Cribbins chap certainly sounds like he's..."

"...When he says 'the Lord'..." interrupted the disciple for the third time, "he's not referring to Satan, you know."

"Good heavens, no...!" confirmed Expectorant, who resisted the urge to give his neighbouring disciple another glare. "No, we're here to enjoy the fresh air afforded us by standing atop this glorious mound, and also to partake in rigorous exercise."

Expectorant proceeded to jump up and down on the spot while starfishing his limbs; his crazed hair dancing above his head like an agitated grey flame. The third time he returned to earth, he deliberately stamped on his continually bungling disciple's foot.

"...Isn't that right, my friend?"

The offending follower nodded through a grimace to affirm his leader's statement as he hopped around on his uninjured foot.

"SAY, YOU GUYS...IT'S THE STONE PILLAR!"

One of the tourists had spotted the monument behind the hopping disciple, and excited cries of *wow* and *oh my* came from other members of the group.

"Will you please step aside, sir?"

Expectorant nervously abided by the request and asked his followers to clear the way.

"Why, what's this...?!" asked another member of the group. "There's apple and tumaydu stains all over it! Jeez, that's no fine way to treat a guy who whooped the Devil's butt!"

"You mean apple and *tomato* stains." mumbled the sore footed disciple sulkily.

"Just look at that huge black storm cloud approaching from the west!" interrupted Expectorant with a pointed arm; his unruly hair again taking on the role of windsock.

As the tourists followed Expectorant's aim, he used his free hand to clout his re-offending follower around the side of the head.

"You call that a black cloud, mister? You ain't seen nothin' compared to the critters we get back home. Why, as sure as young Daisy-Tabatha stood right over there don't bake cornbread as good 'n wholesome as mom, that sure as hell ain't no storm!"

"I do believe you're quite right..." conceded Expectorant. "Our modest island is located in a temperate zone, and I'm sure any wild weather we get is laughably insignificant compared to the great raging storms of Kentucky."

"WHY, TENNESSEE...!" shouted the man who originally shook Expectorant's hand. "DO WE LOOK LIKE GODDAMN *BLUEGRASSERS*?!"

"I should say not!" replied Expectorant with as much vim as he could muster.

"So, are you guys gonna tell us why this stone tribute to the great man is covered in stains from God's finest fruit?"

Expectorant cleared his throat before offering his explanation, as his foot long strands of hair pointed due east and at right angles to his head.

"Well, because none of us had ever heard of this Tim Cratchit fellow you've come to worship, we had no idea that this local custom we keep alive would be considered offensive.

"Every seventh Sunday afternoon, a group of local people hurl various species of fruit at the monument so as to feed this great mound. The nutrition of the fruit seeps down through the stone and replenishes Solsbury Hill to aid it in its continual fight to ward off those who, and I'm sure you'll share our dislike of them, choose to worship the Devil."

"And you certainly wouldn't find us choosing to worship the Devil!" added the unhelpful disciple.

***

Trevor Expectorant led his followers away from Solsbury Hill and back toward Larkhall village.

"Are we in good spirits, dear disciples?"

"We are indeed!"

"Come, let us rest our weary legs awhile."

Expectorant chose a small clearing at the foot of the hill just above the bypass. The five disciples sat cross legged on individual potato sacks and formed a horseshoe before their leader.

"I apologise again for almost giving the game away, cherished leader." mumbled a chastened Sir Leonard Hutton.

Expectorant decided that naming his disciples after vintage English cricketers would help strengthen their resolve and togetherness.

"Thank you, Sir Leonard. I need to keep stressing just how important it is that we don't reveal to strangers that we actually are Satan worshippers.

"Of course, we all strongly believe that the world will soon be no more, and that Satan is our Lord and Master, but we must respect the fact that what we believe may be considered offensive to others.

"When our mortal bodies have breathed their last, we can spend our eternities indulging in all the pleasures our Lord so willingly sponsors. Until the great day arrives, it's courtesy and respect at all times."

"Hear, hear!"

Denise Compton raised an arm of solidarity to accompany her vocal support.

"It means a lot to receive your vote of confidence, Denise. Thank you."

"...None of us would be here unless we were convinced about our beliefs, but we must remain vigilant at all times against incriminating ourselves. Fortunately, I managed to talk our way out of suspicion from our Kentuckian friends, but that's not something I'd enjoy having to repeat."

A sheepish Sir Leonard Hutton aimed his gaze away from his colleagues.

5

THE LURE OF TADWICK

Upon leaving Loadall's house, Graham Curnow decided to return home and put his feet up. He always ended up on a bit of a downer after these visits, and despite the well below normal temperatures for the time of year, he welcomed the brief window of sunshine that began an hour earlier.

Curnow felt sorry for his old chum, as it seemed he'd finally gone right off his chump after a lifetime of filling himself with various narcotics. Loadall's beliefs were hardly unique though, and he briefly entertained the idea that the legend might be worth investigating.

A knock at the door ended Curnow's dabble with the ridiculous, and he instantly regained his optimistic demeanour.

"Sorry to trouble ya mate, but we wuz talking to Barry Loadall and the bloke from the flower shop last night..."

"Oh, don't tell me..." interrupted a smiling Curnow. "they told you all about the local legend, and I suppose you want to hear it straight from the horse's mouth about what I saw?"

Ally Lee and Ronan Rhodes nodded back at the reformed alcoholic.

"Righto, come inside and I'll tell you what I know."

The teenagers stepped inside the modest council house and were offered the living-room's similarly modest sofa.

"Did Barry tell you about what I saw that day in Tadwick?"

"He said you got chased by a ghost doin' shit-loads of cartwheels." answered a slightly embarrassed Rhodes.

"What I apparently saw that day changed my way of life."

"Do you really think you saw a ghost?" asked an excited Lee.

"Well, I've got no belief in anything supernatural to be honest, but I don't categorically know that what I saw that day *wasn't* an illusion.

"I've been an extremely happy person since that day, and so long as I've got enough to survive, I'll be contented. I know the value of life, and the thought of how I acted toward people when I got drunk will ensure, I hope, that I never return to those days."

"Is it true what Baz said that people didn't know when you were really pissed up, and that you never remembered anythin'?"

"Yes, perfectly true. Nobody would have any idea I was drunk until I started being rude and nasty to people. And yes to what Barry said about me having no idea about what I said or did.

"The very odd thing is though, since I became sober, I now remember all the shocking events clearly; take the Larkhall Village Festival two years ago when I had a skin full."

Curnow's expression became mournful as he recalled the shameful incident.

"There was a stall in the Square where local disadvantaged children were exhibiting their artwork, and I told the lot of them that their paintings were utter shite."

Both teenagers tried to suppress their laughter, and Curnow smiled understandingly toward them before he continued.

"I insulted this tiny kid of about seven or eight who was wearing glasses. I said, *I wish you'd learn to paint, four-eyes, this is rubbish.*

"The poor lad started blubbering, and I responded with a V-sign in front of his face. I was always pretty fleet of foot when drunk, and I continued using the gesture as I fled from fist wielding parents."

Curnow was again understanding toward the boys as they this time laughed a little more heartily.

"There are countless examples of how nasty I could be when drunk, but I think the one I've given is sufficient for you to know how glad I am to be sober. If I ever hit the bottle again, you wouldn't see any physical signs, but you'd know straight away from my words."

"Can you tell us where the field is that you ran from?" asked Rhodes to turn the subject toward the purpose of their visit.

"Well, if you want to go there and take a look, be my guests..." Curnow casually responded. "I was a youngster once, and I used to like getting spooked. The older people get, the more they lose their sense of wonder and discovery, so if you feel the urge, I'll wish you good luck and an enjoyable visit. One has to experience fun at your age, though I can't give a guarantee

The Lure Of Tadwick

that the Larkhall Simpleton *won't* be putting on a gymnastic display for your benefit. It's your choice if you want to go ahead and get involved with what Barry's been putting into your heads, although I do get the feeling that curiosity will get the better of you."

***

Ally Lee and Ronan Rhodes began their journey to Tadwick armed with a shared umbrella and two generously loaded joints.

"Well, if we don't see anythin', at least we'll have a good laugh." Lee whispered to Rhodes as they walked past The Bladud's Midriff to exit Larkhall.

"And if we do see somethin'..." added a similarly-excited Rhodes, "we'll have a fuckin' scream!"

Instead of turning right for the extreme ascent of Ferndale Road, the teenagers carried on straight to take the longer but gentler climb of Dead Mill Lane.

The brief spell of afternoon sunshine was now replaced by a sky crammed with constantly evolving grey and indigo clouds. The wind had also strengthened appreciably, and the boys' umbrella had to be handled with skill to counter both that and the swirling rain.

"Fuck me..." Lee shouted above the howling gale. "Just make sure ya keep them fuckin' biftas dry!"

Rhodes responded by loudly patting the tobacco tin inside his jacket pocket as he struggled to keep hold of the umbrella.

"How the fuck're we gonna light 'em?" asked Rhodes.

"With a fuckin' lighter, you dense prick."

"No, twat. I mean how're we gonna light the bastards in this wind?"

"There's a church in Swainswick just past the school. Even if it 'ain't open, it's got a massive fuckin' doorway we can shelter in."

At the top of Dead Mill Lane, the boys were buffeted a few hundred yards along the old highway before turning left to join the country lane that led to Tadwick. The bad weather eased off a little as they approached the halfway point of Upper Swainswick and its tiny school.

"We can spark one up 'ere now it's less windy."

The boys turned their backs to the row of houses opposite the school entrance as the joint was lit.

"Fuck me, dis is da biddly-biddly sheeet." announced Rhodes with a Caribbean lilt after taking his first toke.

"Better not overdo it then, ya screamin' noncester..." Lee responded. "Otherwise we might see the Larkhall Simpleton pole-vaultin' with his own cock."

29

Ronan Rhodes laughed and coughed with equal force as he handed the joint to his mate.

A few minutes later, the boys resumed their journey amid occasional giggling fits. They turned right up the hill just past the school, and after a climb of about thirty yards, turned left to be flanked on either side by the burial grounds of St Crispin's Church.

On the corner of the lane that threaded the graveyards was a signpost that indicated Tadwick was a further mile and a half. The finger of the post was slanted toward the ground as a result of the recent batterings from the elements.

"Should be there in about half an hour." muttered Rhodes.

Lee stood still and grabbed his mate by the shoulder.

"'Ang on a fuckin' minute, didn't Baz say Chatterton wuz buried 'ere?"

"Who the fuck's Chatterton?" asked a cloudy brained Rhodes.

"He's the Larkhall Simpleton, ya thick fuckin' dorkmeister!"

"Shit!" responded Rhodes, whose memory was successfully jogged by his friend.

The wind and rain suddenly returned to its original intensity, and a violent gust wrenched the umbrella out of Rhodes' hand. The boys watched helpless as the umbrella took a crazy parabola over the high hedge of a neighbouring garden.

"You dozy tit, we're fucked now!"

"Ah shut yer face, ya moanin' tosspot."

"We're already wet as fuck, let's see if we can find Chatterton's grave!" Lee prodded enthusiastically.

"Nah, we better head back now the umbrella's fucked off."

"You totally shit-scared woofter!" ribbed Lee, who mocked Rhodes further by flapping his elbows and clucking.

"I ain't scared, twat face!"

"Well let's take a fuckin' gander, then!"

Ronan Rhodes remained silent as he pushed open the gate to the eastern section of the church's graveyard, and dozens of headstones were viewed that were mostly small and basic rectangular slabs tilted at various angles to indicate their age.

"Where's he s'posed to be buried, then?" asked an apprehensive Rhodes.

"How should I know, I'm not the fuckin' gravedigger, am I?"

The teenagers surveyed every headstone in that section of the church grounds without luck. Most of the engravings had been withered away over the years, while the majority of those that could be read dated back to the nineteenth century.

"I've 'ad enough of this!" shouted Rhodes, whose request that they both

The Lure Of Tadwick

shelter in the church doorway was grudgingly agreed to by his friend.

"...We'll never get to Tadwick before it gets dark, so fuck it."

The gates of the two graveyards were directly opposite, and the boys quickly negotiated them to get to the entrance of the small church.

The west facing doorway provided paltry respite from the angry weather, and Lee shouldered the heavy oak door several times with growing annoyance and ferocity. He finally gave up and agreed to Rhodes' original idea of returning to Larkhall. The wind and rain soon nullified the effects of the joint, and they both realised that getting saturated wasn't quite so enticing with a clear head.

"HEY, YOU TWO BLOODY FUCKIN' IDIOTS!"

A thoroughly drenched Dick Joy was holding the bars of the graveyard gate as he stared manically at the teenagers stood in the church doorway.

"WHAT THE HELL ARE YOU PLAYIN' AT? GET OUT OF THERE NOW, CHATTERTON'S ON HIS WAY!"

Joy then sprinted away from the graveyard in the direction of Larkhall. Rhodes and Lee stared at one-another.

"I think we better fuckin' leg-it, mate!"

As the boys were about to flee, they simultaneously spotted the huge headstone directly in front of them.

> RUPERT EDWARD CHATTERTON
> TAKEN SUDDENLY IN TRAGIC AND
> SPECTACULAR CIRCUMSTANCES
> 21st JUNE ONE YEAR - AGED 28
> THOSE WHO ARE CURIOUS SHOULD
> ATTEND TO THEIR OWN BUSINESS
> AND LEAVE WELL ALONE

6

UNEXPECTED REUNION

Sundays were dead quiet these days, and Dave Rensenbrink wondered again about the worth of staying open all day. It was approaching six o'clock, and the pub had been deserted since Dick Joy staggered his way home three hours earlier.

The landlord was interrupted from his scanning of Sporting Life by the return from Cribbs Causeway of his rather more petite wife, who struggled to squeeze through the narrow doors with several bags of shopping.

"Had a nice time, love?"

"If you call getting soaked through waiting an hour for the bus nice, I had a lovely time."

"Ah well, you run yerself a hot bath and relax."

"Has it been like this all day?"

"We had a few come and go. Dick got in a right state again."

"Yeah, I just saw his wife stamping about in the Square. He might have to do a recount of his bollocks when she catches up with him."

Rose clonked her way up the stairs to the right of the bar, and after taking her bath, returned to find the pub still empty of customers.

"I'll look after things if you wanna take the dog out."

Dave Rensenbrink jumped at the chance of stretching his legs and whistled to summon the Doberman over from its blankets in the back room.

"By the way..." the landlord added as he attached Clive's lead. "Dick scared the shit out of the new bloke who lives across the road."

"Bloody hell, as if we're not struggling enough without that piss head frightnin' 'em off!"

"At least he spends a fair bit while he's here, I suppose." Rensenbrink concluded as he and the family pet exited the pub.

A few minutes later, a customer Rose hadn't seen before entered.

"Hello there, what can I get you?"

"House vodka with ice and undiluted orange squash, please."

"Are you okay...?" asked the landlady as she searched for tumbler and tongs. "It's just that you look a little anxious."

"Well, I am a little troubled if I'm to be totally frank. I was in here earlier talking to that Dick chap, and he was saying..."

"Aaaah! You must be the bloke my husband was talking about. I understand Dick gave you a bit of a fright?"

"He certainly did, that's why I've popped back in to ask a few questions."

As Jeremy Bennett-Brewer received his change, the landlady gave him a brief outline of Dick Joy's habits.

"He's been coming here every Sunday for nigh on forty years, and he splits his time equally between the village's three pubs. Wednesdays and Thursdays he's down at the Midriff, Fridays and Saturdays you'll find him in The Blackest Morn, and he's here Sunday and Monday. Tuesdays are his day off."

"Is there anything in what he said about that one eyed fellow and the tin church?" asked a slightly agitated Bennett-Brewer.

"Yep, Chatterton his name is. Ran straight into a stone gatepost, the dozy sod. Mind you, he's always been a bit simple."

The sole customer went a little more ashen as Joy's story was confirmed, and was further ruffled by the landlady referring to a man who died forty years ago in the present tense.

"You talk about him as if he's still alive!"

Rose laughed in a calming manner.

"No, no. I'm only seeing it from Dick's point of view."

It wasn't the satisfactory answer Bennett-Brewer was hoping for, and he struggled to hide his unease.

"What I also found rather alarming was when Dick's wife turned up and said Mr Chatterton was on his way!"

This time the landlady smiled and nodded insightfully before replying.

"When you were a kid, did your mother warn you that if you didn't come home before dark, the bogey man would come and get you?"

Bennett-Brewer nodded back.

"...Well, that's what Dick's wife does when she goes to all the pubs to tell him to get home. Chatterton is his bogey man. For the past forty years,

Dick's been convinced that Chatterton's ghost is haunting him. Sometimes he reckons he hears him wailing, and other times he sees him running past his lounge window."

"Do you think there's anything in it?"

"I think it's all rubbish. As for Dick Joy, he's a known drunkard to everyone in the area. Then there was another drunk, and this one was as chronic an alcoholic as you get. He used to drink in here all the time until he woke up in Tadwick after a two-day bender and got chased by Chatterton."

"Good lord...!" blurted Bennett-Brewer. "And does this chap believe it all?"

"No. He lives a very simple life nowadays, and he reckoned the drink pickled his brain so much he started seeing things. He hasn't gone near booze since that day. Good news for him, but it gave our profits a bit of a hammering."

"So, is it only the alcoholics who get to see these alarming visions?"

"Oh no, people all over the village say they've seen things. Doesn't mean they have, mind you."

Dave Rensenbrink led his dog back through the door, and both were soggy from the incessant drizzle.

"Hello again, old mate!" the landlord greeted his returning customer.

"...Not still worried about rambling Dick, are you?"

"As a matter of fact, I am. I've just heard from your good wife that he keeps seeing the ghost of this Chatterton fellow."

Rensenbrink smiled as he unleashed Clive.

"Look, I told you it was all a load of shite. Dick Joy's got a bloody degree in gettin' arse-holed an' scarin' the customers. He even tells people that when Chatterton's ghost goes running past his window at night, his head flaps back an' forth 'cos of his broken neck!"

Before an even more spooked Bennett-Brewer could respond, the group of six that came in the previous night walked through the door.

"Greetings again, most warm and hospitable publican!"

"Aah, if it isn't the Solsbury Hill brigade...!" Rensenbrink replied with equal verve. "Did you have any luck with yer metal detecting?"

"Alas, nothing but inconsequential scraps."

"No surprise." answered the landlord as he returned behind the bar to pour six pints of Convulsing Cockrell for the group, while his wife and Bennett-Brewer continued chatting.

"...The whole of Solsbury Hill has been metal-detected to buggery. Yer as likely to find treasure down the pans of the public bogs in Larkhall Square."

"Oh well, my mock Tudor mansion is still but a pipe dream!" replied the leader of the group, while the other five members shuffled toward the table in the pub's deepest corner.

"I've got to admire yer resolve though..." added Rensenbrink. "I thought it were only the Devil-worshippers who went up the Hill in these conditions."

Trevor Expectorant shook his head in apparent disbelief as he picked up two pints to take to the corner table.

"Absolutely scandalous some of the things people get up to."

"Anyway, you go and sit down, and me and the wife'll bring the rest of your drinks over."

"Strange bunch." whispered Bennett-Brewer, as landlord and landlady returned to the bar after delivering the pints.

"They're those Devil worshipping fruit 'n nut cases I told you about earlier..." the landlord whispered. "Couldn't be more bleedin' obvious if they all wore t-shirts that said *WE WORSHIP THE DEVIL.*"

As it was, Expectorant and his clan were dressed with rather more orthodoxy than during their Solsbury Hill mission earlier in the day.

"Dave, what do you reckon made the one-eyed chap run into that gate post?" asked Bennett-Brewer.

"Well, I don't think it was anything he saw. He was always a bit retarded though, and epileptic too. That might have had something to do with it."

"What the bloody hell are you on about...?" snapped the landlord's wife. "Have you ever seen an epileptic having a fit? Hardly makes them get up and take a hundred yard run up at a stone gatepost!"

"I suppose not..." Rensenbrink responded. "In that case, perhaps he actually did see the Devil an' Witchfinder givin' it what for inside the tin church."

***

"You don't think they suspect us do you, glorious leader?" asked WG Grace in hushed tones.

"Don't you worry about a thing, WG." Expectorant whispered back in a calm and sensitive manner.

"Our leader has never let us down before, and we must retain full trust." Sir Jack Hobbs loyally interjected.

"I'm very touched, Sir Jack."

Trevor Expectorant placed a grateful hand on Hobbs' shoulder, and was pleased that his decision to make him his second in command was further vindicated.

"Trust me, dear disciples..." the group leader added, "as long as we continue to be successful in not drawing attention to ourselves, we have absolutely nothing to be worried ab..."

"HEY Y'ALL! SAY, IS THIS THE PLACE WHERE WE CAN GET US SOME REAL OL' ENGLISH REAL BEER?"

Expectorant and his followers were alarmed as they heard the unmistakeable bellowing from the other end of the pub, and each aimed their reddened face at the table.

"Old English beer is our speciality!" replied a jovial Rensenbrink, aware that the pub coffers could be nicely swelled by the incoming tourists.

The group leader shook hands with landlord, landlady, and Jeremy Bennett-Brewer.

"Gee, is your English weather always so darned horrible?"

"I'm afraid it is, hardly a day without rain these last two months." answered Rose, before recommending the group leader try a sample of Spasming Scarecrow.

"This is our best-selling beer, hope you like it."

"Wow! Sure looks nothin' like anythin' we get back home!"

After taking a good gulp, the group leader's face contorted in disgust.

"WHOA! THIS STUFF'S HOTTER THUN FRESH BISON CRAP!"

"Should always be served at room temperature." the landlady matter of factly responded.

At the table in the far corner, Trevor Expectorant and his followers decided to make a break for it. To get to the door, they had no option but to shuffle past the Americans.

"Keep your heads down everyone," whispered Expectorant, who hoped the ongoing beer debate would help make their departure unnoticed.

"WE SURE CAN'T DRINK THIS ENGLISH BEER, TASTES LIKE IT'S BEEN LEFT OUT ON THE PORCH WI' THE FIRE-FLIES ALL DARNED SUMMER!"

As Expectorant's group trod quietly behind the tourists, Sir Leonard Hutton was tapped on the shoulder.

"Say YOU, whaddaya think about this here, HEY, IT'S THE CRICKET GUYS FROM SOLSBURY MOUN'AIN!"

Expectorant's heart sank, and he decided to respond before Hutton had a chance to put his foot in it.

"Well I never, how lovely to see you all again!"

For the second time that day, Expectorant shook hands with all six American visitors.

"HEY, BARTENDER! THEM GUYS WERE THROWIN' BAD FRUIT AT THE OL' STONE PILLAR. SAID IT WAS THE TRADITION OF THIS HERE VILLAGE!"

"Yes, it is."

Expectorant was puzzled but thrilled at the response from behind the bar, though his relief was short-lived as the landlord turned his cynicism and suspicion toward him and his followers.

"So, you lot are not only metal detecting cricketers, but you also keep our traditions alive, do you?"

Stood behind his leader, Iftikhar Ali Khan - Nawab of Pataudi, panicked.

"Should anybody ask, we're all cricketers preparing for an overseas tour by partaking in a rigorous bonding session."

"Where we'll also be telling the natives in no uncertain terms not to worship the Devil!" added Sir Leonard Hutton with a prodding finger.

"SAY, WE DIDN'T SEE US NO DOGGONE METAL DETECTORS, AN' THAT SURE AS HELL AIN'T NO LIE!"

"They were all packed-up in our rucksacks by the time your group appeared." answered Expectorant.

"JEEZ, AND THERE WAS ME THINKIN' THOSE THINGS ARE THE SIZE OF HOOVERS!"

"We have the latest fold away models..." Expectorant gingerly added. "Anyway, it's been delightful seeing you all, but it's time for us to go."

The Devil-worshippers were swiftly herded by their leader out into the evening drizzle.

"Now there go some real strange bunch o' folk! We go up the moun'ain to worship Thomas Crabbings, an' it don't seem right to me that those guys throw apples and tumaydoes about where Crabbings hung the Devil's ass out to draaah!"

"You do realise..." began the landlord as he re-addressed the leader of the American group. "that accordin' to the legend, it was Crabbings' arse that was hung on the washing-line?"

"Say, I sure never knew the English were *this* crazy!"

"And that the Devil turned Crabbings into the stone pillar. People who throw fruit at the pillar are lovers of the Devil, just like that lot you've just been talkin' to."

"WHOA! And those guys were so darned courteous, too. Still, they'se gonna have their asses fried real good 'n golden when the Lord calls 'em!"

The leader of the group turned his attention toward the silent onlooker sat at the bar.

"Pardon me for asking, sir, but are you crazy too?"

Before Jeremy Bennett-Brewer could reveal his bemusement, a flustered Jemima Joy appeared at the door.

"I'VE SEARCHED FUCKIN' EVERYWHERE, AND I STILL CAN'T FIND MY FUCKIN' DICK!"

7

ABORTED MISSION

As soon as Lee and Rhodes had left his house, Graham Curnow became concerned for their welfare. It was out of character for Curnow to dwell on things, but he regretted not trying to dissuade the teenagers from visiting Tadwick.

The whole legend was probably hokum, but Curnow was troubled by the fact that a fair few respected locals were happy to recall unusual phenomenon they'd witnessed. Mrs Mordent from the haberdashers was a case in point, and she'd never tire of informing those who asked about the occasion years ago when she saw the Devil and Witchfinder Crabbings playing what appeared to be *leapfrog* in her garden. Then there was the local carpenter who was awoken by strange sounds downstairs. When he investigated, he discovered the Devil and Crabbings swaying suggestively on top of one another in the rocking chair he'd recently constructed.

Curnow's experience in Tadwick was the rock bottom moment that finally told him to get his act together, but he realised that his own success story was the exception to the rule. Too many locals refused to leave their house after dark, and he'd never forgive himself if the youngsters were to receive more than they bargained for.

***

It was hard to make out any noise above the wind and rain, but Ally Lee thought he registered the sound of distant wailing.

Aborted Mission

"Fuckin' 'ell, can you 'ear what I'm 'earin'?!"

Ronan Rhodes nodded as the blood drained from his face. The boys were statues for several seconds, which was long enough for them to note that the incoherent wailing was coming from the direction of Tadwick.

"Fuckin' great!" shouted Lee sarcastically as he again read the threatening epitaph on Chatterton's grave.

The troubling noise was getting nearer, and the pair finally broke free of their dithering. They scrambled toward the graveyard gate, and just before reaching it, Rhodes lost his footing on the saturated ground and struck the sharp corner of a slanted headstone with a shin.

Ally Lee decided to open the gate before attending to his injured pal, and Rhodes continued moaning in pain as Lee pushed and pulled at the gate with growing frustration.

"THE FUCKIN' THING WON'T BUDGE!"

Finally realising how much pain his friend was in, Lee crouched down to cajole Rhodes into regaining his feet.

The approaching wailing was now interspersed with angry but indecipherable shouting.

The fright felt by Rhodes was enough motivation to get up and ignore his pain. Ally Lee abandoned further attempts to open the gate and put his arm around Rhodes' shoulder to help him hobble back toward the church.

The wailing and cursing became deafening as Lee again shouldered into the heavy door. This time it gave way with such ease, he went sprawling flat on his front along the stone floor of the church's interior.

"GET INSIDE, YOU PRICK. NOW!!"

With a moan of pain, Rhodes limped through the door, and Lee got up to slam it shut with his back. The dreadful weather brought about an early twilight, and the boys could see little inside the church.

"Right, let's get under one of them benches." whispered Lee as the sounds outside came to an abrupt halt.

The teenagers rolled under the pew they were nearest to, where they remained in frightened silence for several minutes.

"This is the last fuckin' time I go anywhere with you, ya clumsy cunt." Lee whispered.

"Well 'ow the fuck did I know we'd hear the ghost of a spazzer?" Rhodes protested as the pain in his leg began to fade.

A few more minutes of silence went by before both boys heard whistling that consisted of two notes continuously repeated.

"What the fuck's goin' on now?"

For the next few minutes, the teenagers could clearly hear the volume of the whistling rising and falling, as if whoever was producing it was completing slow circuits around the church. The two alternating notes made an unpleasant and grating sound that heightened the boys' fear, and as the whistling returned to full intensity for the third time, it stopped.

Lee and Rhodes were lying on their stomachs as they stared at the door side wall of the church. Both viewed the slow developing of an image cast from the opposite window, and a head and shoulders silhouette with its head tilted severely to the left came into focus.

"Oh shit my spats, it fuckin' IS Chatterton!"

As soon as Rhodes finished his jittery whisper, he began to blubber, which triggered his friend into following suit.

The head of the black silhouette began to swing like a pendulum, before gradually becoming fainter and vanishing. The boys stared at each other through reddened eyes.

"What the fuck're we gonna do?" Rhodes finally asked after several seconds of silence.

"We've just gotta stay 'ere 'til he's gone."

"How're we gonna know he's gone?"

"How the fuck should I know when a ghost's fucked off, ya bell end."

The boys remained led in silence underneath the pew for almost half an hour, in which time nightfall had arrived to fill the church with total blackness.

Ally Lee decided enough was enough and rolled out from under the pew.

"I'm gettin' fucked off with this!"

Ronan Rhodes was a little more apprehensive but agreed that it was time to make an exit.

"Nothin's happened for ages now..." Lee began. "c'mon, let's get out."

Although both were still frightened, time had recharged their levels of rationality, and each began to wonder whether the joint and their expectations had conspired to produce a Curnow style hallucination.

"Remember what Baz said last night...?" muttered Rhodes with a slightly more courageous volume. "The stuff we've been smokin' is the wildest gear 'ee's ever 'ad!"

In a stoned flashback to their state of about an hour previously, both boys laughed.

"Not only that..." a progressively more confident Lee went on. "Curnow also said that Dick Joy's the maddest bloke in the village an' always scarin' the shit out of everyone."

Both boys giggled as they played blind man's buff to get to the church door. Just as Lee's scrabbling right hand located its large brass ring, the church was violently rattled by a huge crash on its roof.

Lee and Rhodes scampered back to their original hiding place in a fresh state of terror, and a few seconds later, they both heard the muffled crackling of an irate voice.

A rhythmic thumping began on the roof that sounded to the boys like the stamping feet of a jumping man. Both put their hands over their ears to try and block out the deafening sounds, and the lumpy stone floor of the church began to tremble. They removed their hands as soon as they realised it made no difference, and both blubbed more heartily as the crazed anger in the crackling and fizzing voice upped even more.

The trembling beneath Lee and Rhodes halted after a few moments, and everything went silent.

Lee got up from the floor and screamed at the unseen entity that he assumed produced the noise above them.

"WHY DON'T YOU JUST FUCK OFF, YA MAD FUCKWIT?"

To the relief of both youngsters, Lee's desperate outburst was followed by nothing other than continuing silence.

"Look..." Lee addressed his friend as he rolled out from under the pew for the second time, "so we've seen the fuckin' ghost of Chatterton, but we can't stay here the whole fuckin' night!"

Rhodes was also fright wearied and agreed that they had to be brave and make an exit whatever they might see.

"Yeah, yer right. I'm not 'anging around waitin' for him to appear. D'ya remember what Baz said 'e looked like?"

"Too fuckin' right, mate..." answered Lee. "Six foot seven, built like a brick shithouse, and 'is face smashed to fuckery!"

The boys were filled with fresh urgency as Lee again located the church door's brass ring. As he began to turn it, a shaft of light flooded the pew they'd just removed themselves from. The light was coming through the window adjoining the door, and both youngsters silently froze. After a few seconds, they took a few backward paces as solid footsteps approached from outside. Lee and Rhodes clung to each other in fear of whatever it was that was attempting to enter the church.

A heavy creaking accompanied the slow opening of the huge door, and the boys were momentarily blinded by a pure white dazzle.

"I take it you didn't quite manage to make it to Tadwick?" uttered a smiling Graham Curnow as he shifted the torchlight toward the church floor.

8

GREETINGS FROM TENNESSEE

Barry Loadall looked up at the *Hair Bear Bunch* clock on the wall and saw the time approaching nine-forty. Apart from Curnow's midday visit and attending to an early evening customer, he spent the day alone. He took advantage of the brief afternoon break in the weather to pop down the convenience store and stock up on pastries and confectionery. Loadall's attempt at offsetting the dietary drawback of this type of refuelling was a fridge permanently stocked with several varieties of vegetable juice.

After simultaneously sucking two rubber tubes from two bongs, Loadall suffered a coughing fit that forced a reluctant visit to the lavatory. After getting on all fours to properly rid his lungs of their freshly produced waste, he sat back down after a detour to the kitchen to soothe his chest with a beaker of pressed radish.

Loadall pondered his heritage, and although being born into wealth and privilege, wasn't at all sorry when he was ostracised by the family. He knew what his calling was, and it certainly wasn't pheasant shooting or berating the butler. Being generously bankrolled into keeping his mouth shut about his blue blood underlined his complete lack of regret. Dear Aunt Minerva was the only close relative who stood by him, and he continued to receive regular visits from her. Three decades on, her gift of the clock on the wall was still going strong. Also recalled was her gift of the Zorro slippers; twenty years old, but still as comfortable as ever. Despite being treated as never having grown beyond childhood, Loadall was enormously fond of Minerva, and proud of the austere and chaste life she'd led.

Loadall was jolted out of his thoughts by a loud rapping at the front door.

"Sir, I hope you will excuse me for imposing myself on you on such a dirty night."

The bleary-eyed host was surprised by the man's American accent and enquired upon his business.

"Myself and a group 'o friends are visitin' yer beautiful country to pay tribute to the great Thomas Crabbings, and we heard from the bartender in the pub that you know everythin' ya could about this here village."

"Well, well, well," Loadall responded. "I was quite unaware that Larkhall had achieved such fame across the pond."

"Hell yeah! Ma dear ol' paw – Lord rest his good soul, told me all about it after bein' stationed near these parts durin' the war."

"I see. Well in that case, please step inside and away from the gaze of the Devil."

"Sir, I thank you for yer real warm courtesy."

After a swift and vigorous salute, the tourist stepped inside.

"What the hell is that smell?"

"Oh, I'm growing some exotic and rather perfumed flora." answered a casual Loadall as he moved the bongs to behind his armchair.

"...May I enquire as to how much you know about the history of our village?"

"Sir, you are very welcome to do so. Me and my colleagues are good God fearing folk who're in search for the truth about Solsbury moun'ain."

"And where are your colleagues now?"

"Why, they made their way back to the guest house along the ol' highway."

"And what do you know about the medieval flirtations between Crabbings and Satan?"

Loadall followed the question by resting his long chin on joined hands.

"From what was passed down to me from ma paw, the Devil and Wyvern came to the village to spread mischief 'n evil. The local guys got theirselves the best witchfinder they could buy to kick 'em outta town, and in the name o' the Lord, that's just what he did on top o' the moun'ain."

Loadall remained silent for a few seconds before giving his response.

"I'm sorry to disappoint you, but I'm afraid that the story adhered to around these parts is that Mr Crabbings lost the battle, and that the stone pillar of Solsbury Hill is his remains after being slain by the very Devil itself."

"So those guys we saw throwin' bad fruit at the stone pillar were fer sher Devil worshippers?"

"I am most sorry to compound your misery, but yes, most certainly. Desecrating the pillar is an anti-Crabbings custom that predates us by several generations."

"...I must state however," continued Loadall, "that anti-Crabbings pilgrims travel to Solsbury Hill from the furthest corners of the kingdom, and that their views do not necessarily reflect those held locally."

Loadall's guest shook his head in bewilderment.

"Well how d'ya like that? I just can't make it all out. As sure as the Lord is ma witness, our world is bein' ravaged by a foolin' an' a meddlin' Satan."

"If I may play devil's advocate for a moment," began Loadall after a brief coughing fit.

"...I'm not so sure that Satan is quite the villain he's been so vehemently portrayed as throughout history."

The American guest stood-up to point accusingly at Loadall.

"WHY, YA GOOD FOR NOTHIN' LOVER OF ALL THINGS HORRIBLE 'N UNWHOLESOME!"

"Please, please, please..." responded the host calmly. "I'm not saying that to insinuate that your own chosen deity isn't worthy, it's just that many in this village claim to have encountered Satan, and some say his negative public persona is wildly off the mark."

"AH JUST CAN'T PUT UP WI' NO MORE OF THIS BULLSHIT! YOUS GONNA BE SENTENCED TO ONE GODDAMN DEEP FRIED ASS ON JUDGEMENT DAY!"

The guest kept his finger on Loadall until he finished his tirade, and then made his way toward the door.

Loadall stood up as quickly as his sunken armchair allowed.

"WHEN YOU OPEN THE FRONT DOOR, YOU WILL BE CONFRONTED BY A SIX-FOOT-SEVEN-INCH GHOST WITH A POOR EXCUSE FOR A FACE."

The American froze in reaction to Loadall's sudden shouting. He stood still for a moment before eventually turning around.

"Hell, did I hear you right, sir?"

"That depends on what you think you heard." Loadall unhelpfully replied as he returned to his usual docile self.

"...May I politely ask you to resume your seat?"

Loadall accompanied his request with an inviting arm.

The guest complied and returned to the armchair with a face even redder than before.

"Thank you."

"...The people of this village go about their business in a friendly and harmless way. However, if people choose to interfere with the genuine and deeply held beliefs of a few locals, then Satan really can become unpleasant; perhaps as much as his fiercest critics believe.

"Over forty years ago, a mentally retarded man was nonchalantly going around the village being vocal in his support for Thomas Crabbings. Although he was backward, he had enough sense to know better.

"The final straw for many was when he spent several days riding his bicycle through Larkhall using a megaphone to extol Crabbings' virtues. Many people warned him that he was asking for a judgement, but he just laughed it off in true simpleton style.

"The Larkhall Village Festival was taking place around this time, and as part of the celebrations, the beer garden of The Blackest Morn housed a trampoline for the enjoyment of local youngsters. The weather was as foul as it is at present, and while parents and children were celebrating inside the pub, the characteristically stupid Chatterton was seen bouncing with glee while being buffeted about by the wind and rain. At the zenith of each jump, he shouted the witchfinder's name. A few people inside the pub were becoming disturbed as they viewed Chatterton's antics through the window."

The host took a big swallow of radish juice before continuing.

"He then began performing somersaults on the trampoline whilst wailing Crabbings' name even louder. The next thing, Chatterton screamed, and his body gradually bounced to a halt. One of the pub's customers said he saw a missile of some sort clatter into Chatterton's head, and he ran out through the wind and rain to check on his state of health."

Loadall tilted his head to frown at his guest over the top of his round glasses.

"Of course, he was completely soaked through, but that was the kind of attention seeking idiocy he was famed for. When the first aider turned the unconscious Chatterton onto his back, he found that his left eye was tilted upwards so that only half of his pupil and iris was visible. A huge bruise circled the eye, together with fragments of splattered, overripe apple."

"JUST WHAT THE HELL IS GOIN' ON AROUN' THIS CRAZY PLACE?" demanded the American.

Loadall carried on as if his guest was mute and invisible.

"Despite losing the sight of his left eye, the fool continued being a bigmouth for several months after, until he received what many viewed as his comeuppance after breaking into the tin church of Bailbrook Lane.

"If you know what's good for you, you'd best stay put and not cause a commotion; unless, of course, you fancy a dead of night visitation from our resident retarded spectre."

Loadall's living room was wobbled by three loud thumps on the front door. He looked up at the clock and saw that it was ten o'clock sharp.

"One thing I will say for Chatterton, he was always an impeccable timekeeper."

9

THE GUEST HOUSE SIGHTING

"Sir Leonard, I really wish you'd cut your perishing toe nails!"

To economise on their weekend visit, the head of the clan had booked three double rooms to be shared in pairs, and he was beginning to wonder if Hutton was a good choice as his bed mate. After the exhausting trudge to the top of Solsbury Hill, together with the stress caused by Hutton's bird-brained contributions in their dealings with the Americans, Trevor Expectorant wanted nothing more than a good night's kip.

"I do apologise for inadvertently digging them into your calves, wise leader; it's just that I'm sure I saw a ghostly figure on the landing earlier, and it's making me a touch jittery."

Expectorant wearily turned around in the dark to face his disciple.

"Sir Leonard, we are sheltered under the generously circumferenced umbrella of Satan's love, and there's no way He'd desert us and allow such visitations."

"I'm sure you're right, lauded one. Perhaps it's a case of my senses working overtime as a result of today's pilgrimage?"

"Of course they are. Now let's get us some sleep, because we all have to be up at the crack of dawn to begin the working week."

"Before we settle down to again attempt sleep, cherished leader, would you mind if I switched the light on?"

"Oh, if you must." answered a resigned Expectorant as he buried his head face first into a pillow.

"WAH!!"

Within a second of Hutton switching on the bedside light, he switched it off, and snuggled up to his leader while pulling the duvet up to completely cover them both.

"What the blazes has got into you now?"

Expectorant could feel Hutton's body trembling, and as a result jumped out of bed to turn on the main light. The frightened disciple immediately pulled the covers back over his head as his leader stood agitated in his carrot and leek patterned pyjamas.

"Has...has...has it...has it gone now?" asked Hutton in a muffled voice.

"Sir Leonard, you really must pull yourself together!"

"But I saw it looking through the window, lovely leader!"

"Saw what?"

"I saw something staring through the window!"

"What do you mean, something?"

"The head and shoulders of something looking through the window!"

Hutton briefly popped his head out, and despite seeing nothing, quickly re-submerged.

Expectorant was now aware that Hutton was seriously scared. He returned to bed and spoke to his disciple sympathetically.

"Look, Sir Leonard, you have nothing to fear while you have the support of both myself and the Devil. May I remind you of the courage and determination displayed by the great man whom I named you after?"

Expectorant could make out a brief nodding of the head underneath the duvet.

"...A fresh-faced lad of twenty-two walked out to bat against the might of the Bradman inspired Australians at The Oval in 1938. Did this young Yorkshireman shy away from this ultimate examination of his character and technique?"

This time Expectorant detected a shake of the head beneath the duvet.

"...No he didn't. Instead, he treated the sun-kissed crowd to a world-record innings of 364!"

Hutton gradually began to calm down, and his trembling lessened in response to his master's soothing and upbeat words.

"...Not only that, but the legendary man returned after the war with one arm shorter than the other, though it didn't stop him captaining his side to a memorable victory in Australia in 1954-55!"

The disciple now felt relaxed enough to lift his head above the duvet to give thanks.

"Now then..." continued Expectorant, "do you really think the real Sir Leonard Hutton would be so scared if he were in your situation?"

The Guest House Sighting

"Absolutely not...!" declared the reinvigorated follower. "Why, he'd dismiss any spectral visions with the same dismissiveness he showed the Australian bowlers in 1938!"

"Now we're speaking the same language!" beamed a delighted Expectorant.

"...Let's now turn the light out, forget about what you thought you saw, and let us gain a sleep deep enough to make Satan proud!"

Expectorant returned to bed after switching off the light, and with an emphatic tone, offered his disciple more comforting words.

"Even if there was a ghost, you have absolutely nothing to fear while I'm here."

Both men could hear a rustling sound emanating from the corner of the room, followed by a quiet and high-pitched wail. Expectorant and Hutton whimpered as they slowly and tremblingly pulled the duvet over their heads.

***

It was dark by the time Dick Joy turned off the old highway to join Dead Mill Lane. He'd run most of the way back from Upper Swainswick and was spent and saturated. He was troubled by the thought of being confronted with an apparition of the flappy necked Chatterton, and also by the retribution his wife would be dishing-out when he got home.

Joy's house was just behind The Bladud's Midriff, and the pub's illuminated facade became visible as he reached the foot of the lane. He poked his head out from the side of a bush just in case Jemima was stomping about looking for him. The coast was clear, and Joy bounded across the road to bypass the pub.

With a sigh of relief, Joy saw no light in the house. His hope was that the longer it took for his wife to find him, the more chance of her anger being lessened to manageable and non-physical proportions. Before Joy put his key in the lock, he crouched down to peek through the letterbox just in case the outsized silhouette of his wife was lying in wait. He saw nothing and proceeded to turn the key. As quietly as his drunken state allowed, Joy swung the door open and turned on the light. He was confronted by an unusually pristine kitchen, with a handwritten note left on an otherwise empty table. Joy gulped as he picked it up.

You useless drunken prick. When I catch up with you, I'm going to knock you into the middle of next week. I'm in the house somewhere, and I'll jump out on you when you won't expect it. You know I'm too fat to fit under the beds, so at least that's one place you won't have to look.

Dick Joy's worst fears were confirmed as he pulled out the wooden chair directly in front of where the note was left. He noticed a PTO at the bottom together with the possibility of her hiding behind the drawn curtains of either room, they were the likeliest lairs for an ambush.

After turning on the light to the spare bedroom, Joy was relieved to see the floor length curtains undrawn. To provide confirmation, he lifted the defunct fishing rod from the nearest corner and poked each curtain. He drew a blank either side and turned his attention to the wardrobe.

Dick Joy took a deep breath that inspired a minor burp, and quickly pulled both doors open before covering his face with his hands. A few seconds went by before Joy opened his eyes and again used the dusty rod to verify that the wardrobe was unoccupied.

Only the master bedroom remained, and Joy became more confident that Jemima was merely trying to scare the shit out of him. He switched on the light and replicated the search he took of the spare room. The result was again negative, but as Joy stepped back onto the upstairs landing to begin guarded celebrations, he felt a tremendous weight fall on him from above.

After a brief flailing of limbs, Jemima Joy had pinned her husband flat on his back. She quickly straddled his chest and squashed the inside of his elbows with her knees.

"I knew you'd be too much of a drunken cunt to remember the attic."

10

THE TWO BLADUDS

Barry Loadall opened the front door to be confronted with Graham Curnow, flanked by the teenagers who'd visited the previous evening.

"I found this pair of upstarts inside St Crispin's Church in a bit of a state."

"That is excellent news...!" replied Loadall with unusual excitement. "Please do step inside. I'm currently entertaining a trans-Atlantic guest who's asking some rather provocative questions about our locale."

The trio of new visitors entered Loadall's lounge and were given a cold and wary look by the American, who successfully hid his relief that none of the new arrivals were hideous apparitions.

Ally Lee and Ronan Rhodes were pallid and in a state of delayed shock. They were requested to sit either end of the sofa, while Curnow was offered the emergency seating of Loadall's yellow and black striped deckchair.

"SAY, ARE YOU GUYS DEVIL-LOVIN' CRAZIES, TOO?"

Loadall turned to wag a finger at his original visitor.

"Now, I've already warned you about pouring scorn over local beliefs, and you are putting yourself very much in harm's way with your continued militancy and aggressive probing."

Graham Curnow decided to weigh in.

"Come along now gentlemen, we aren't going to get anywhere unless we respect each other's points of view."

Curnow became the definition of diplomacy since beating the bottle, and he turned to the American and smiled courteously.

"I apologise on behalf of Larkhall and our country as a whole for our woeful weather!"

"That's real kind of you, sir. The weather sure wasn't this bad when I came here as a kid."

The ears of both the host and Graham Curnow pricked-up at the revelation, and Loadall was first to question his overseas guest.

"So, you're not a complete stranger to these parts?"

"Hell, no! As I told you before these other guys got here, my paw was stationed near here durin' the war; a place up right real high by the name o' Charmy Down."

"I understand Charmy Down Airfield was only opened for the war, and closed down as soon as it finished?" Graham Curnow enquired.

"You don't need to tell me that, sir. When I was knee high to a southern cicada, paw decided to take me on a vacation to show me where he flew his Mustang. It was many years after the war, and I remember the place bein' empty and full o' weeds. Why, the only thing left was the goddamm control tower, and even that was nothin' but a stone shell!"

"That must've come as a great shock and disappointment to both yourself and your father." sympathised Loadall before he took a sip of courgette juice.

"I don't think paw was too worried about it at all, 'cos he had a local sweetheart durin' wartime. I guess he came back to see if she was still there. Mom died the moment I took my first God given breath, so I'm sure all was levelled with the good Lord."

"Yes, I've no doubt it was!" seconded a smiling Graham Curnow.

"Paw confided in me not so long ago; said this lady sweetheart of his lived somewhere just below Solsbury Moun'ain."

The host's tuneful doorbell chimed.

"Please excuse me, gentlemen."

Barry Loadall opened the door to be greeted by two dishevelled looking men.

"Good evening to you, Mr Loadall."

"And what can I do for you two troubled fellows?"

"Oh dear, is our appearance one of persons failing to disguise their fear from the unpleasantness of the incident that occurred not more than thirty minutes previously?"

"I'm afraid you have both failed quite spectacularly."

"That's because we've just seen a really flippin' scary ghost!" added Sir Leonard Hutton as he half hid behind his leader.

Hutton's head popped out from behind Expectorant's shoulder to add

The Two Bladuds

a postscript.

"...Although it had absolutely nothing to do with any form of Devil worship, which of course both of us would never contemplate."

Despite again being irritated by his disciple's lack of subtlety, Trevor Expectorant nodded in full agreement.

"Would you both like to come inside?"

Instead of following Loadall toward the lounge, Expectorant took a couple of paces back from the doorstep and gazed up at the heavens with a look of wonder.

"My word, Sir Leonard; as sure as Colin Cowdrey and Peter May's astonishing rearguard blunted the potent West Indian bowling-attack at Edgbaston in 1957, there's a UFO hovering right above our humble heads!"

The weather had improved to the extent of leaving a clear and starry night as Hutton craned his neck to look due north in great anticipation. The sky was scanned fruitlessly for several seconds before Expectorant used his middle finger to powerfully flick his disciple's Adam's apple.

"OWWW!"

"If you continue to be so slovenly in the disguisement of our true intentions, then there's plenty more where that came from!"

Expectorant then prodded his bumbling disciple inside.

The two new arrivals were greeted by a lounge full of guests, and Expectorant bade them good evening.

"WHY, YOU DECEITFUL SHINERS OF SATAN'S SLACK 'N HAIRY BUTT-HOLE!"

The American leapt from his seat to confront the pair, before Graham Curnow diffused the situation with more diplomacy.

"Let's not have any hostility, I'm sure these two people would have no intention of applying any type of polishing agent to the tradesman's entrance of Satan."

Curnow looked at Expectorant to seek confirmation.

"Why, absolutely not indeed, good sir!"

Expectorant then turned apologetically to the American, who grudgingly returned to his chair.

"I'm very sorry you feel that way, sir. Our weekend has been filled with innocent and harmless activities such as metal detecting and rigorous bonding sessions for an overseas cricket tour. Worshipping the Devil wouldn't cross our minds in an eternity of thinking."

"Who's the Devil?" asked Hutton while scratching his head quizzically.

"You must excuse my friend..." Expectorant fumed. "Sometimes he requires a little shock therapy."

Expectorant dipped his right hand inside the back of Hutton's trousers, grabbed the top of his underpants, and savagely pulled them in the direction of the ceiling.

Through Hutton's cries of discomfort, Expectorant addressed the room with a face reddening from effort.

"Please don't be alarmed, good people. He's as right as rain once I've dispensed his prescription."

The harsh treatment dealt by Expectorant was enough to snap Ally Lee and Ronan Rhodes out of their state of shock, and both giggled.

"Yes, well..." piped up Curnow as he looked at Expectorant. "I must say that's quite the most unconventional treatment I've ever seen, although I'm in no doubt that you know what you're doing."

Hutton turned toward Curnow as he busily re-arranged himself.

"Yes indeed, he's quite the best doctor I've ever had!"

"Now then..." began Loadall as he eyed the new arrivals. "you mentioned on the doorstep that within the past half hour, you experienced a spectral visitation. Could you enlighten us further?"

Expectorant answered immediately to prevent Hutton getting a word in.

"Well, we were at our guest house changed and ready for bed. I'd gone to the en-suite bathroom to perform my nocturnal ablutions, and suddenly I heard a cry of fear from my friend here, who needless to say was studying the Bible at the time. I rushed out to see what caused the commotion, and, lo and behold, we both saw this quite appalling face staring at us through the window."

"And was the head of this quite appalling apparition tilted at a quite appalling angle?" enquired Loadall.

"Yes, I'm afraid it was." confirmed Expectorant, who then used his index finger to make the shape of a sideways cross on his upper body.

"FUCK ME, THAT'S WHAT WE SAW IN THE CHURCH!" declared Lee, as his friend nodded in enthusiastic agreement.

Despite the strong evidence that Chatterton's ghost was real, the boys felt great excitement rather than fear.

"Which guest house are you currently residing in?" Loadall asked Expectorant.

"The Pilgrims' Playground."

"Ah yes, that place is synonymous with apparitions of Chatterton." Loadall stared at the American.

"And where are you staying, my good man?"

"Why, me an' ma friends are at the Bladud's Head along the ol' highway." Ally Lee looked at Loadall with curiosity.

"How come there's a Bladud's Head and a Bladud's Midriff?"

"Well, a few centuries before the Romans arrived, King Bladud was

The Two Bladuds

alleged to have created the hot springs of nearby Caervaddon through his own magical powers. Bladud was regarded as the local hero, but at some stage he riled the locals, and his execution was ordered by the village elders.

"He was beheaded at the location of where the Bladud's Head guest house is situated. King Bladud's genitals was then severed from his lifeless body and catapulted down the steep hill of where Ferndale Road now stands. The Bladud's Midriff public house is purportedly built on the site of where his genitalia came to rest."

Lee and Rhodes again giggled, before Rhodes turned toward Loadall.

"I still don't understand why it's called The Midriff?"

"Apparently, King Bladud's personal dimensions were so impressive that when he was at his most regal, his length would bisect his entire midriff."

"Besides..." added Graham Curnow. "it would hardly be acceptable to name the pub *Bladud's Cock & Bollocks*."

In contrast to the hilarity displayed by the teenagers, the American put an exasperated head in his hands before looking around the room with bewilderment.

"I DO DECLARE YOU GUYS HAVE ALL GONE KOOKY!"

Without a further word, he got up from the armchair and left the house by slamming the front door behind.

Completely unfazed by the sudden departure, Barry Loadall turned toward Expectorant and Hutton.

"How did you know my name?"

"The landlady of our guest house told us..." Expectorant replied. "She said you're the local expert regarding terrifying apparitions."

"I am most humbled to be held in such high esteem..." answered Loadall as his face creaked into a partial smile. "Perhaps you'd like to sit down in the recently vacated armchair? No doubt our fiery American friend has left it warm and cosy."

Expectorant took the seat, while Hutton sat cross legged at his master's feet.

Graham Curnow glanced at the clock on the wall.

"My word, is that the time?"

"Yes, it is." the host responded stone faced.

Curnow glanced over to Lee and Rhodes.

"I think it's about time I got you two whippersnappers back home safely."

"Yes, I think it is."

Trevor Expectorant decided that it was also time for him and his disciple to leave.

"We have to be up first thing in the morning, so I think it's time we were also on our way."

57

"Yes, I think it is; and I'm very pleased to hear that neither of you subscribe to worshipping the Devil..." Loadall added. "because that's the one thing that truly angers the quite appalling apparition you witnessed."

11

THE AUGMENTED-FOURTHS

"Now then, who can tell me what I mean by the word *pitch*?"

Jeremy Bennett-Brewer folded his arms and leant them on the desk to await an answer. After a few seconds, a hand slowly raised from the back of the class.

"Sir, I'm afraid I'm unable to tell you what you mean by the word *pitch*."

"Thank you for that erudite interjection, McCaulder, one that typifies your boundless enthusiasm and thirst for the subject."

A month after starting at the school, the teacher decided that constantly getting agitated with this acne ridden adolescent would lead to nothing more positive than raising his own blood pressure, and that laid back sarcasm was more therapeutic.

"*Pitch* is the word we use to describe how high or low a musical note is, and the difference of pitch between notes is what's known as an *interval*."

Bennett-Brewer strode across to the piano and repeated the notes of C and C sharp several times.

"Now, this is what we call an alternating minor-second interval; an interval of pitch so ghastly and filled with menace that one can only anticipate doom."

"Sir?"

Bennett-Brewer took an elongated blink of wariness to prepare for whatever silly question McCaulder decided to throw at him.

"Isn't the augmented-fourth an even more ghastly interval?"

The teacher's face lightened with both delight and a touch of shock at the musical knowledge shown by his most troublesome pupil.

"Well, well, McCaulder. I honestly never thought that a scallywag such as your good self would be such an authority on these matters!"

McCaulder reacted by flamboyantly straightening his tie and giving his classmates a look of exaggerated pomposity.

"I jolly well think this chap deserves a round of applause."

The star pupil stood to gleefully acknowledge the class.

As the clapping died down, Bennett-Brewer played the notes of F and B one after the other, and then crunched the two notes together.

"Goodness me, did one ever hear such a foul and devilish interval?"

"One should jolly well say not!" answered McCaulder to mimic his teacher.

Mr Bennett-Brewer joined in with the class mirth at McCaulder's cheeky reply, before he explained the significance of the augmented-fourth.

"In less enlightened times, composers could be imprisoned for using this unpleasant interval, and I for one find it most discomfiting. This hideous tritone became known as *diabolus in musica* – 'the devil in music.'"

For the first time since taking up his new teaching position, Bennett-Brewer sensed that the whole class was becoming interested in what he was saying. This sudden fascination, coupled with the unlikely musical knowledge shown by Marcus McCaulder left the teacher feeling uneasy. He made a mental note of asking McCaulder to stay behind at the end of the lesson.

"You shall now hear an excerpt from Liszt's Dante Symphony as an example of how composers deliberately used the augmented-fourth interval to evoke a devilish mood.

"As this piece attempts to paint a picture of a journey through hell and purgatory, full use is made of unpleasant melodies and naughty harmonies, rising and falling semitones, minor-sixths, and of course, our old diabolical chum, the augmented-fourth."

Bennett-Brewer pressed the play button on his ancient but faithful cassette recorder, and the first movement of the symphony whirred into action. The teacher sat on the edge of his desk and scrutinized the class as the dissonant music unfolded.

Bennett-Brewer was both pleased and disturbed to see the looks of concentration and fascination on every pupil's face. Even Bobby Stainrod, the gangly class bumpkin, swapped his usual empty-headed look for one of wonder.

About two minutes into the symphony, the teacher turned his head to see light drizzle clinging to the windows. One of the perks of teaching in this classroom was having an unfettered view of Solsbury Hill, and even amid the direst weather of the past month, the famous landmark was always clearly visible.

As a foreboding descent of strings marked a particularly unpleasant section of the symphony's first movement, Bennett-Brewer turned back to the class and saw Bobby Stainrod slump forward on his desk to rest his head against his arms. The teacher made eye contact with Stainrod's desk mate and received assurance through expression that Stainrod was okay.

Bennett-Brewer again looked outside and saw Solsbury Hill become noticeably less visible through the low cloud that had now swamped the valley. The apologetic drizzle had suddenly become a sheeting horizontal torrent, and as the teacher again returned his gaze to the class, Bobby Stainrod sprang up from his desk and ran from the classroom. Despite Stainrod's famed lack of coordination, the class was shocked to see him veer left and right as he made his journey from the back row. As the classroom door was slammed shut, Bennett-Brewer hurriedly switched off the cassette recorder and leapt from his desk. He pointed at the single pupil in the room who'd attained the status of school prefect.

"LANGRIDGE, YOU'RE IN CHARGE."

Bennett-Brewer left the class behind to begin the search for the troubled boy.

In the absence of the teacher, the whole class including the prefect shot from their desks and jostled for places against the rain battered windows.

Several minutes and several fruitless enquiries with staff later, Bennett-Brewer returned to the classroom resigned to the probability that Bobby Stainrod had absconded from the school.

"BACK TO YOUR DESKS. NOW!"

It was the first time in his decade long teaching career that Bennett-Brewer had displayed anger toward his pupils, who took no notice and continued to stare through the windows.

"I SAID, GET BACK TO YOUR DESKS!"

After a pause of a few seconds, the children grudgingly returned to their seats, with several giving their teacher stony glares.

Bennett-Brewer glanced at the classroom clock and saw that a minute of the school day remained.

"RIGHT...THE LOT OF YOU, GET OUT OF MY SIGHT!"

The teacher again surprised himself at his bad temper and took a moment to compose himself. He noted that the exiting pupils wore sullen looks; all except the class comedian bringing up the rear.

"McCaulder...can you stay behind for a moment, please?"

The rain was easing, but the gloom continued to thicken, and Bennett-

Brewer was startled enough to jump when he looked outside to see that Solsbury Hill had vanished. Apart from the immediate vicinity of the school grounds, the only building around the Larkhall valley visible to the teacher was St Swithin's church, and of that, only the four tower turrets and flagless flagpole penetrated the bleakness. Bennett-Brewer stared at the peculiar vision for a few seconds, and that was long enough to view the remains of the church fade to nothing. Just before vanishing, the teacher could make out the top half of a figure stood behind the tower parapet.

"What a ghastly day, sir!"

The short space of time it took to witness the church being swallowed left Bennett-Brewer in daydreaming mode, and he jumped again when Marcus McCaulder snapped him out of it.

"Yes indeed, Marcus. I think we can jolly-well wave goodbye to the cricket match against King Bladud's school this evening."

"What do you want to see me about, sir?"

"Well, first of all, can you shed any light on why Bobby Stainrod suddenly ran from the class?"

"I'm not sure, sir. I remember him running out of the class a few times when our old teacher was 'ere. Always seems to do it when the weather gets bad."

"Do you think he was upset by the music?"

The teacher stared anxiously at McCaulder as he unplugged the cassette recorder.

"Yeah, that and the weather. Stainrod was in a special school before he came here, and they reckon he went a bit mad a few years ago."

"And who exactly are *they*?"

"Everyone in Larkhall."

"I see. It's not a term I like to use, but do you have any idea why Stainrod went a bit mad?"

"He lives up by the tin church on Bailbrook Lane, and they reckon the church is haunted."

"Haunted by what, exactly?"

"I dunno. Me dad says the church has been locked for years. My dad knew Stainrod's dad, and he reckons Stainrod's dad tried to break in with a few mates when they were kids. My dad says all the kids who were there went a bit mad after that."

"Yes, well I'm sure there's a rational explanation for all of it, and that Bobby will be fine." answered Bennett-Brewer with little conviction.

"...McCaulder; the main reason I asked you to stay behind was because I found the musical acumen you displayed earlier rather odd."

McCaulder smirked mischievously before the teacher elaborated.

The Augmented-Fourths

"...And the reason I found it rather odd is because in the music theory test last week you answered just three questions out of twenty correctly. For someone who memorably answered the question 'How many beats is a semibreve worth?' with 'Half as many as a breve, whatever that is,' I'm a bit surprised that you should know so much about intervals."

The teacher wound the electrical lead around his cassette recorder in preparation for going home.

"Not that surprising, sir, lots of people round here know the augmented-fourth is the interval of the notes whistled by the Larkhall Simpleton."

Jeremy Bennett-Brewer's ancient but faithful cassette recorder crashed to the floor and broke into several pieces.

12

THE FEATHER-RUFFLING CLERGYMAN

The Rector of St Swithin's knelt in front of the altar and offered his troubled private thoughts to The Almighty.

Victor Carping had taken up his current role the previous autumn; head-hunted specifically for the task of reversing the year-on-year dwindling numbers of Larkhallians requiring spiritual replenishment of the more traditional kind.

Carping had been a rousing success at his previous placement in the sleepy Wiltshire village of Wombwell Derriads, and was seen by many as a high flyer destined for the top of the ecclesiastical tree. Carping knew that the Church had to move with the times, and was aware that modern society was turned off by threats of eternal damnation and perpetually scorched nether regions. Of course, the ancient fuddy-duddies were aghast at Carping's modern methods of recruitment, but his view was one of if you stand still, you move backwards, and are soon out of business.

The young Reverend became the talk of West Wiltshire. Turning up for services on rollerblades and juggling pickled eggs while delivering sermons were just two examples of his novel attempts at wooing the locals. Soon, the houses of Wombwell Derriads were emptied for every Sunday Service and Evensong. People travelled from as far afield as Hampshire and Dorset to view the performances of the man billed as 'The Rollerbladin' Rev,' and

The Feather-Ruffling Clergyman

even the crusty old theologians had to concede defeat against the irrefutable evidence of massively swelled congregations.

Even so, Carping was still very much a polarising figure within the Church, and hot-headed disagreements between conservative and liberal bishops of various diocese were known to spill over into fist fights and Chinese burns. Although many traditionalists were won over by the sheer numbers pulled in by Carping, for others, there had to be a limit on moving with the times, and resignations followed when the radical reverend produced his thesis, *The Devil: Is He Actually Quite Nice?*

Though he accepted that the title of his dissertation was deliberately provocative, Carping's point was that while certain human behaviours such as excessive drinking, gambling and fornication have been seen through the ages as trademarks of devilishness, was it really that harmful provided the participants weren't harming others? For Carping, any kind of love was alright, and so long as all involved were willing and able, then all was fine and dandy. His assertion that God is sympathetic toward anybody who tries to treat others nicely curried much favour with the villagers of Wombwell. Carping also went on to explain that it was his belief that nothing got The Almighty's goat more than acts of wickedness being carried out in His or Her or Its name.

When accused of gimmickry with his pickled egg routine while sermonizing, Carping claimed that it was a physical analogy explaining how hard it was to juggle life's responsibilities while trying to retain goodness. Eggs were a symbol of new life, and it was down to each person to decide how the pickling process of life experience and circumstance would shape them. Performing the sermons on rollerblades was his way of further emphasising the balancing act required to achieve and maintain righteousness.

Although this explanation was enough for some of the old schoolers to cut Carping some slack, they were soon goaded when his response to a parishioner's question made the front page of the local paper. *PULL THE OTHER ONE!* screamed the headline; which was the alleged reply of the reverend when being asked about the feeding of the five thousand. Carping contended that making so few loaves and fish go such a long way would've been a logistical nightmare that should be treated with caution, and perhaps a pinch of salt.

No matter how much revulsion Victor Carping inspired from his hard-line colleagues, even they had to grudgingly admit that he had huge powers of persuasion. After confronting the author of the sensational article, the journalist humbly acknowledged that his headline misquoted Carping, and the ambitious young hack willingly volunteered to let parishioners pelt him with pickled eggs as a penance.

Victor Carping's physical dexterity and coordination wasn't limited to juggling pickled eggs; he excelled at several sports during his school and university days. He was a good enough footballer to have been offered apprentice forms to sign at AFC Devizes-Mendes, and as a cricketer, was a hard-hitting batsman who still held the school record for most runs scored in a season. He earned scratch golfer status aged fifteen, and on one particular school sports day, threw his javelin so far that it went way beyond the field and almost impaled the school chaplain. In recent times, this incident was used by Carping's most vocal detractors as evidence of his anti-Christian leanings, and some went as far as to allege that he'd formed a fruitful relationship with the Devil.

Things were going well for Carping, and one of the great joys of his St Swithin's placement was experiencing the rich views of the surrounding hills and valleys offered from the tower. Gorgeous vistas were few and far between over recent weeks, and even if the rain and mists were regular spoilers, the fresh air always did him the world of good. Clambering up the iron steps of the spiral staircase was exercise enough, and the dividend received by his lungs on reaching the top of the tower always boosted his soul. As his meeting with the old dears from the Larkhall Jams, Marmalades & Preserves Society was still an hour distant, he decided on another visit to the tower.

Victor Carping took a deep breath before hitching up his cassock and leisurely ascending the fifty-odd rungs to the top of the tower. On arrival, he poked his head above the parapet and scanned the hills and valleys of Larkhall and its surrounds. He looked to the north and saw a bright blue sky dotted with fluffy white clouds. *This is a bit more like it!* Carping whispered to himself as he exaggeratedly filled his lungs and rubbed his hands. Turning to the south, his feeling of rejuvenation was nipped in the bud by seeing a monstrous blanket of cloud swirling over and slowly enveloping the elevated woodland of Bathampton Down. The television transmitter on top of the Down was quickly eaten up by the meteorological bruise of black, mauve and creamy yellow.

The Rector's upbeat mood was replaced by one of trepidation, and within seconds, the top half of Bathampton Down had disappeared, with the cut-off point a near perfect horizontal line. In a few moments, St Swithin's church, the Sun, and the whole of the Larkhall valley was swallowed, and the thick cloud continued to smother the northern hills of the village. Carping could make out nothing apart from the odd light peering through the gloom from the secondary school classrooms halfway up the nearest hill.

For a minute or so, light drizzle fell upon the tower before the heavens burst spectacularly, and the young cleric was drenched within seconds. Enough was enough, and Carping decided to make a hasty descent. Much to

The Feather-Ruffling Clergyman

his displeasure, the Rector felt a numbness in his entire lower half that prevented his legs from working. The light breeze blowing from the southwest suddenly became a horizontal gale, and Carping's plentiful and formerly well-groomed hair was violently pulling at his scalp in the north easterly direction of the school.

Above the dreadful noise of the howling gale and hammering rain, Carping heard two alternating notes which seemed to emanate from inside his skull. The notes were horribly dissonant and rose in volume and vibration until the spooked clergyman felt his head would burst. Clamping his hands as forcibly as he could against his ears in a futile attempt at gaining relief, Carping's eyes registered a strange vision of haze emanating upwards from the school building a few hundred yards distant. The Rector started to tremble as the haze began to form into the shape of human head and shoulders. The head began to tilt to the left, where it stayed for a few seconds, before swinging metronomically left and right. Carping let out a silent shriek in response to the alarming vision, and before he could close his mouth, it vanished. Within a few moments, the wind eased, and the sky cleared. Carping took his hands away from his ears and made his way unsurely down the staircase.

13

MISHAP IN SYDNEY GARDENS

Dave Rensenbrink opened the doors to his free house at five o'clock Monday evening. The weekend had been fairly fruitful with the American tourists and Devil worshippers stopping by, but weekdays were still quiet, and the landlord decided that from now on the pub wouldn't open until early evening. Apart from the odd local tradesman popping in for a lunchtime pint, weekday afternoons were as good as write offs. Besides, the permanent Monday residence of Dick Joy didn't begin until shortly after five.

Shortly after five, Dick Joy shouldered the door open to become that evening's first customer. He sported multi coloured black eyes.

"Bloody hell, mate, how the fuck did ya manage to get those bastards?"

"Evenin', Dave. Oh, it's that bloody bike o' mine. I was comin' down the hill, then I had to screech the brakes on 'cos some soddin' mother duck an' fuckin' ducklins were crossin' the road, and I went flyin' over the handlebars an' hit me head against the bastard railings above the brook."

"Sounds nasty. Yer missus said she was gonna give you a right clobberin' when she came in yesterday, so glad the real reason is very believable."

The landlord's reply was totally deadpan, and Joy couldn't detect his sarcasm.

"That's right, Dave, she's all piss and wind. You'd 'ave to send a rocket up to get to the far side of 'er mouth, but when it comes down to it, she wouldn't dare lay a finger on me. And as for that bloody gurt arse of 'ers, each 'alf' has a different fuckin' postcode!"

Mishap In Sydney Gardens

Rensenbrink was pleased to see another customer walk through the door.

"Ah, it's the music man from down our way!"

"Double vodka with ice and undiluted orange squash."

The landlord noticed Jeremy Bennett-Brewer looked agitated, and it wasn't like him to do away with the pleasantries.

"You alright, me old mate?"

"No, I'm not bloody alright, mine host!"

Bennett-Brewer continued his sudden lack of cordiality by slamming a five-pound note on the counter.

Rensenbrink served the vodka and gave the teacher his change.

"Christ, yer shakin' like a shittin' dog!"

Bennett-Brewer took a sip of his drink with a trembling hand before he spoke.

"I've never taught a lesson before where the class was so enraptured."

"Well, that's pretty bloody good, innit?" questioned Dick Joy, as he neared the end of that day's debut pint.

"No, it isn't pretty bloody good." answered Bennett-Brewer with uncharacteristic snappiness.

The teacher was so ruffled, he didn't notice Joy's black eyes.

"...Last lesson of the day, I was talking about musical dissonance."

Dave Rensenbrink raised his eyebrows as a gesture to prod his customer into explaining what he meant in simpler terms.

"Musical dissonance is music that's not very tuneful and usually designed to put the wind up one's clappers. Anyway, I was playing the class a very dissonant piece of music, and they all became strangely intrigued. Usually when I play them any music, they're messing about chattering or playing slapsies, but I was most unnerved by how interested they became."

"If it stopped 'em pissin' around, you should be celebrating!"

"Normally I would be, but this music was pretty ghastly."

The teacher stared at Joy and Rensenbrink in turn.

"...Do you two know the boy Bobby Stainrod?"

Dick Joy responded slurrily before tackling his second pint.

"Yeah, I knew his dad. Steve Stainrod was Chatterton's best mate."

Jeremy Bennett-Brewer drained his glass before offering it to the landlord.

"Do the honours, mine host."

***

Victor Carping had calmed down a little as he stepped off the final rung of the spiral staircase. About thirty minutes later, and after he changed into fresh attire, he walked toward the church's main door, where he was greeted by old Mrs Mordent from the haberdashery shop.

"Good afternoon, Rector."

"And a good afternoon to you, Mrs Mordent."

"Why, Rector, are you feeling a bit under the weather? I must say, you do look a little bit at sixes and sevens."

"I've just had a bit of a long day, Mrs Mordent. I'm afraid I got caught up in that most unpleasant little storm we had earlier. I took such a drenching, I had to change my cassock and under-vitals!"

"Oh, you do make me laugh, Rector! You get the whole church smiling, and I'll bet you're making all the young ladies go weak at the knees!"

"I do my best, Mrs Mordent!"

The pair were joined by Mrs Tanning, a widow of forty years.

"Mrs Tanning...!" The Rector beamed. "I do so trust that you will be wooing Larkhall with your mouth watering preserves?"

"I should coco, Rector! I've never known the gooseberries to be so sweet and tender this time of year!"

"Well, perhaps there are some things that welcome the horrid weather of our rather disappointing and dispiriting spring!"

Victor Carping led the old ladies toward the catering annexe near the north transept of the church.

"I must say, Mrs Tanning..." began the Rector. "it does fill the heart with toasty warmth that a lady widowed so many years is so full of life and purpose!"

"Well, we wouldn't have given Hitler such a good clip round the ear if we'd all been sitting about moping and whining, would we?"

"That's right, Mildred!" agreed Mrs Mordent as she poked her walking stick forcefully through the air.

"He was king of the allotments, was my Jack..." Mrs Tanning continued. "Beetroot, swede, tomatoes, potatoes, and nobody in the whole of Somerset grew broccoli that flowered like my Jack's."

"He sounded very much like the outdoor type, Mrs Tanning, and we all know how growing our own vegetables helped keep Mr Hitler away!"

"Oh yes, my Jack wouldn't've allowed that troublemaker anywhere near his fruit and veg."

Mrs Tanning's smile turned into a frown.

"...Just a pity my old Jack couldn't keep the weather away, an' all. One day, he went up the allotment to prune the broccoli, and his friend on the next patch reckoned he never saw our Jack look so proud. They flowered so well that year, and our Jack asked his friend to have a look. 'You're the broccoli king of Larkhall, Mr Tanning, let me shake you by the hand!' his friend said. 'My sprouting broccoli is for all of Larkhall to share!' my Jack responded. Anyway, soon as he said it, the weather turned bad and the wind started whipping up. Jack's empty seeding-bucket was lying nearby, and a huge gust came out of nowhere so-said his friend. The bucket flew up and knocked our Jack on the back of the head. He fell forward and was stone-dead with his face in the broccoli."

"I'm terribly sorry to hear about your Jack's tragic accident." replied Victor Carping as he laid a hand on the widow's shoulder.

"I'M NOT SORRY!" snapped Mrs Tanning with an energy that defied her years, while the Rector removed his hand as if he'd received an electric shock.

"...That old bastard never had any time for me, and it served him right. He was a proper miserable old sod."

The broad-minded Rector felt uncharacteristically embarrassed, and went a bit red.

"...I was glad to be rid of the cantankerous old so and so. He wasn't much between the sheets either; I didn't get seen-to once the last ten years he was alive. The only things he cared about was getting the right soil for his radishes, or when he was going to force his perishing rhubarb!"

Victor Carping was both mightily shocked and tickled by Mrs Tanning's explicit revelation and had to cover his mouth with the sleeve of his cassock to smother a giggle.

"...On top of that, I never liked my Jack since he became too friendly with that village idiot what killed himself."

***

Dick Joy was seeing double by the time he finished his sixth pint.

"I reckon that should do ya, young Dick. Best get yerself on home, lad."

"Aaaah, shut yer cakehole, yer gurt fat cunt."

"Look, you best get goin', you silly sod. An' make sure you don't get any more black eyes that *weren't* caused by yer missus."

Dick Joy got up from his stool and stood to face the landlord on wavering legs in the posture of a drunken gunslinger.

"You mark my words..."

Joy used a stabbing finger for each word before falling silent. He went to sit down again, but crashed to the floor and was spread-eagled on his back.

The landlord waddled through the bar hatch and invited Bennett-Brewer to help him get Joy to his feet.

"Grab 'old of 'is arm, and we'll drag him to the back room."

Amid incomprehensible mumblings and tips of shoes scraping across the parquet flooring, Joy was deposited in an old armchair beside the dozing Clive. Within seconds, dog and human were united in peaceful sleep.

Returning to the bar, the publican and teacher were confronted by the sight of the Rector from St Swithin's church.

"If it's not the Rector Carping..." Rensenbrink remarked with surprise. "What brings you to our humble alehouse?"

"I've had quite a something of a day, I don't mind telling you. Please furnish me with a schooner of sweet sherry, good sir."

Jeremy Bennett-Brewer resumed his seat next to the standing Rector.

"Are your flock giving you a bit of aggro, Vic?" asked the landlord.

"You could say that Dave. Not intentional on their behalves, I'm sure, but I've just been chairing a meeting with the old jam and marmalade making ladies in the church."

"Well, that'll explain you wanting a sweet sherry. You better watch it before you start knittin' pullovers and reekin' of cat piss."

The Rector's return smile was a little forced as he began to detail host and fellow customer of the day's events.

"I climbed the steps to the church tower earlier, and while I was up there, I've never seen the weather change so abruptly."

"Was this about half past three?" asked Bennett-Brewer.

"Yes indeed."

"I'm pleased to hear it, I thought I was seeing things when I saw someone standing up there from the classroom window. When the weather suddenly turned, the church tower was the only thing I could see, and even that vanished a few seconds after."

"That's funny..." Carping replied. "When that bad weather came, the only thing I could make out from the tower was the lights from the school classrooms."

Victor Carping asked the landlord to give the music teacher another vodka.

"I may not be your traditional Rector..." Carping began. "I like to think I have a very open mind when it comes to the unknown, but what I saw from the church tower was enough to make your teeth itch."

Jeremy Bennett-Brewer took a grateful sip from his fresh glass as he allowed the Rector to expand.

"...The weather changed in a finger click. When I looked to the south, I saw the most monstrous cloud sweep over Bathampton. I've never seen a sky consisting of such horrid colours, and it soon spread along the valley and over the church. As it made its way north, the whole landscape disappeared; all that was except for the lights of the school shimmering through the gloom.

"I thought I was imagining it to begin with, but above the school build-

Mishap In Sydney Gardens

ing, I saw a silhouette develop."

"Ah, that'll be Chatterton..." the landlord nonchalantly responded. "It was his head and shoulders, with his head swinging from side to side, unless I'm very much mistaken?"

"YES, that's EXACTLY what I saw!" confirmed the Rector.

Dick Joy returned from his brief sleep and staggered down the two steps from the back room to the bar. He was still demonstrably drunk, and swayed a little as he resumed the stool he vacated a few minutes earlier.

"It's ok, Mr Rensenprick..." slurred Joy as he held up a hand of conciliation. "I know my limits, so...I won't touch another fuckin' drop...tonight."

Dick Joy observed the fresh sight of the local Rector dressed in full regalia beside him.

"You off to a fancy dress, you silly cunt?"

The question was offered light heartedly, and publican, teacher and churchman responded with laughter, though Bennett-Brewer's jollity was manufactured in response to the latest hairy revelation involving Chatterton. He turned to face Carping.

"I'd be lying if I said I wasn't extremely perturbed by the vision you just described, Rector. The weather came over all horrible in the blink of an eye, and I was teaching the class about some of the more horrid sounds composers use to evoke nasty moods."

Dick Joy's head slumped forward to rest against his chest while sat upright with arms folded. He began to snore lightly, and the others thought it best to leave him to it. Bennett-Brewer continued to describe the events of earlier.

"I was playing the class a recording of Lizst's Dante Symphony."

Landlord and rector remained silent, and the only noise came from Dick Joy's contented dozing.

"...As the symphony was playing, that boy I was talking about earlier, Stainrod, shot up from his desk and ran from the school; Lord knows where he got to. Dick was saying earlier that he knew Stainrod's father."

"Oh yes, I knew that lad's father alright."

The three other residents of the bar turned with surprise toward Dick Joy, who was now speaking coherently after his micro sleep.

"He was Chatterton's best mate, was Steve. Maybe they were close 'cos Stainrod was a bit backward as well, and they both loved takin' dares and getting into danger. I remember years back goin' to Sydney Gardens with 'em and a couple of other kids."

"Oh, is that the Sydney Gardens where Jane Austen used to visit?" asked Bennett-Brewer.

"Yeah, she lived right opposite in one o' them posh houses. Course, she were around before they built the canal and railway that goes through there now."

For the first time in his long career as a pub customer, Dick Joy asked for a glass of water.

"...Not long before Chatterton's left eye got fucked up, a few of us went down Sydney Gardens. Let me think, there was me, Chatterton, Roy Swindlehurst – he was the local bully, Steve Stainrod, and a lad called Garrett; he was a bit smaller than the rest of us."

The pub was still empty apart from the presence of landlord, teacher, cleric and paper boy. Three pairs of eyes were fixed on Dick Joy.

"Chatterton was quite a few years older than the rest of us, but he preferred spending time with the younger kids 'cos his mental age was closer to theirs. Anyway, we all walked through the main gate of Sydney Gardens, and Chatterton said, 'let's have a game of chicken on the railway line!'"

Joy mimicked Chatterton's disabled speech theatrically, before continuing as a sober narrator.

"Me, big Roy Swindlehurst and Stainrod were all up for a dare, but little Charlie Garrett wasn't too keen. The rest of us pointed at him and clucked like chickens. The poor little sod would either have to do as we said, or get his lights punched out by Swindlehurst if he didn't."

Dick Joy again impersonated Chatterton's speech,

"Ya little chicken shit fucker! Tell ya what, the rest of us'll play chicken with the trains, but we'll let ya off doin' it, but ya godda do somethin' else instead, or Roy's gonna deck ya!"

"That poor Garrett kid was really shittin' 'imself, 'cos Swindlehurst was itchin' to give someone a good panning. Chatterton told Garrett that he'd have to climb over the small stone wall onto the railway and lay ten big stones on the track. The rest of us searched for large stones nearby, and when we found them, we threw 'em at Garrett. We didn't throw 'em hard at him – just hard enough for him to still be scared enough to do the dare. A few seconds later, the nearest train track started to fizz, and a train was due through the tunnel any second. We all grabbed hold of Garrett and pretended we were gonna lift him over the wall. The poor little bastard was terrified, and he was bloody relieved when we just stood there holdin' him and laughin' as the train went by. As soon as the track stopped fizzin', we told Garrett to get on with his job. Swindlehurst stood in front of him with a clenched fist as a reminder of what'd happen if he didn't do what we asked. As he climbed over the wall, the rest of us laid the ten big stones on top of it, and Garrett had to place all ten of them a yard apart along the nearest rail."

Dick Joy took a dainty sip of water as the other three remained silent

Mishap In Sydney Gardens

and all-ears.

"...The wall in front of the tracks is about three foot high, and was easy enough in them days for a small kid to get over – 'specially as the wall had gaps carved-out in the middle so he could get a good foothold. We could all see that Garrett had tears in his eyes as he laid the stones on the track, but we were such nasty bastards that we mocked him by pointing at him and pretending to cry. Not only that, but we told him if his fingers touched the rail, he'd get a thousand volts up his arm and 'ave to 'ave it amputated. He was white with fear. He had his back to the far tunnel as he was layin' the stones, and we told him the signal in the tunnel went green when it was still yellow. He laid the last stone, and was really panickin' when he got back over the wall away from the track."

Joy resurrected the speech of Chatterton; this time with more volume and wildly flailing arms.

"NEXT ONE COMIN'LL BE THE EXPRESS TO PADDINGTON! THEM STONES MIGHT DERAIL THE FUCKER!!"

"...Next thing, Chatterton then goes a bit mad with excitement and starts makin' daft spazzy noises. Then he starts jumpin' and prancin' and cartwheelin'. When we saw Chatterton act like that, it wasn't just Garrett, but all of us who got worried. The train before was the slow one that turned off along Sally in the Wood, but next one would be doin' near a ton by the time it got to the end of Sydney Gardens."

Victor Carping interrupted Joy's story,

"I visited Sydney Gardens for the first time only last week. I noticed the stone wall in front of the railway is fenced off all along."

"Yeah, and they only just got round to doin' that. Talk about lockin' the stable door after the horse fucked off, and about forty fuckin' years too late.

"Anyhow, we all stood a few yards in front of the wall waitin' for the train to arrive. I was imaginin' it pulling-out of Bath Spa and gettin' to Sydney Gardens a minute or two later. It was starting to go dark by then, and we all peered over the wall and got even more excited when the signal in the tunnel really had gone green.

"The tracks started to hiss, and all of us except Garrett were gettin' really excited. The poor little bugger was fully cryin' by the time the train lights hit the curve of the tunnel, and I reckon he knew summat was gonna go wrong.

"We were all lined up side by side about a yard apart just behind the wall as the train approached. If my memory hasn't fucked me up, stood left to right was Chatterton, me, Garrett, Swindlehurst the bully, and Steve Stainrod at the other end.

"The train roared past, and we could hear the screech as the wheels went over the stones. It was like a fuckin' firework display with all the sparks. Through all the screechin', I 'eard a deaf'nin' ping, and I was scared shitless the train was gonna crash into the wall and kill the fuckin' lot of us.

"Anyway, the train carried on okay, but when I looked to my right, Charlie Garrett was layin' on his back. Course, that 'ping' I 'eard was one of them stones shot sideways and up from the rail and through a gap in the wall. That stone smashed him full in the face, broke his neck, and killed him straight off."

14

PHEROMONE-FUELLED ELEVENSES

Whitsun half term provided the chance of a welcome break for Jeremy Bennett-Brewer. Easter had come early this year, and the eight-week term that followed had left him drained. The mostly foul weather during that time, allied to the various strange happenings and stories hardly lifted his spirits.

Bennett-Brewer decided that he'd exercise restraint with his drinking, at least for holiday week. Living less than fifty yards from the pub didn't help, and it had now become habitual to have a few vodkas in the evenings to de-stress. Apart from the fact that visiting the pub so often took a big hole out of his finances, he was regularly being spooked by Dick Joy. Now that the local Rector had added his own scary chapter to the Chatterton saga, the teacher decided that giving the pub a miss wouldn't do any harm.

He'd asked Dave Rensenbrink where he could find out more about the local legend, and was directed toward Barry Loadall; who in turn recommended he visit the old man from the old cottage along Bailbrook Lane. Bennett-Brewer decided to give that option a miss, as he wasn't particularly keen on visiting the location where the local ghost decided to shatter his face.

Bennett-Brewer felt rejuvenated by the thought of the week of leisure ahead, and it was enough for him to become sceptical that there was anything odd about the village. The fact of the matter was that he himself hadn't witnessed anything untoward. Looking out of the classroom windows and seeing the weird weather blanket the whole of Larkhall was certainly strange, as was Bobby Stainrod suddenly running from the class. At the end of the day, he hadn't seen anything overtly scary, and Stainrod was found safe and well, even if he was mostly surly or mute for the rest of that week.

Bennett-Brewer decided that his holiday would be just that. Seven days of simple relaxation, and complete avoidance of anything to do with local superstition.

***

Mrs Mordent and Mrs Tanning loved nothing more than catching up on the local gossip inside the café in Larkhall Square. While Mrs Tanning had long since retired, Mrs Mordent still helped out at the haberdashers three days a week. As Monday was one of her free days, she arranged to meet her old friend for tea and cake at eleven.

Mrs Tanning was thumbing through a booklet of knitting patterns on the corner table when Mrs Mordent shuffled through the door.

"Morning, Mildred."

Mrs Mordent waved her walking stick in the air to accompany the greeting.

"Hello, Else. How's the rheumatism?"

"Oh, I'm not letting that bother me."

Mrs Mordent smiled and made her way slowly toward the counter to order a cup of tea and slice of Battenberg cake. Upon joining her chum at the corner table, Mrs Tanning looked admiringly at Mrs Mordent's plate.

"Battenberg was always my Jack's favourite. He used to put a slice of it on top of his bread and dripping of a morning; said it set him up for the day good and proper."

"Oh yes, Mild. All this blessed 'watch what you eat' stuff is a load of hogwash. I was chatting to Doris from the dry cleaners at the bus stop, and she was saying how her Albert always starts the day with lard and golden syrup on toast. He's over eighty now, but he still gets out and about every day."

"All down to pot luck, Else. When your number's up, it's up, and I don't care for all this looking after yourself palaver. What's the good of denying yourself a bit of what you fancy if the Lord decides to run you over with a bus?"

"Or get clonked on the back of the head like my Jack." replied Mrs Tanning wistfully.

"You knew old Nobby Cundick who used to work for the gas board?"

Mrs Tanning again nodded.

"...Well, he was smoking forty a day when his doctor told him to stop. Up until then, he didn't have a care in the world. Anyway, he took the advice, gave up the fags, and sure enough, within a month he dropped dead while he was crossing the road. It was only by the Lord's good grace that he didn't get run over, too."

"Just goes to show, Else. I'm not going to spend the rest of my life worrying. The Almighty has plans for all of us, and He'll decide when it's the right time for us to toddle-off."

Mrs Tanning glanced-up to see a young man enter the café, and then leant over to whisper to her friend.

"I haven't seen this young fellow before."

"Nor me." Mrs Mordent whispered back.

"...He's got a nice face. Ooh, if I was forty years younger!"

Jeremy Bennett-Brewer turned from the counter with his black coffee and flapjack to make his way to the only empty table – situated next to where the whispering old ladies were sat. The café always did brisk business during late mornings, and Bennett-Brewer soon realised that not only was he the sole male customer, but that the dozen or so females, including the woman behind the counter, were various shades of post-retirement age.

Mrs Tanning turned toward the new customer.

"I hope you don't mind me asking, but you're new to these parts, aren't you?"

"Of course I don't mind you asking! My name's Jeremy, and I moved to Larkhall a few weeks back; I teach at St Saviour's Secondary."

"Well, it's always lovely to see new faces!" Mrs Mordent replied gaily.

"...Especially a face as nice as yours!" added Mrs Tanning.

The teacher felt slightly uncomfortable but was in no doubt the compliment was made innocently.

"I hope those young scoundrels aren't giving you the runaround!" Mrs Tanning continued.

"No, they're alright. I used to teach kids from rough areas before I came here."

"Well, their loss is our gain!" enthused Mrs Mordent.

Bennett-Brewer smiled bashfully back.

"I do enjoy the peace and quiet of Larkhall, it's almost like stepping back in time. It's so nice that the supermarkets and combines have been kept out."

"Oh, we don't let outsiders push our shopkeepers out willy-nilly...!" Mrs Mordent answered proudly. "The haberdashers where I work has been around nigh on two hundred years, and it's still a family-run shop."

"That's the kind of thing that makes me glad to have moved here!" the teacher beamed.

Jeremy Bennett-Brewer was now feeling completely at ease, and just one day into his holiday, had erased all thoughts about any dodgy village happenings.

"Oh, you've come to the right place, alright..." Mrs Tanning confirmed. "If you're looking for peace and quiet, this is the place to be, and no mistake!"

"You really must visit the haberdashery shop sometime!" invited Mrs Mordent.

"Yes, I'll make a point of doing so...although my sewing and knitting skills probably leave a bit to be desired!"

The aged population of the café suddenly laughed heartily, and Jeremy Bennett-Brewer was puzzled by the mirth.

An elderly lady with a blue hair rinse at a nearby table addressed Mrs Mordent with a smile.

"By crikey Else, if I had a handsome young thing like that in my shop, I'd pull down the shutters and put-up the half-day closing sign!"

More hilarity ensued, and this time the laughter moved up a notch. Bennett-Brewer suddenly returned to pre-holiday unease.

Mrs Mordent turned toward the old lady serving behind the counter.

"What do you reckon, Pearl?"

"What do I reckon, Else? I reckon I wouldn't mind delving into my Christmas stocking and finding *that* inside!"

The bar of the communal laughter reached a new height that bordered on hysteria, and the teacher's face turned scarlet from sheer horror. His discomfort was eased when the laughter hushed in response to a local builder bustling through the door. He ordered a hot baguette and coffee to take out, and within a minute, he was gone. The chorus of laughter started again and lasted for several seconds.

"I must say..."

The words were spoken by a pink haired old lady sat next to the one with the blue hair rinse, and Bennett-Brewer prepared himself for more inappropriate attention as he turned to face her.

"...I reckon an hour spent havin' me ticket punched by this cheeky young buck would finish me off!"

The teacher desperately wanted to be elsewhere but was powerless to move.

Another old lady walked through the door, and she was immediately addressed by Mrs Tanning.

"Hello, Flo...what do you reckon about this young thing sat next to us?"

Mrs Tanning accompanied her question by pointing at Bennett-Brewer. "COR! I'll tell you what, you don't get many of them to the pound!"

The latest visitor to the café then addressed its single male customer.

"You'd better keep your hand on your ha'penny being sat next to old Mild, she may just put you across her knee. Tanning by name, tanning by nature!"

The entire population of the café bar the unfortunate music teacher again exploded into laughter.

"I haven't had any since my Bertie popped off..." continued Flo. "He was a right useless bugger in that department. What we need in Larkhall is more life creating young stallions!"

Jeremy Bennett-Brewer's pallor turned from scarlet to heart attack mauve as more hilarity filled the café.

"I really must be on my way."

The lone male held up an apologetic hand.

"Surely you don't need to go just yet, do you?"

Mrs Tanning gently rested her hand on Bennett-Brewer's shoulder, before giving it a sensual squeeze of encouragement.

"I'm afraid so, there's a few things I need to do."

"Oh, I'm sure those things can wait..." interjected Mrs Mordent. "You're on holiday, remember?"

"Yes, but time and tide wait for no man."

Another burst of laughter swamped the café, before a sudden hush descended.

The old lady from behind the counter walked toward the teacher's table wearing a frown that suggested she felt badly let down. She pointed a hostile finger at Bennett-Brewer.

"I don't believe for one moment that you have anything important to do."

The rest of the café nodded in agreement while wearing stern expressions.

"I'm with Pearl..." added the lady with the blue hair rinse. "Just exactly what is it that you need to be getting on with?"

Various grunts and mumblings of *hear, hear* resonated around the café, and every pair of eyes were fixed on the teacher. He was feeling rather panicked and said the first thing that came into his head.

"Oh, er...I need to pay my paper bill before the shop closes."

"But it's only half eleven...!" Mrs Mordent protested. "The paper shop doesn't shut 'til half five!"

Pearl was still standing in front of Bennett-Brewer, and she folded her arms slowly to show her dissatisfaction.

"Are you seriously trying to tell us that it's going to take six ruddy hours

The Wyvern & The Witchfinder

to get across to the paper shop and pay your bill??"

More grunts of approval greeted Pearl's question, and was this time accompanied by a few fists banging lightly against tables.

The teacher was lost for words, and again blurted out the first thing that came into his head.

"Well, after I've paid the paper bill, I've got to..."

Bennett-Brewer experienced speech paralysis once again, and every old woman in the café followed the example of Pearl by folding their arms to display communal distaste at his wriggling and slithering. This led to more panic, and the teacher shot up from his seat, wore an expression of shocked remembrance, and theatrically declared that he had to return home immediately because he'd left the iron on.

For the final time, the café exploded into hilarity, and Bennett-Brewer rushed from the table toward freedom, but not before two separate old hands and fingers had managed to pinch a buttock each.

15

PHEROMONE-FUELLED JOURNEY

That afternoon, and after the double therapy of a soak in the bath and meditating to the most soothing and least ominous Vaughan Williams' symphony he could find, Jeremy Bennett-Brewer thought again about the amorous attention he'd received from the old ladies in the cafe. The medicine of the bath and music wore off quickly, and the teacher returned to being unsettled at his apparent animal magnetism toward the elderly.

Bennett-Brewer spent a long time torturing himself about whether he should seek answers to this latest uncomfortable episode, or forget about it and carry on in bliss free ignorance. As he completely failed in his attempts to rid his mind of what happened that morning, only the first option was viable.

Now his task was to choose where he was to seek the answers from. One thing he was adamant about was avoiding the pub; not only was he determined not to cloud his mind with booze, but Monday was one of Dick Joy's evenings of residence, and the possibility of listening to another of his hair-raising reminiscences was unlikely to be the precursor to a refreshing night's sleep.

The only option left was Barry Loadall, and the teacher decided to pay him an immediate visit. Despite that act of positivity, Bennett-Brewer was nervously flapping to the extent of digging out the false beard from his amateur dramatics days to disguise himself. Being accosted by several elderly women troubled him as much as the Chatterton stories, and he became paranoid that more of them could be prowling about. After a few deep breaths, the front door was closed, and the teacher sallied forth. He slowly swung his falsely bearded face left and right along the road to look out for hot blooded pensioners. The coast was clear and Bennett-Brewer marched quickly toward his destination. The closer he got to Loadall's front door, the calmer he became, but his heart sank when he spotted an elderly lady approach from the top half of the street where the drug dealer resided. The lady plodded along very slowly with the aid of two walking sticks, so at least the chances of him being chased or having his behind touched up were remote.

Although the teacher convinced himself that the beard put years on him, a fresh wave of paranoia hit. He again recalled his acting days and decided to adopt a Richard the Third hunchback posture. If the beard wasn't enough, then walking with a hunch and limp would surely extinguish any last vestiges of attraction.

The old lady and teacher took a long time to reach each other halfway up the street.

"Good evening!"

Bennett-Brewer returned the pleasantry with the deepest bass voice he could muster, and the old lady looked at him quizzically.

"...I haven't seen you round these parts before, are you new to the area?"

"I don't actually live here..." replied the teacher as he plundered his deepest tones. "I'm a travelling salesman, and I've visited every house in the village today."

"This is quite a big village, you know."

The heavily disguised teacher detected a certain disapproval in the old lady's voice.

"...I wasn't born yesterday. There's hundreds of houses in Larkhall, and I don't for one minute believe that you could've managed even a couple of dozen with that nasty limp of yours."

Jeremy Bennett-Brewer was more unnerved than ever but kept up the act.

"Fortunately, a good friend of mine generously agreed to carry me from door to door. He's a former middle-distance runner and weightlifter, and you wouldn't believe how quickly he got me around Larkhall today."

To Bennett-Brewer's great surprise, the old lady was totally satisfied with his explanation, but his relief was fleeting as he felt his beard coming loose at the left sideburn. He reacted by pushing his left palm against it and keeping it there for several seconds.

"I must say, I do like your beard!"

"That's very kind of you."

Pheromone-Fuelled Journey

The physical effort of speaking in his lowest possible voice was proving hard work for Bennett-Brewer, but he reminded himself that he had to make every effort to avoid radiating irresistible pheromones.

"I must say, I do like a man with a deep, husky voice. Add that to the beard, and it's the kind of thing make makes me go weak at the knees!"

The disguised man's eyes widened with alarm.

"...Would you mind if I had a little stroke of your whiskers?"

"Some other time I'd be delighted madam, but I'm currently battling against toothache, which is why I just pressed my left hand against my cheek."

"I am sorry to hear that, and I do hope it gets better very soon!"

"Thank you for your good wishes."

"Nothing better than being serviced in the bedroom by a man with a beard, though it doesn't half tickle!"

The teacher was horrified by what he'd just heard, and desperately tried to banish the image of the old lady being orally pleasured.

"I really must be on my way; I've just remembered I've left something cooking in the oven."

"And during the war..." the old lady continued regardless. "I had more Yank servicemen than Eisenhower!"

Another wave of horror hit Bennett-Brewer as he tried to expand on the excuse for making his exit.

"I really do have to go. My dinner will be far hotter than I'd like unless I get home in a few minutes."

"But I thought you said you weren't from round these parts?"

"Er...that's right! Because I'm a salesman, I'm staying at a local guest house; and because I'm on a tight budget, I get a discount if I cook my own dinner."

"But you said you had to return *home*. A guest house is only home to the people who own it, so are you sure you're telling me the truth?"

"Yes I am sure that I'm telling the truth, madam, though I understand your suspicion."

Bennett-Brewer's voice was becoming hoarse, and he hoped the act wouldn't have to continue for much longer.

"The house I've just left has a telephone. How about you come back to the house, telephone the guest house and ask them to switch the oven off for you?"

The teacher could only stare back in disbelief.

"...While you're on the telephone, I could rustle up something hot and tasty, and that'd save you a trip back to the guest house."

The old lady fluttered her eyelashes before continuing,

"...It'd be a chance for us to get to know each other better, and I'm sure you'd know how to look after a neglected woman who needs the cobwebs blown away from her..."

"AAAAAAAAAAAAARGH!"

Bennett-Brewer feigned injury by crouching to rub his shin.

"Oh dear! You're in no fit state to be walking back to your guest house. If you wait a few minutes, I'll telephone for an ambulance, and I'll stay in the ambulance with you and make sure you get back safely."

"Oh, it's nothing; I'll soon walk it off. Just a touch of Agent Orange I picked up in 'Nam."

The old woman ignored Bennett-Brewer's response. She turned and clacked back the way she came with her walking sticks, before stopping and turning around.

"What's the name of the guest house you're staying at?"

Without answering, Bennett-Brewer suddenly got up from his crouched position and ran as fast as he could up the street and away from the old woman.

As soon as he turned the corner, Bennett-Brewer pressed his back to the wall. After regaining his breath, he popped his head out to see if the old lady was out of sight. The first couple of times he looked, the old lady appeared stationary. Eventually, after half a dozen head-pokes over the space of a few minutes, she was gone. Bennett-Brewer warily trod back toward Loadall's house, and his eventful journey finally reached its conclusion. As he was about to ring Loadall's bell, the door suddenly opened, and a balding, middle-aged man walked out clad in a pin striped suit and sparking shoes. Barry Loadall's latest customer shyly acknowledged Bennett-Brewer's presence before making his way shiftily down the pathway.

Loadall himself appeared, informed the teacher that the departing customer was a leading local Rotarian, and held the door open invitingly.

"What's the thinking behind your rather clumsy and unimpressive false beard?"

In the aftermath of his latest episode of inadvertently stoking the fires of elderly lust, Bennett-Brewer had completely forgotten he was still wearing it.

"Oh...I do apologise!"

The ginger beard was quickly removed, and Bennett-Brewer headed toward the tatty armchair in the lounge.

"...It's all rather embarrassing, and I'll try to explain it in good time."

Loadall sat down in the opposite armchair and looked Bennett-Brewer up and down with fascination. "Are you here for business or pleasure?"

"Oh, don't you start as well...!" the teacher blurted with great agitation.

"I've just spent the day fending off old ladies. It was like a bad dream; I was even propositioned by two ladies sat next to each other in the café with pink and blue hair rinses. Like being accosted by a pair of liquorice bloody allsorts."

Loadall uncharacteristically burst out laughing, but his hilarity was soon replaced by a violent coughing fit as his lungs gave another reminder of their displeasure. Bennett-Brewer got up to give his host several hearty slaps on the back. It did the trick, and after giving thanks to his makeshift nurse, Loadall returned to his usual serious self.

"I must say, you do seem rather flustered, Jeremy."

"So would you if you'd just become the pin-up boy for every OAP in the village!"

This time Loadall remained stone faced.

"I understand your obvious discomfort, Jeremy. It can't be much fun to have your backside pinched by members of the elderly fraternity."

"How did you know about that??"

"I had a visit from Mrs Mordent earlier, and she told me all about it."

The teacher gulped audibly before he replied.

"I wouldn't have thought you two would be friends."

"She's more of a customer than a friend."

"God almighty, please don't tell me she's a stoner as well as being a sex maniac!?"

"Please calm yourself, Jeremy, her usage is purely for medicinal reasons. She suffers from rheumatism, and there's no way she could be termed a recreational user."

Barry Loadall wore his sternest expression.

"...Having said that, Mrs Mordent is renowned for assembling the longest, fattest, most intricately designed and most heavily loaded joints in the whole parish."

Jeremy Bennett-Brewer reacted by rolling his eyes with shock and disapproval before sinking his head into his hands.

"...Every year there's a spliff designing competition as part of the Larkhall Village Festival, and Mrs Mordent won it twenty-nine years in succession."

The teacher's face remained in his hands.

"...Eventually she got banned from entering so others would have a chance."

Bennett-Brewer looked up slowly.

"So, are all the old ladies in Larkhall fruity druggies?"

"Oh no. As I just said, Mrs Mordent only uses my wares to help with pain relief."

"But you can't tell me she's had rheumatism over all the years she's been winning the spliff competitions?"

"Not at all. She only started after she peered-out through her kitchen window many years ago and saw the Devil and Witchfinder physically unionising in her back garden."

The teacher again sunk his head into his hands.

"...Around these parts, people have a very different perception of the Devil from the accepted norm. Our friend Rupert Chatterton wouldn't have any of it. Everything was one or the other to him, and his simple mind made him a slave to the puritanical Thomas Crabbings."

Bennett-Brewer reluctantly lifted his head from his hands.

"He sounds like a pretty ghastly fellow."

"You didn't state whether you meant Chatterton or Crabbings sounded ghastly, but the answer is yes for both."

"After Chatterton died, many diaries were found in his house. He had the handwriting style and spelling of a five-year-old, so no easy job working-out what he was saying. He would often write about locals who were openly hostile toward Crabbings, and he detailed exactly what he planned to do with them. It didn't make for pretty reading in any respect."

Somewhere in the distance, both men heard a grumble of thunder. Barry Loadall stared out of the window in the direction of Tadwick before he returned his attention to Bennett-Brewer.

"Jeremy, I understand the fear you must be feeling about Chatterton's ghost, and also your discomfort at being the subject of unwanted attention from elderly ladies."

"Yes, well you'd hardly need to be the psychic of the century to know that."

Loadall studied his guest intently.

"Things can get a little unpleasant when some of us speak ill of Chatterton, so we shall need to tread carefully."

Bennett-Brewer turned around to see light rain fall against the window while the sky became noticeably darker.

16

SIX GOOD TURNS

Harry Trundle was a familiar sight to the residents of Keynsham. Familiar as he was, he wasn't necessarily the most popular. Still, he had a job to do, and if he wasn't there to do it, the town would soon become a gridlocked maelstrom of lost tempers and tooted horns.

Trundle thoroughly enjoyed his job. He got plenty of fresh air and miles in his legs from prowling the streets, and even if he was occasionally on the receiving end of irate words and invitations to bare knuckle fights, he never forgot just how important his role was in keeping this little corner of north Somerset functioning.

Fifty-eight minutes earlier, Trundle had scanned the vehicles in the car park next to the town library and noted any that were flirting with a ticket. As he returned to the scene, he discovered a vehicle still parked two minutes past its expiry time.

Harry Trundle prided himself in not taking pleasure from issuing parking fines, and instead saw himself as championing the people of Keynsham by ensuring there were fair shares for all with the competitively priced town parking. Every morning before leaving his house for work, Trundle reminded himself of the duty he was performing for the town.

The good folk of Keynsham deserve better than certain people trying to take advantage of the already-generous parking allowances and fair prices offered them!

Those words were writ large on Harry Trundle's refrigerator, and that mantra was recited aloud each morning as he reached for the milk.

Trundle felt a little sad as he affixed the latest penalty notice to the latest windscreen, and fervently hoped the owner would understand that Keynsham would be happier place if people didn't push the boundaries of fairness.

A middle-aged man came scampering toward his guilty vehicle with several books tucked under his arm.

"Oh, I'm so sorry. I was waylaid by reading a real page turner in the library."

Harry Trundle smiled at the man.

"Firstly, may I say how pleased I am that you enjoyed your visit. Those of us who love a good yarn are always on the lookout for that elusive unputdownable read, and I'm delighted that Keynsham Library has provided you with such a spiritual boost."

"That's very kind of you to say so." replied the man, who was struggling to regain his breath after his hurrying.

The traffic warden soberly explained the necessity of his work.

"It's always disappointing when I have to issue a penalty notice, but I'm sure you understand that everyone who parks their car so as to enjoy the wonders of Keynsham do need to abide with the regulations clearly detailed by several notices."

"Yes I do, and it's a fair cop. I'll learn from this regrettable incident, and from now on, I'll never park longer than the law allows."

It wasn't often that a car owner on the receiving end of a parking fine was so contrite, but it was this kind of acceptance that reminded Harry Trundle that this job was his true Earthly vocation.

"It fills the heart with gladness that you have learnt your lesson, good sir."

"And my heart is filled with gladness also that there are people like you who diligently ensure that this inspirational town is shorn of car park hogs."

Trundle smiled again at the apologetic man, then whispered into his ear.

"If you pay the fine within seven days, you'll receive a fifty percent discount."

The man beamed a smile, then stretched both arms to grab the right hand of Trundle to shake it passionately.

"Why, that is good news indeed!"

The two men exchanged a happy farewell as the driver clambered into his car.

Harry Trundle felt invigorated by this positive episode. He looked down at his watch and noted that he was an hour away from finishing work. He'd then make his way to Midsomer Norton high street for an important

Six Good Turns

meeting.

***

"Morning. I'd like a return to Nibley-under-Edge, please."

Charles Ubley smiled at his newest passenger.

"Certainly, young fella m'lad; though I should point out that for a mere twenty pence extra, you could secure yourself a 'Somerset Day Pillager,' which allows you to ride on as many buses as your heart desires for twenty-four hours from my issuing of the ticket."

"That sounds good value for money!"

"Too right it's good value for money; just think of all the historic places of wonder that are within the approximate thirty-mile radius served by our omnibus company!"

"Well, I've got plenty of free time today, and I'd be a fool to myself if I didn't take advantage of this generous deal!"

"You obviously know a bargain when you see one. If you'd kindly cross my palm with five of your Earth pounds, I shall issue you with your multi layered ticket to ride!"

"Oh, for Christ's sake...!" spluttered an impatient old man who'd recently boarded. "Is this a private party, or can we all bloody join-in?"

Charles Ubley turned around to face his unhappy passenger.

"I'm sorry you feel that way, sir. Time is a relentless beast, and one we should never attempt to cheat."

"But I've got to get my bloody prescription, otherwise I'll be wearin' a wooden bleedin' overcoat before the day's out!"

"Time will ensure we'll all be moving on to the next world sooner or later, sir. What cannot be denied is the health benefits of having a spring in your step and a song in your heart."

The elderly man reacted with a spoilsport scowl as he stared aimlessly through the window.

"...As you're past retirement age, doesn't it please you that you can ride as many of our buses as you like without having to delve into your hard-earned pension?"

The old man continued to stare through the window and responded only with a sulky grunt of *s'pose so.*

"...How about we sing an old tune together that rekindles the music hall spirit of yesteryear?"

This time the chirpy bus driver received a half smile, and Charles Ubley struck while the iron was hot by bursting into song.

"My old man said 'foller the van'..."

The old man's eyes lit up, and then sprang to his feet while pointing at the driver.

"...And don't dilly dally on the way!"

Apart from the amused passenger who'd just boarded, the other two occupants of the bus were a retired couple, and they joined-in as the previously sour old man conducted along with animated arms.

> "...Off went the van with me 'ome packed in it, I walked be'ind with me old cock linnet
> But I dillied and dallied, dallied and dillied; lost me way and don't know where to roam..."

The final line of the old knees-up ditty was followed by a communal OI! together with elderly arms punched in the air.

"Are we feeling better now, sir?"

"Too bleedin' right, Drive!"

Charles Ubley was delighted at the old man's sudden exuberance, and after issuing the young man's day ticket, whistled all the way through the rest of his shift as he turned his attention toward the evening summit in Midsomer Norton.

***

Rolf and Teresa Slad were the first twins to be employed as cleaners of Bath's flagship public toilets. At the age of fifty-four, neither twin had married or had children, so both could retain their focus on doing the job they'd performed since leaving school to the best of their ability.

"I tell you, sis; when the hard-working people of Bath, together with the constant influx of tourists spend their hard-earned cash in local shops and boost the local economy, the very least we can do in return is to make sure that any lavatorial visits they make be ones of cleanliness, comfort, and of little fuss."

"You're preaching to the converted, bruv..." replied the female twin, as they marched regimentally toward the city centre's main convenience to begin their shift. "Lavatorial needs are no respecters of class, creed or wealth. Whether it be a homeless person sadly cut adrift from society, or a chairman of the board helplessly caught short during his or her lunch break, they all deserve the very best."

Within moments of the pair opening the public toilet at seven-thirty, a man came through the door and whispered a *good morning* to the male twin, who was stood primed with his mop and bucket. His sister was busy making sure the female section of the toilets sparkled.

Six Good Turns

"Sir, it is a good morning, and I wish you an enjoyable visit!"

The man locked himself inside one of the cubicles, and emerged a few minutes later visibly refreshed.

"I must say, the toilet I performed my daily duty on was absolutely spotless; and that, allied to the powerful flushing system, has indeed made my visit an enjoyable one!"

"Delighted to hear it, sir...!" Beamed Rolf Slad. "The daily duty should be one of the most enjoyable of all Earthly experiences, and my aim is to do everything in my power to ensure that's the case."

The man returned a nod of approval and whistled a merry tune as he began to wash his hands. He used the heel of his palm to push the soap dispenser, which to his displeasure yielded nothing. He tried the other three dispensers but drew a blank from each. He turned to the male attendant who was busy mopping the floor.

"Oh dear, I'm afraid that all the dispensers are out of soap."

"I can't apologise enough, sir."

Rolf Slad immediately dipped into his lavatorial bag of tricks and produced the necessary replenishments. Within a couple of minutes, all the soap dispensers were fully stocked.

"Sir, I'm sorry to say that the person who was on yesterday's evening shift was a young lad just out of school, and he's obviously a bit wet behind the ears."

"That's not a problem..." answered the man in an understanding tone. "Sometimes younger people can be a little lacking in empathy; what with their raging hormones, youthful curiosity, and zest for adventure. It's understandable that they can sometimes forget about the more mundane bread and butter aspects of performing their duty."

"Thank you for being so understanding, sir. I'll have a word with the young lad, though I won't be too hard on him. For all we know, he could be experiencing the angst of young love, and tasks such as replenishing soap dispensers can sometimes take a back seat when dealing with the mixed-up emotions all youngsters feel as they begin the tentative journey toward finding that elusive life partner."

"If that is the case..." answered the man as he swamped his hands with soap. "then please send him my good wishes. If I had a pound for every time I've had my heart broken I'd be a rich man, and I wish him well as he journeys through the peaks and troughs of life."

"Sir, you are a gentleman!"

As the man held his hands underneath the hot air dryer, Rolf Slad sneaked a couple of soap sachets into the top pocket of his jacket. He then whispered into the man's ear from the corner of his mouth.

"We're all friends here, sir, you can have these on the house."

The two men shook hands as the attendant produced a crafty wink. Rolf Slad felt an enormous sense of wellbeing as he envisaged his twin sister and himself making the trip to Midsomer Norton high street later in the day.

***

"Good evening sir, and what can I do you for?"

Colin Drysdale leant his arms on the counter and awaited the customer's order.

"Evening; I'd like two cod and chips, two fishcakes, and a tub of your mushiest peas."

"Your wish is my command, sir. This is the finest fish and chip shop in the whole of Somerset, and as you can see behind me, we are stocked to the proverbial rafters with all the items one would wish and expect from any fish shop worth its salt."

"I'm very impressed. Good fish and chip shops are hard to find these days, and it's hard-working people like you who deserve to be named in the New Year's Honours List."

"I'm very humbled, sir!"

Colin Drysdale beamed a proud smile before relaying the order to his young assistant. Returning to his customer, Drysdale's face became serious.

"Sir, I'm very touched by the positive impact my fish and chip shop has had on you, but the real heroes are those brave men who defy the elements on a daily basis to make sure that we all have the option of having a nice piece of fish on our plate of an evening."

"That's very true."

The customer returned the serious expression of the proprietor.

"...I hadn't given it much thought before, but what those valiant fishermen must go through to earn a living; keeping the swooping gulls away from their catch, ice on the rigging, bitter nor'easterlies and so on. It all makes me feel rather inadequate and unworthy."

"Now, now, my good man, let's not have any of that kind of talk!"

Colin Drysdale reached over the counter and lifted the man's spirits by gently pinching his cheek.

"...I've no doubt that your Earthly duties are of great importance also."

"Well, I'm not sure that lollipop men can be mentioned in the same breath as our heroic fishermen."

"I beg to differ, sir!"

Colin Drysdale wagged a finger of disapproval at his downcast customer.

"...Ensuring that children cross the road safely and get to school in one piece is a noble duty. The children of today are the industry captains of tomorrow, and this country would be on its knees without vigilant folk like you who ensure they make it to adulthood."

"Why, thank you for that kind compliment."

"Not at all, sir. Neither of us would be here today if we'd been run over and killed by motor vehicles, and that's due in no small part to the previous generation of lollipop men and women who selflessly championed our safety."

The young assistant handed his boss the customer's order.

"...Here we are sir; but before I wrap your mouth-watering feast, this evening has already produced an impressive volume of golden scrumps. What say you to me filling a bag to the brim with these delightfully haphazard chunks of fallen batter?"

"Not half!"

Colin Drysdale was as good as his word, and soon handed the customer his order and tasty bonus.

"I really can't thank you enough! Not only have you made me feel good about the job I do, but kindly adding those scrumps takes me right back to my childhood!"

"And just you remember..." replied Drysdale passionately. "that childhood of yours could have been cut short if it wasn't for the brave folk of your profession."

The reinvigorated customer tucked the hot paper package under his arm and prepared to leave.

"I'm absolutely delighted with the service I've received this evening, and I can't wait to tell people about the wonder of this shop."

"And on behalf of all the staff dedicated to the success of *Cod Only Knows*, I can assure you that you'll always receive a warm welcome here."

The satisfied customer turned and left, and Colin Drysdale reminded himself that tomorrow was the single day of the week that the shop was shut. He'd take advantage of his day off by making his way to Midsomer Norton high street.

***

Midsomer Norton stands close to the Mendips a few miles southwest of Bath. Notable both for its high street being bisected by the narrow River Somer, and also the reminder of the town's importance to the old Somerset coal fields by being overlooked by a huge volcano shaped heap of slag.

Watkinson & Sons Greengrocers was one of the most celebrated and successful shops along the high street, and it sold nothing other than locally grown produce. Customers came from as far as Gloucestershire to the north,

Wiltshire to the east, and even day trippers who crossed the Severn from South Wales.

Behind the counter, a huge poster was displayed that detailed the mission statement from the founder of the business. The poster was headed by a grainy black and white photograph from the 1870s of the owner cradling several species of vegetables and fruit in his arms.

As proprietor of this store, I have the most humbling responsibility to provide the blessed people of Midsomer Norton with nothing but the finest reapings from this area's fertile soil. It is my sincere and unwavering aim to ensure that every single item I sell be tended and nurtured with the same diligence, care and devotion as a mother tending and nurturing her infant child.

I hereby declare that I regard each item I stock as having sprouted from my modest loins, and that a blighted potato or ruined radish would pain me as surely as being bereaved of a dear relative. Come! Come! All you good people of the fine parish of Midsomer Norton. Come! Come! Please do stop, browse, buy and taste the produce I view as my very own cherished offspring.

Your profoundly obedient servant,
Ephraim Spencer Perceval Watkinson

The latest offshoot of the original owner, Trevor Watkinson, glowed with pride as he read his great-great-great-grandfather's words for the umpteenth time. The current owner was now two decades into his tenure, and every morning without fail he'd stand in front of the poster, read its inspiring words, and dab his eyes with tissues in response to the burden of responsibility he felt toward catering for the steadfast folk of the town.

The tinkling of the bell announced that day's first customer.

"Good morning, Mr Watkinson. I dare say the weather seems to be taking an upward turn!"

Mrs Trifling was one of the town's oldest residents, and had been a regular visitor to the store since making her debut appearance as a babe in arms ninety-four years previously.

"Why, it does appear to be quite so indeed, Mrs Trifling!"

Mr Watkinson followed his reply by bowing respectfully.

"...One mustn't be too full of ire for the recent unpleasantness we've experienced from the heavens; after all, the radishes do so love temperate moistness, and I'm old enough and ugly enough to know quite well enough how our Mrs Trifling does so love a succulent radish!"

"That is quite so, Mr Watkinson."

Six Good Turns

Mrs Trifling rummaged around inside her wicker basket.

"...Though I'm afraid, as you can see, many of the radishes you sold me yesterday have split, and as a result, my beloved son is refusing to speak to me."

Mr Watkinson turned pale as he laid eyes on the dismal state of Mrs Trifling's recent purchase.

"Why, Mrs Trifling, I am so sorry to hear about these substandard radishes, and my apoplexy leaves me no option but to humbly quote the Bard, inasmuch as I am bound upon a wheel of fire, and that mine own tears do scold like Bolton lead."

"...The single ambition that drives me from my bed each morning is to provide seamless goodness and quality for every generation who dwell in our ancient settlement."

"That is very good to hear, Mr Watkinson. I know you care deeply for your stocks of vegetables, and also that this is my first complaint."

Mr Watkinson's face adjusted to a self-loathing pink, and he submissively nodded his head during Mrs Trifling's reply.

"Believe me, Mrs Trifling, if I could turn back the clock, I would. Nine decades and fifteen prime ministers have come and gone since you first visited this store as a helpless infant, and I was rather hoping that the entire span of your Earthly existence would be free of vegetable related glitches."

Mrs Trifling rested her hand on the proprietor's shoulder to offer her sympathy.

"There, there, Mr Watkinson; accidents will happen, you know."

Mr Watkinson cracked a smile of gratitude, while the old lady's face turned serious.

"...However, such is my son's yearning for the plain radish, I fear that unless they're replaced immediately, his mood will remain sullen, and that history may repeat itself after his dear old father took his own life after being confronted with bruised sprouts; though I should say also that this incident happened many years before you began running the store."

The owner of the shop solidified his posture and wore an expression of unstinting duty.

"My store and suicide make very uncomfortable bedfellows, Mrs Trifling, and your radishes shall be replaced IMMEDIATELY!"

Trevor Watkinson trod with purpose toward the box of radishes with the same scooper used by the illustrious founder of the store.

"We had a fresh new consignment delivered early this morning, Mrs Trifling!"

Mrs Trifling nodded with approval as Mr Watkinson filled a huge brown bag to the brim with moist-yet-firm radishes. He placed the bag in Mrs

Trifling's basket.

"...As a further gesture of my remorse, may I fully fill your basket with only the finest crab apples?"

"You may indeed!" replied the delighted old lady.

"I have been serving you for many years now, Mrs Trifling, and in that time, I have become wise to certain nuggets of useful information. One of those informative nuggets involves knowing how much a devotee of apple pie your son is!"

"Trust you to be so knowing and considerate, Mr Watkinson!"

"My advice to you, Mrs Trifling, is to bound home immediately with much haste and hand hoisted skirts. For my replenishment of your basket will be eyed by your son, and that in itself will assuredly keep the black dog of his mood at arm's length."

"Mr Watkinson, you are the pride of Midsomer Norton!"

"Mrs Trifling; may I bid you farewell, and trust that warmth and reconciliation feature prominently in the dealings between you and your son this fine morning!"

Mrs Trifling returned a cheery goodbye and left the store in high spirits.

The rest of the day saw good trade, light hearted banter, and no further complaints. Two minutes before official closing time, four men and a woman entered the store together. Watkinson closed the door, looked left and right along the high street, turned the *open* sign around, and pulled down the blind.

17

STORE-ROOM SATANISTS

Jeremy Bennett-Brewer continued to stare through the window and saw the figure of Graham Curnow scuttling up the path toward the front door. Before Bennett-Brewer had a chance to notify his host, Barry Loadall leapt with unusual swiftness from his armchair and opened the door before Curnow had a chance to jingle the bell. As Curnow entered the lounge, he greeted the teacher in an uncharacteristically subdued manner.

"Oh, hello Jeremy."

Bennett-Brewer returned the greeting, and though he was grateful for the extra company, was struck by Curnow's lack of enthusiasm.

"...Looks like I've made it just in time."

Curnow removed his waterproofs and sat himself down on Loadall's battered sofa.

"...The sky's turning very dark, and I could hardly see Solsbury Hill by the time I arrived."

"Graham is a keen rambler." Loadall informed Bennett-Brewer.

"...So where have you been today, old friend?"

"Well, I was planning a route from the start of the canal in the city centre through to Dundas Aqueduct."

"From your intonation, I gather you didn't manage to see the plan through?"

"No Barry, I didn't. The weather started out pleasant enough, but began to turn a bit sour as I got to the part of the canal that goes through Sydney

Gardens."

Bennett-Brewer addressed Curnow with unease.

"Oh gawd, I hope you managed to make it through Sydney Gardens in one piece!"

Barry Loadall replied on behalf of Curnow,

"Well, he looks in one piece to me, Jeremy."

Loadall turned his attention back to Curnow.

"I must say, Graham, you don't seem your usual effervescent self this evening."

"Indeed, Barry; that's all due to me taking the rather stupid decision to take a detour from the canal to explore the rest of Sydney Gardens."

Loadall stared at Bennett-Brewer.

"Another thing Graham likes to do is watch the trains speed through the Gardens."

A loud crack of thunder made Bennett-Brewer jump, while Loadall and Curnow remained unmoved.

***

"Thank you all for coming today, and I trust that you're all in high spirits?"

"Yes we are, Mr Watkinson!" chorused his five followers.

Trevor Watkinson led his disciples through to the storeroom at the back of the shop. As part of the process of turning them from humble working people into devoted followers, Watkinson handed cricketing clothing to each. From that point on until further notice, they were to be known by their devilish pseudonyms.

"I am now becomest Trevor Expectorant, and I anoint Earthly omnibus driver Charles Ubley as my devoted follower, Sir Jack Hobbs."

Expectorant made the shape of a sideways cross over Hobbs' torso, before completing the metamorphosis by smearing his forehead with the symbolic blood of overripe tomato.

"...I, Trevor Expectorant, anoint Earthly warden of the traffic Harry Trundle as my devoted follower, Sir Leonard Hutton."

Expectorant performed the same ritual with the other three followers; lavatory attendants Rolf and Teresa Slad became WG Grace and Denise Compton respectively, and chip shop owner Colin Drysdale was now Iftikhar Ali Khan - Nawab of Pataudi.

"...The reason I've called this Extraordinary General Meeting is because the time is approaching where the planets will be aligned for judgement day."

Store-Room Satanists

Trevor Expectorant scanned the faces of his five disciples to look for any signs of diffidence. He found none, and the pride he felt caused his eyes to moisten.

"...I really don't know what I've done to deserve such wonderful and dedicated followers as you wholesome folk!"

"I'm sure I speak for all my colleagues when I say that we all feel likewise..." answered Expectorant's deputy, Sir Jack Hobbs. "I was like a ship without a rudder before my eyes were opened to the possibilities of the next world."

Hobbs then addressed his fellow disciples.

"We all do Earthly jobs that are considered mundane, but thanks to our smashing leader, we now have a purpose. I now address the persons who hop onto my bus with much cordiality and understanding. We all believe that treating people with unstinting niceness is the key to a successful and fulfilling afterlife."

"I'll second that!"

Denise Compton's exuberance was even greater than that of Hobbs.

"...WG Grace and I always used to wear a scowl while cleaning the public lavatories, but now the sun continually shines after crossing paths with Mr Expectorant!"

"If I may be allowed to add my two-penneth worth?" asked Iftikhar Ali Khan.

"Two-penn'orth granted, Ifty." smiled Expectorant.

"I used to get very downcast running my fish shop; what with the ever-spiralling cost of cod, my temperamental deep-fat fryer, etcetera. I needed my life to take on a new meaning, and Mr Expectorant has given me that new meaning!"

Trevor Expectorant raised his arms to the heavens in approval, and invited his disciples to feast heartily on stock that had just passed its best-before date.

***

"Before you continue, Graham..." Bennett-Brewer began. "I would like confirmation of what I've heard from others; namely that you don't subscribe to the local legend, or indeed to the alleged hauntings by Chatterton."

Graham Curnow answered with an expression indicating that he now wasn't so sure.

"Oh crikey." responded Bennett-Brewer, before he again looked through the window to notice that the rain had become a little heavier.

"The reason I'm now not so sure is because what I experienced in Sydney

Gardens earlier was with a clear and sober head. Back in those terrible days of my alcoholism, I was capable of seeing anything, whether desired or not."

Loadall got up from his armchair.

"Before we go any further, gentlemen, how about I fix your favourite hot beverages?"

"Well, I'm not sure that a steaming black coffee will erase my sense of foreboding, but I am rather parched." affirmed Bennett-Brewer.

"And a steaming mug of Ginger & Moroccan Mint won't do me any harm." added Curnow.

A few minutes later, Loadall returned from the kitchen with Curnow's usual drinking vessel and a mug for Bennett-Brewer displaying a cannabis leaf with the words, *I'M WELL AND TRULY FUCKED!*

"A present from Mrs Mordent." Loadall informed the teacher.

For the third time during his visit, Bennett-Brewer put his head in his hands. Eventually, he looked up and warily invited Graham Curnow to detail his earlier experience.

"Well, I was strolling along minding my own business, and even though the weather wasn't exactly clement, I was filled with the joys of springtime. As I walked toward the gate from the canal to the main part of Sydney Gardens, I had an irresistible urge to explore this playground of the Georgian elite.

"I made haste from the gate down the sloping hill that leads to the bridge that goes over the railway. I crossed the bridge, came down a further incline, and sat myself down on one of the benches in front of the tracks. It was at that moment that the rain and wind upped the ante.

"I'm always well prepared for foul weather, as you can see from my rugged waterproofs drying out on the hat stand."

A low rumble of thunder accompanied Curnow's pointed finger.

Bennett-Brewer sighed with trepidation, though he was desperate for Curnow to continue.

"...The railway runs for about three-hundred yards through the Gardens, and rather than remain stationary to be bullied by the weather, I decided to walk the path that runs parallel to the tracks through to the far end."

Loadall turned to Bennett-Brewer.

"Have you visited Sydney Gardens yet, Jeremy?"

"No, and after what I heard from Dick Joy, it's not exactly high on my wish list."

Graham Curnow took a sip of herbal tea before continuing,

"I must say, even when the weather's agreeable, it is a rather spooky walk along the pathway. There are two bridges inside the Gardens that span the railway, and both have archways over the path that divide it into three equal sections. The archways are always covered in graffiti, and I noticed a particular message left on the first: *RIP wee Charlie Garrett.*"

Jeremy Bennett-Brewer widened his eyes on hearing the name of the boy whose freak death was witnessed by Dick Joy and his friends many years earlier.

"...When I reached the archway of the second bridge, I saw exactly the same message scrawled on it. I then walked through the arch to join the final third of the pathway, and although I've walked it many times over the years, this was the first time that I noticed the tower of St Swithin's clearly visible through the tunnel at the far end. Although the church is the best part of a mile away, my eyesight was good enough to notice a figure stood behind the parapet of the tower. I could hear the tracks begin to hiss, so I stood still to watch the express to Paddington roar through. As it disappeared through the far tunnel, I looked again toward the church tower, and noticed that the figure was replaced by a glowing light. I eventually reached the end of the pathway, and for the third time saw the same *RIP wee Charlie Garrett* chalked on the wall of the far tunnel. This time, there was another message underneath."

Curnow pronounced the badly-spelt message phonetically, "Good ridunce to the littel cunt."

***

"On the last day of the Larkhall Village Festival, the grand cross of Mars, Pluto, Saturn and Uranus shall be formed, and it is imperative that we are there to witness what we all hope will be the end time."

The disciples nodded excitedly.

"...I want you all to make sure you can take the day off on Sunday, June fifteenth."

"Oh dear..." whispered Sir Leonard Hutton as he held a troubled finger to his lips. "I'm afraid I've used up all my holiday allowance until August!"

"Fear ye not, Sir Leonard...!" Expectorant replied. "I am prepared to write a sick note under my Earthly name of Trevor Watkinson for all those who may struggle arranging absence from their employment; I would write one for you, Sir Leonard, but you've overlooked the fact that you don't work on Sundays, anyway."

Hutton glanced bashfully around the room as his air-headedness was again exposed. Expectorant addressed the other four.

"...In any required sick notes, I shall explain that my parsnips were unknowingly blighted by root knot nematodes, and that absence of any disciple from their place of work be due to continual visits to the lavatory. I

The Wyvern & The Witchfinder

have no idea if root knot nematodes cause bowel woes, but I'd hope it would sound plausible to any employer."

"I must say I'm quite relieved..." answered WG Grace. "Fortunately, Denise and myself have several days of holiday to take, but it's nice to know we have the safety net of knowing that continual visits to the lavatory would be like a busman's holiday for us."

Expectorant smiled and turned his attention toward Iftikhar Ali Khan.

"Is the coast clear for you, Ifty?"

"Oh, don't you worry about me, glorious leader. My young assistant is coming on a bundle, and I've no doubt my fish shop will be left in capable hands."

Expectorant nodded cheerily, and finally addressed his trusted left-hand man.

"How about you, Sir Jack?"

"I've always got a few days of holiday up my sleeve for the summer months, so you can pencil me in."

"That's great news...!" Expectorant responded. "Naming you after cricket's all-time leading run scorer shows just how highly I regard you!"

The four other disciples took it in turns to high-five Hobbs.

"I'm glad that we all know the score, and it simplifies things greatly that there's no need for me to unnecessarily blight the good name of my parsnips!"

Sir Jack Hobbs interjected,

"Let there be no doubt that Mr Expectorant is quite the most humble and selfless leader we could wish for. It's nice to know that sick notes won't need to be produced, but being prepared to put a dent in his own reputation as high-class fruit and vegetable proprietor by inventing phantom illnesses due to his stock goes way beyond the call of duty."

"Very kind words, Sir Jack, although whatever the damage to my reputation if I did have to write those sick notes, it won't be very important after the world has ended."

The disciples mirrored their leader's sober expression.

***

"It gave me quite a start to read that illiterate anti tribute to that poor young boy..." added a sombre Curnow. "As soon as I read it, I looked through the tunnel again toward the church, and noticed that the glow from the tower parapet was getting brighter and a little bigger."

The loudest thunderclap of the evening followed, and startled Bennett-Brewer into spilling hot coffee over his groin.

"AAAARGH!"

Loadall got up from his chair, went to the kitchen, and returned with a cloth for the teacher to wipe himself down.

"A most unfortunate accident, Jeremy..." uttered Loadall. "Though having hot coffee spilled over your intimate parts is no doubt preferable to having old ladies attached to them."

Bennett-Brewer didn't see the funny side of Loadall's comment, especially as it was delivered in a way that inferred it wasn't meant to be amusing.

"Scorched intimates notwithstanding, may I continue?" smiled Curnow as he asked permission.

"Please do." invited Loadall, while the teacher mopped himself down in silence.

"The weather became even filthier, and the tower of St Swithin's faded almost to nothing. Through the gloom, I could make out the orange glow grow larger, and then I saw a blinding flash of light; far too spectacular to be lightning, and because it wasn't followed by a rumble of thunder, I knew it was something quite different. I blinked my eyes a few times to regain proper vision, and I saw a bright orange ball of haze fill the tunnel, then make its way slowly along the railway line, all the way through to disappear into the depths of the tunnel at the other end of the Gardens."

The rain was now hammering against the lounge window, and another rumble of thunder inspired Barry Loadall to lift his face skyward with a half grin.

"...I continued to look along the track into the far tunnel for several seconds, and then I noticed the gloom in the tunnel slowly brighten with the returning glow. I saw another blinding flash, and after again blinking several times to clear my vision, saw the orange glow re-emerge from the tunnel.

"This time, the fuzzy glow seemed to be bounding along the tracks in a circular motion, and it approached at quite a rate of knots."

"Jesus!" Bennett-Brewer exclaimed, as he again put his head in his hands.

Curnow smiled understandingly.

"To my alarm, as the glow got nearer, I could see it take on the form of a cartwheeling man. I got pretty scared and ran up the steps that adjoin the tunnel away from the tracks. I could now only see a tiny section of the railway from the top of the steps, and I was dreading what might soon be appearing in front of me."

"And was your dread well founded?" a serious Loadall asked Curnow, while Bennett-Brewer's face remained in his hands.

"Yes it was. Within a few seconds, the orange glow stopped on the track at the bottom of the steps and turned into the unmistakeable form of Chatterton. It became even more dreadful when I saw his facial features slowly develop. His face was broken beyond recognition, and his head began to tilt sideways. Mercifully, the appalling sight vanished in a couple of seconds, and I was also grateful that the weather suddenly took a turn for the better and the sun appeared."

"So..." added Curnow as he turned toward Bennett-Brewer. "that answers the question as to why I'm now not so sure that Chatterton is a figment of my imagination."

18

TEMPTATION OF THE TIN CHURCH

"You're a complete piss-pot and a total twat...what are you?"
"I'm a complete piss-pot and a total twat, my sweet."
"Good."

Jemima Joy placed the plate of fried eggs on toast on the kitchen table, then clenched her fist to perform a *doughny* on her husband's head.

Mrs Joy briefly left the kitchen to pick up her handbag from the lounge, and Joy raised both arms and flexed his fingers to mimic strangling her. He hurriedly put his arms down as she returned to the kitchen. Mrs Joy plonked her handbag on the table, leant her palms on its surface, and leaned toward her husband.

"Why is it you always have to get pissed and blab that fuckin' mouth of yours?"

"I haven't said a word my love, honest!"

Mrs Joy stepped toward the draining board, picked up a saucepan, and returned to clonk her other half forcibly on the crown of his head.

"Do you think I'm totally bloody stupid or something!?"

The question was left unanswered as Mrs Joy returned the pan to the draining board, stamped out of the house and slammed the front door shut. As Dick rubbed his sore head, he used his other hand to aim an obscene gesture at her through the door. He kept his hand in position a little too long, and his wife spotted it as she passed the kitchen window. She reacted by again clenching her fist, and then running a finger across her lips in a zipping motion as a warning to her husband to keep his mouth shut. She eventually walked away from the house after producing a final threatening scowl.

Bloody-fuckin' fat-arsed old fuckin' sow, Joy whispered to himself before tackling his breakfast. As it was Wednesday, he had an appointment with The Bladud's Midriff, and as his wife would be away for the whole day visiting her sister on the other side of town, decided that he'd take advantage by visiting the pub as soon as it opened. Joy's alcoholism decreed that he only needed the bare minimum of food to keep him alive, and he disdainfully pushed his breakfast away after one mouthful.

***

The Bladud's Midriff was a free house, as were the other two pubs that adorned Larkhall. The fact that none of the village's pubs were owned by breweries was a source of local pride, and occasional tentative approaches from corporate representatives met with fierce hostility. After a heated battle with the local council several years earlier, the landlord was forced into taking down the pub sign that depicted a huge scrotum with the crowned head of King Bladud hovering above it. The city council argued that a two-foot-square depiction of male genitalia would upset the tourists of Bath, while the locals counter argued that visitors to the city were unlikely to stray that far from the centre, and even if they did, this was exactly the type of quaint olde English eccentricity they'd delight in.

The new sign for the pub resulted from a reluctant compromise between pub and council that displayed a much larger illustration of King Bladud's head and crown, together with four much smaller scrotums in each corner.

Late-morning weekdays were almost always free of customers, so the landlord made use of his free time by playing darts. Malcolm Dawkins was pretty handy with the arrows, and after his first two darts hit the treble-twenty bed, composed himself for the final throw. Just as the last dart was released, he was put off by the creaking of the bar door and skewed it wide of the mark. The agitated publican turned around to see Dick Joy shuffle toward the bar.

"A broken fuckin' clock's got better timing than you, ya frizzy, short-arsed twat!"

"Sorry mate, didn't mean to fuck things up."

Dawkins' disappointment with his aborted maximum soon faded as he returned behind the bar to pour a pint of hard scrumpy for his unexpectedly early customer.

Although Dick Joy's black eyes had faded over the few days since his latest battering, they were still very noticeable.

"Christ, Dick, how the hell did you end-up with those shiners?"

"Honestly Malc, you couldn't make it up if you bloody tried. I was in the hardware shop lookin' for a new blender, and that old bat Mrs Mordent came in with that stupid little fuckin' dog of hers. Anyway, the bloody thing got tangled up in my feet, and I tripped forward and stepped on two rakes at the same time, and both handles whacked me eyes."

The landlord nodded his head in strained agreement. Even by Joy's drunken standards, this was a whopper of breath-taking proportions due to Mrs Mordent not even owning a dog.

"Fair enough mate, though you do look as if your missus has given you a good seein' to!"

"Quite the bloody reverse, pal!"

Dick Joy used a stabbing finger to emphasise his conviction.

"...I was the one givin' her a good seein to. I gave 'er such a good tubbin' last night, she were walkin' round in circles this mornin'!"

The landlord failed to supress a mocking chuckle in response to the absurdity of Joy's libido claims.

"'...Ere, you ain't takin' the piss Malc, are ya?"

Joy lifted his pint only half-jokingly as if to tip it over the landlord's head if his answer wasn't satisfactory.

"Course not, me ol' chum! I know you can put it about a bit, and I'd never doubt that you're capable of turnin' yer missus into a cripple."

"Too bleedin' right, Malc! Honestly mate, when I finished with 'er last night, she 'ad a minge like a wizard's sleeve!"

"I take it yer missus is away for the day?"

"What makes ya say that?"

"Well, you wouldn't be in 'ere so early if she weren't, would ya?"

"You sayin' I'm scared of 'er?"

Malcolm Dawkins decided not to answer and instead shook his head with amused incredulity.

"You fuckin' ARE piss!"

Dick Joy drank the final two-thirds of his pint in one, got up from the barstool and kicked over several tables and chairs before storming out of the pub.

***

On each corner of Larkhall Square stood the café, the chemist, the butchers, and The Blackest Morn public house.

As opposed to Larkhall's other pubs, The Blackest Morn was never short of custom. Due to its position in the very heart of the village, its fame as being the oldest pub in the area, and its sheer size, it was a favourite for both the locals and passers-by.

Ally Lee and Ronan Rhodes both had the day off, and the pair arranged to meet in the pub lounge to begin their day of drinking. The time was approaching midday, and already the pub was doing good trade with about a dozen customers. The latest to arrive were greeted by the landlord.

"You pair of wazzocks not working today?"

"Nope!"

Ally Lee followed his excited answer by asking for two pints of rough cider.

"We're gonna get rat arsed!" added Ronan Rhodes with equal excitement.

"Yeah, well don't you two over bloody do it." warned Terry Pensford; the latest in a long line of Pensfords to have run the pub.

Just as the landlord was about to expand on the dangers of overdoing it, Dick Joy stumbled through the door to illustrate his point.

"There you go..." Pensford whispered to the boys from the corner of his mouth. "If he ain't a warnin' to you two about turnin' into pissed up pricks, I dunno what is."

As soon as Pensford finished his whisper, he looked-up at the approaching Joy and noticed his fading black eyes.

"Someone's been in the wars, I reckon!"

"You can bloody say that again, Tel...!" Joy responded as he took a barstool next to the teenagers. "I were up Solsbury Hill with me binoculars doin' a spot of bird-watchin', and then some twat on a bike who weren't looking where he were goin' crashed into me, knocked me forward, and as I hit the ground, the binoculars jammed against me eyes."

The landlord, teenagers, and the other few patrons scattered around the bar struggled to hide their amusement.

"You bastards takin' the piss?"

"Course not, Dick!"

Joy mumbled a grudging okay to Pensford before tackling his scrumpy. A pub regular raised his voice from the end of the bar.

"What the fuck are ya doin' in here today, it 'ain't the weekend, is it?"

"None of yer fuckin' business, ya nosy cunt!" Joy answered aggressively.

"He's only bloody in 'ere cos his missus it out for the day!" re-prodded the regular.

Before Joy could respond, the whole pub except for the landlord and newly-arrived teenagers burst into laughter.

Another customer decided to rib Joy further.

"Where's she gone Dick, off to get a mousetrap for yer cock?"

Again the whole pub laughed, and this time Lee and Rhodes didn't bother to attempt hiding their amusement.

Dick Joy remained silent for a couple of seconds before downing the final two thirds of his pint in one. As he got-up from the barstool, he used a horizontal arm to karate chop the double magnum sized vodka bottle half-full of charity coins off the bar. Lush carpeting ensured the bottle stayed in once piece, and after a few seconds of shocked silence, the customers again burst into merriment. Joy further announced his departure by kicking over the two empty tables and several chairs on his way to the exit.

"Fuckin' 'ell, Tel...!" whispered Ally Lee to the landlord, as he and his friend got on all fours to help return the coins to the bottle. "D'ya reckon Dick's lying about how he got his black eyes?"

Terry Pensford laughed heartily.

"Course he's bloody lying, you dozy little turd. Dick's been knocked about by Jemima for as long as anyone can remember, but ya gotta admire his imagination. I remember the time years back when he came in with his arm in a sling, and he told everyone he caught a massive fish, but when he reeled it in, his arm got broke 'cos the fish got really angry and kept flapping against it."

Both boys laughed as they were informed of Joy's state of denial.

"Why does his missus keep battering him?" asked Lee.

"It goes back years. Dick's wife is a few years older than him, and when Dick was about twelve or thirteen, his missus was gettin' porked by Chatterton."

Lee and Rhodes' eyes lit up with excitement and they invited the landlord to continue.

"...Chatterton was hated by everyone around Larkhall, and when word got about that Dick's missus was gettin' shafted by him, people started avoiding her. Every time Dick gets pissed, he keeps goin' on about Chatterton, though she only gets violent with him when he starts tellin' people new to the area. I've heard that Dick's been tellin' that new teacher in The Wyvern all about Chatterton, an' 'is missus is gettin' fucked off with it.

"She worshipped Chatterton, an' she blames Dick for gettin' him to unlock that tin church up Bailbrook and gettin' his face smashed up."

"Fuck me...!" blurted Lee. "Where d'ya reckon Dick went when he left 'ere?"

"I dunno. There's somethin' strange going on though, 'cos in the forty-odd years he's been comin' in here, can't remember him comin' in on a Wednesday before."

"D'ya reckon he's gone to The Wyvern?" asked Rhodes.

"Well, Sundays 'n Mondays are his days for drinkin' in there, but if he's just come in here on the wrong day, maybe he's gone somewhere else on the wrong day."

***

Rose Rensenbrink reversed her husband's decision to keep their free house shut during weekday afternoons. Any custom was better than none, and she successfully reasoned that the pub needed every scrap of trade it could get. Dave Rensenbrink decided to make use of his day off by walking Clive, and then popping down The Midriff to discuss trade with Malcolm Dawkins over a few pints.

Twelve-thirty Wednesday afternoon, Rose was delighted to see Ally Lee and Ronan Rhodes enter.

"Hello lads, what can I get you?"

"Two Witch Rogerer's please." answered Lee.

As Rose poured the pints, she asked the teenagers what their plans were for their day off.

"We're gonna get shit faced!"

"And why not." Rose responded, hoping that they'd achieve their ambition before leaving the premises.

"Has Dick been in?" enquired Rhodes.

"Nope, won't be seein' him before Sunday. Wednesdays he goes to The Bladud's."

"We've just come from The Blackest Morn, and Dick was in there."

"You sure?"

Rose handed over the two pints to the nodding boys with a puzzled look.

"...Well there's a turn up for the books. In all the years we've served Dick, I've never known him to break his routine. Sundays and Mondays he's here, Wednesday and Thursday it's The Bladud's, and it's The Blackest Morn Fridays and Saturdays. You could set your clock by him."

"That's what Terry Pensford reckoned too..." replied Lee. "He said it's the first time he ever saw Dick in there on a Wednesday."

Mrs Rensenbrink handed Rhodes his change.

"That's really odd; not just Dick going there on a Wednesday, but also not waitin' until the evening. His wife makes sure of that."

"His missus is away for the day, apparently."

"How d'ya know that?" the landlady asked Ally Lee.

"Well, as soon as he came in, the rest of the pub started takin' the piss out of him, and they were sayin' he wouldn't've dared come in if his missus weren't away."

"You wouldn't fuckin' believe what happened." Rhodes added.

Temptation Of The Tin Church

The boys took hearty swallows from their pints as Rose invited them to continue.

"Dick got right shitty with ev'ryone takin' the piss out of him..." Lee answered. "'He knocked over the massive vodka bottle on the bar and booted over the tables and chairs on his way out!"

"Crikey, that's not like Dick. I know he sometimes gets a bit lippy 'n lairy, but I've never known him get physical."

After a moment of silent pondering, the bar door opened, and a contrite Dick Joy plodded furtively toward the bar.

"Hello Dick...what're you doing in here on a Wednesday?"

"Hullo Rose, m'love. Alright lads?"

Joy received understanding smiles from the landlady and the teenagers, who could see from his defensive posture that he was full of regret.

"Just give us a half of best, Rose love."

"Everythin' alright, mate?" asked Ronan Rhodes as he held a concerned hand on Joy's shoulder.

"Yeah, I'm alright lads, and cheers for askin'."

Rose Rensenbrink was the latest publican to comment on the nasty faded bruises around Joy's eyes.

Joy took a sip of bitter before gazing ruefully at the landlady and both teenagers.

"Well, I went to Weston-super-Mare the other day, and I was looking out to sea through one of them telescope things they got on the front, and some kid whacked a football into the back o' me head."

The boys burst into laughter in response to the story being completely different to the one they'd heard from Joy a few minutes earlier in The Blackest Morn. The landlady glared at Lee and Rhodes in anticipation of Dick getting shirty and storming out of the pub.

Joy in turn glared at the boys, and they reacted with nervous silence. After a few seconds, he turned his glare to the landlady, then looked down into his half-pint. After a deep breath, Dick Joy eventually came clean.

"It's no good, I can't keep talkin' bullshit all me life."

Rose and the teenagers raised their eyebrows in unison.

"...Me missus did this, just like she's been doin' it for the last forty years."

The other three feigned surprise before they allowed Joy to continue.

"I dunno why the fuck I married her in the first place, she's had me by the short 'n curlies ever since she found out I was one of the kids who was there when lover boy smashed himself up."

"D'ya mean Chatterton the spaz?" asked Ronan Rhodes insensitively.

"Yeah, I do mean Chatterton the spaz."

Joy drained the remainder of his glass and asked for a pint of his usual tipple of rough cider and blackcurrant.

"That's more like our Dick!" beamed Rose Rensenbrink, who was pleased that Joy's flirt with moderate drinking was over.

***

After taking Clive to the park and having a couple of pints at The Bladud's Midriff, Dave Rensenbrink returned to his pub to discover Dick Joy sat upright on a barstool with arms folded and snoring contentedly. His wife smiled from behind the bar, while Lee and Rhodes returned tipsy grins.

"It is Wednesday today, innit?"

Rose nodded back.

"Well I'll be buggered."

The landlord unleashed Clive, and the dog merrily trotted toward the back room for its afternoon nap. Rensenbrink spoke in a hushed voice to avoid waking Joy up, and recommended the teenagers do the same.

"...That's the first time he's been here on a Wednesday. I've just been in The Midriff, and Dawkins told me he popped in just before I got there. Said Dick got right nasty and started kickin' over 'is tables!"

"We were down The Morn before we got here..." mentioned Ally Lee in a slurry whisper. "and he was bootin' over the tables 'n chairs in there, an' all!"

"Fuck me...!" exclaimed Rensenbrink quietly. "He never goes to The Morn on a Wednesday, either."

"D'ya know anythin' about the tin church?" Rhodes asked Rensenbrink with youthful relish.

"Yeah, plenty, though I'd steer well clear if I were you."

"Dick says no-one's been in there for forty years."

Dick Joy suddenly returned to consciousness and answered on behalf of Dave Rensenbrink.

"Nobody's dared try an' get in ever since I were a kid and saw Chatterton smashed-up."

"D'ya reckon we could break-in?" a mildly drunk Ally Lee asked the landlord.

"If you got yourselves the right tools, yeah, though you'd better think carefully."

"We have thought carefully, ain't we?" Lee gazed at his pal to seek confirmation.

"Have we?" answered Rhodes apprehensively.

Dick Joy rose from his barstool and invited Lee and Rhodes to join him on a trip to the hardware store to obtain the necessary tools for the job. Both boys agreed to curtail their drinking, though Rhodes was less enthusiastic than his mate.

19

UNORTHODOX SERMON

Victor Carping was determined to go ahead with his latest sermon, although he was well aware of how divisive it might prove. After much gnashing of teeth, Carping finally settled on the sermon title of *Let's Invite Satan in for a Refreshing Cuppa*.

The Rector of St Swithin's braced himself for fiery communications from the Church hierarchy, but he felt it was about time that The Devil's point of view was given a sympathetic hearing. The main thrust of Carping's argument was that everybody had the capacity for good and evil, and that if Satan was continually being dissed and disapproved of, then it was hardly surprising that He took umbrage and behaved in a beastly manner.

Thirty minutes before Carping's scheduled appearance, the pews of the church were full to capacity, with dozens of curious locals forced into standing. St Swithin's had never known such numbers attend, and Carping viewed that as ammunition enough against the inevitable cries of orthodox protest.

As Carping affixed his rollerblades, he silently prayed to whatever entity was in charge of his Earthly existence for understanding and compassion. The young Rector then took a deep breath, reached for his jar of pickled eggs and decided it was too late for turning back.

The expectant buzz from the congregation suddenly turned into riotous applause and wolf whistling as Carping appeared from the front of the church and glided through the central aisle clutching the two-kilogram jar to his chest.

***

The retired vicar of Nibley-under-Edge was as unyielding and inflexible as any churchman in the country. While most of his former colleagues were busy watering down Biblical teachings and encouraging analogy rather than literal revelation, Adam Abrahams became more and more enraged with every concession the Church made in the face of science and reason. Whilst he grudgingly accepted that the Earth revolved around the Sun and wasn't at the epicentre of the known universe, that's as far as it went for bowing to science. For him, it simply wasn't good enough that blind eyes were turned against folk coveting their neighbours' asses, or them revelling in secular materialism at the expense of spiritual obedience.

Abrahams had kept every newspaper cutting he could find involving Rector Victor Carping, and every now and then he leafed through his scrapbook to top up his hatred of the man who appeared no more God fearing than the coldest atheist.

Nothing aroused the ire of Abrahams more than the article from the Nibley Mercury headlined *Give Him A Break!* – in which Carping told a reporter that Satan was the victim of a two-millennia old witch hunt. To add insult to injury, the article was accompanied by a photograph showing Carping warmly embracing a person dressed in a traditional devil costume.

The ex-vicar of Nibley made sure he got himself a good place for Carping's latest sermon. Although he'd witnessed a couple of the Rector's previous heretical chunterings, Abrahams decided to keep a low profile. The damage to the Church was becoming irreparable, and the time had now come for him to physically intervene.

Abrahams strategically placed himself on the end of a pew at the back of the main aisle, and as the roar of the congregation announced Carping's arrival, braced himself to do what he had to do.

As Victor Carping elegantly glided past Abrahams, the enraged former churchman stepped out from the pew and into the aisle.

"YOU HERETICAL CHUNTERING SHITBAG!"

Abrahams followed his shriek of rage by running after Carping and attaching both hands to his back to give him an almighty shove toward the altar. The rest of the congregation let out confused gasps as Carping sped along the aisle while struggling to keep the pickled egg jar clamped to his chest. The Rector's powers of co-ordination were severely tested, but he finally regained full balance as he rapidly wheeled along. Even so, he was powerless to slow down, and a heavy impact with the altar table seemed unavoidable. Carping braced himself for the collision, but at the last moment decided to see if his schoolboy gymnastic skills were still in rude health.

The altar table was three foot high, and proved the perfect height for the speeding Rector to clamp his left palm onto its surface and successfully perform a one-handed handstand for several seconds as his right arm successfully held the jar against his chest. After a moment of astonished silence, the congregation burst into ecstatic applause in response to Carping's incredible feat of strength and balance.

A hush slowly descended as Carping continued to balance motionless. Gravity caused his cassock to gently flop down to blanket the entire upside-down form of his upper body and head; revealing boxer-shorts emblazoned with a caricature of The Devil shaking hands with Jesus. Only the first few rows of the congregation were close enough to turn their heads upside down and make out the details of the Rector's underwear, and several of them turned behind to pass on the news. Very quickly, the whole congregation was informed of Carping's illustrated smalls, and more cheering and clapping spread throughout the church.

The only person unimpressed with the audacious spectacle was Adam Abrahams, and the ex-cleric struggled to free himself from the half dozen church goers who'd performed a citizen's arrest in the centre of the aisle.

All eyes were fixed on Victor Carping as he finally let himself fall slowly back from the altar table and land perfectly on stationary rollerblades. The Rector rounded off his gymnastic display by gracefully turning one hundred and eighty degrees to face the congregation, performing the splits, and raising his left arm in triumph while the right still clutched the two-kilo egg jar.

Carping held the pose for several seconds amid ecstatic cheering and flashing cameras. After finally returning to his feet and rearranging his cassock, the Rector requested the arresters of Adam Abrahams to march him up to the altar.

The conservative and liberal churchmen stared at each other in silence in front of the altar table, before Carping requested Abrahams to sit in one of the front pews. Several parishioners left the pew to make way for the retired vicar, and joined the many already standing at the back of the church.

Carping climbed the steps to the lectern with an agility and elegance that defied his rollerbladed feet and jar clutching. The St Swithin's Rector then cleared his throat and patted the microphone.

"Parishioners of our wonderful church, I welcome you all most warmly; and may I extend this welcome to the retired vicar of Nibley-under-Edge."

The congregation buzzed with curses and booing before the Rector held up a hand.

Unorthodox Sermon

"Please, please good parishioners, we are here to show love and understanding toward everyone. Whether it be Satan Himself or an irked former member of the clergy, our cup of charity must be overflowingeth."

This time a respectful silence followed, while Adam Abrahams had calmed down to the extent of his face fading to its natural colour. The persons sat either side of Abrahams were ready to restrain him should he attempt a sudden dash toward Carping.

The Rector unscrewed the top of the jar and removed four pickled eggs. He began to juggle as he continued his sermon; much to the delight of his audience apart from Abrahams, who was busy muttering angrily to himself.

"People of Larkhall, it is now time to renounce centuries of displeasure aimed at those alleged not to be on the Lord's narrow path of righteousness."

A communal hum of appreciation and acceptance followed.

"...Our way MUST be one of compromise and compassion toward those we previously reviled and wished to be toasted in the depths of hell."

"BOLLOCKS!"

Adam Abrahams' yell was loud enough to be heard by the entire congregation. Carping remained calm enough for his juggling rhythm to remain unbroken, while another chorus of disapproval was aimed at the ex-churchman's latest intervention. Carping decided to hold out an olive branch.

"What we must never lose sight of..." began the Rector as he shifted his focus between the congregation, Abrahams and his juggling. "is that all points of view must be heard. I now extend the hand of friendship to my enraged former colleague and invite him up to explain his position."

More cheers greeted Carping's throwing down of the gauntlet, and Adam Abrahams agreed to be escorted up the steps to the lectern as Carping nimbly made way. The cheers gradually died away and turned into an excited hush as Abrahams cleared his throat.

"Firstly, may I thank the Rector of St Swithin's for allowing me to have my say."

A courteous silence greeted Abrahams' opening statement.

"We live in a world of moral decay, a world where people openly snigger at the Lord's teachings."

The congregation remained silent.

"...Anybody who smirks in the face of God's ways shall find their backsides endlessly punctured!"

Abrahams then thumped his fist against the lectern, and the proximity of the microphone caused a deafening bang. More discontent spread through the pews, before Mrs Mordent rose from the second row and pointed an accusing walking stick at the ex-vicar.

"I'm fed up with people like you trying to put the wind up us! Why should fuddy-duddy old buggers like you tell us that we shouldn't be having a nibble of whatever we fancy?"

Certain words were emphasised by stabs of the walking stick, and the old lady's statement was backed by hearty cheering from the rest of the church. Several of them urged her to continue blasting Abrahams, and she readily accepted.

"...Just look at the state of you! You're such a sour faced old sod, and that's all because you've spent your whole life denying yourself and being bloody miserable!"

More cheering followed from the congregation, and the ex-churchman's face re-reddened with rage.

"DON'T YOU TELL ME HOW TO LIVE MY LIFE, YOU WRINKLED OLD TROUT...!" Abrahams bellowed back. "AND DON'T YOU COME MOANING TO ME WHEN YOU BEGIN YOUR SENTENCE OF EVERLASTING TORMENT!"

Mrs Tanning stood to show solidarity with her friend.

"AND DON'T YOU TELL *US* HOW TO LIVE *OUR* LIVES, BIG EARS!"

Laughter and cheers greeted Mrs Tanning's retort, and Abrahams reacted by self-consciously smoothing his ears that stuck out almost ninety degrees. The jollity caused by his humiliation made Abrahams shake with rage.

"AH SHUDDUP, YOU DEVIL-LOVING OLD SLAG!"

Mrs Tanning produced a pickled egg from her pocket, and for an old lady, threw it with surprising force and accuracy. The ex-vicar took a direct hit to the middle of his forehead.

A few of Victor Carping's helpers had been secretly handing out pickled eggs to the congregation as Abrahams began his tirade. By now, most of the first three rows were armed.

Abrahams swayed on his feet trying to recover from the blow to the head, then raised his right fist toward Mrs Tanning while being closely chaperoned by several parishioners.

"...YOU'LL BE LAUGHING ON THE OTHER SIDE OF YOUR FACE WHEN SATAN WORKS ALL MANNER OF FIERY OBJECTS UP YOUR SAGGY OLD ASS!"

The whole church was incensed by the ex-vicar's latest threat, and Abrahams held up both arms in defence as pickled eggs flew at him from all angles. He continued to damn the congregation while occasionally pausing to duck and weave against the onslaught.

"...SATAN WILL BE USING HIS OWN...OW!!... TRUSTED FORK...

Unorthodox Sermon

TO PRICK YOUR BLASPHEMING... SPHINCTERS... AS YOU ALL... WRITHE AND... OW!!... TWIST IN THE BIGGEST AND... HOTTEST FURNACE HE... OW!!... OW!!... CAN IGNITE!"

Victor Carping suddenly appeared in front of the lectern and held out his arms to the congregation as a gesture to say enough was enough. The former vicar of Nibley-under-Edge was then taken down from the lectern as a final pickled egg caught him a glancing blow to the top of his balding head.

Abrahams was a blur of flailing limbs and monstrous obscenities as he was manhandled down the steps and through the aisle to the main door. As his humiliated opponent vanished from view, Carping re-climbed the steps to the lectern with the same elegance and assurance he'd achieved earlier. He re-tapped the microphone to make sure it still worked properly after Abrahams' fist-thump.

"Comrades, brothers and sisters, may we all rejoice in the expelling of that pitiful and embittered creature, and embrace with much warmth and compassion our supposed enemy; the very Devil itself!"

The whole congregation stood, raised their arms skyward, and yelled *Oh my Lord!"*

20

BACKFIRING BLACKMAIL

On their way to the hardware store, Dick Joy and the teenagers discussed which day was best for visiting the tin church. They decided on the coming Sunday afternoon, and none of them felt impatient about waiting a few days.

"Hello Dick, 'ow's 'ee goin'?"

"Alright, Willie?"

"Who're these two varmints you've dragged in with ya?"

Joy remained silent as the boys introduced themselves.

"What're you all after, then?" enquired the store owner.

"Well..." began Joy. "these two wanna take a look inside the ol' tin church."

"You realise it's got chains 'n padlocks all 'round it?"

"Course I do, that's why we wanna borrow yer biggest bolt cutters!"

The store owner looked Joy up and down with disdain and incredulity.

"You must be fuckin' jokin'!"

The conviction of Willie Woodman's brief reply stunned Joy and the boys, and they could only stare back in disappointment.

"...First, I'd be shut down if word got about I lent specialist equipment to a walkin' piss pot like you."

Joy stared innocently back at the store keeper, while the other two struggled not to laugh.

"...And second; I'm not gonna play any fuckin' part in openin' that church."

Willie Woodman glared at Dick Joy.

"...If you and these two kids wanna poke about, that's your bloody funeral, but don't expect me to help you out."

Lee and Rhodes decided that was that, and agreed to go back to the pub.

"You comin', Dick?"

"Yeah, but give us a few minutes."

As soon as the teenagers left, Willie Woodman leant over the counter to pull Dick Joy by the lapels and bring his face to within a few inches of his.

"Listen to me, you pissed-up wanker, I'm asked all the time to do a job on that church, so don't you fuckin' come it with me!"

Such was the desperation of Joy to get hold of the necessary tools, it overrode his desire to get back to drinking. His desperation also gave him a sudden shot of courage and conviction.

Woodman let go of Joy, and the two men stared at each other for a moment before Dick broke the silence.

"Look mate, we've known each other for years. I know we 'ain't always got along, but if you don't help me out, I might just let it slip about the time I saw ya in the back room hooverin' somethin' ya shouldn't've been hooverin'."

The store-owner's face went red with a mix of shame and anger. He again pulled Joy toward him by the lapels.

"You wouldn't fuckin' dare!"

Woodman let go of his irritating customer in the desperate hope that his aggressive response would disguise his fear and force Dick to abort his nasty threat.

"I dunno if I would dare, but I also dunno what yer missus would say if she knew. Is that a chance yer'd wanna take?"

***

Jeremy Bennett-Brewer stewed for a long time about the wisdom of visiting the old man from the old cottage, and by the time Sunday arrived, his battle between curiosity and fear had been narrowly won by the former. It was such a close-run thing that he could only make the decision on the spin of a coin. The teacher was full of nagging doubt as he closed the front door behind.

Bennett-Brewer's trepidation gradually eased as the Sun burned away the light cloud to produce a warm and pleasant early June morning. He made his way along the road that ran parallel to Lam Brook toward The

Bladud's Midriff. As he passed the pub to begin the steep climb up Ferndale Road, the teacher paused for a few seconds to steel himself.

The hill of Ferndale Road was so steep, Bennett-Brewer had to place his hands on his thighs to help with his balance and endurance. Thankfully, it was only a short climb until he reached the old A46 highway. He stood still for a few moments to regain his breath as he contemplated the further climb ahead. Not a single vehicle passed Bennett-Brewer as he paused, and as he eventually crossed the road, found himself at the bottom of Bailbrook Lane. The first part of the lane was as steep as Ferndale Road, and again the teacher clamped his palms to his thighs for assistance.

The Sun vanished from view as Bennett-Brewer crossed the part of the lane that doubled up as a bridge high above the A46 bypass. At this point, sightseers to Solsbury Hill would turn left and walk parallel to the dual carriageway deep below. Bennett-Brewer continued straight along Bailbrook Lane and was grateful that the uphill gradient was beginning to flatten out.

Finally, the old cottage was reached, and the teacher was struck by how pleasant and innocuous it appeared. The lawn was beautifully manicured, and a kaleidoscope of colour was produced by an endless array of ripened flora. The Sun appeared again to turn the stonework honey coloured and make the cottage an even more appealing sight. Bennett-Brewer smiled to himself as he thought what a delightful subject for a jigsaw puzzle it would make.

Carrying on the extra hundred or so yards to the tin church wasn't part of Bennett-Brewer's plan, but he felt a sudden compulsion to do so. He thought that if he was brave enough to visit the old cottage and seek answers, he may as well do the double.

Bennett-Brewer left the cottage behind, and as the lane finally became level, he spied the tin church looming at the end of a picturesque row of houses. The continuing sunshine lit the church to turn the rust orange, and as he reached the gate, was greeted by a KEEP OUT! notice.

The teacher was stood with hands on hips as he leant back to view the upper part of the church. He noticed a worn weather vane that featured a blackened depiction of a figure with high crowned hat and an accusatory outstretched arm and finger. The weather vane creaked audibly as it was lightly nudged around in the westerly breeze.

The wild foliage around the steps to the church was saturated from two months of heavy rainfall and entirely hid the main door. Bennett-Brewer decided to straddle the padlocked gate and attempt to reach the entrance. He gingerly lifted his left leg over and felt the sole of his shoe rest on a raised and curved slice of metal. The teacher was startled to look down and see a half hidden and badly rusted mantrap awaiting a clumsy step.

Bennett-Brewer gulped and turned red, then delicately slid his foot out of harm's way. He swung his right leg over the gate to straddle the mantrap and found himself within the church's tiny grounds.

The few steps leading up to the entrance was awash with overgrowth and litter, with various packets and cans bleached white from years of sun. Bennett-Brewer kicked them clear while using both arms to plough a path. After a bit of slipping and sliding, he found himself at the door to the church. The door was very basic and made of cheap but thick plywood that gave the impression it was a temporary fix. Attached to its handle were three padlocks and three metal chains.

The teacher smiled when confronted with the impossibility of opening the church door; not that he had the merest urge to try and get inside. He thrust out a hand of curiosity to yank at one of the chains to test its strength. As he pulled for the third time, the sound of what appeared to be a clenched fist thumping against the door from the other side startled him. Bennett-Brewer removed his hand in shock and fright, and immediately decided to vacate the premises. Even though the main gate was only a few yards away, his panic ensured that the return journey was more challenging. The overgrowth seemed to come alive, and Bennett-Brewer became more tangled the more he thrashed his limbs. Eventually, he swished his way clear, and after narrowly avoiding the mantrap for the second time, used his pumping adrenalin to vault the gate with room to spare.

Bennett-Brewer staggered over to the stone wall on the other side of the narrow lane to regain his breath and senses. After a few seconds, he returned his gaze toward the church, and saw the figure on the weather vane creak around slowly and come to rest with its arm and finger pointing straight at him.

***

"Are you sure we should be doin' this?" asked Ronan Rhodes.

"Dunno, but I'm fucked if I'm leavin' without gettin' inside." responded Dick Joy with uncharacteristic purpose.

"Stop being a scared knob end...!" Ally Lee mocked his mate. "Can't go back now, an' Willie'll be waitin' for us with 'is chain snappers!"

"Look lads, if either of ya's got cold feet, yer better fuck off now and leave me to it."

Joy looked at the boys sternly as he awaited their answer.

"Nah, I'm not gonna miss this!" blurted Lee excitedly.

"Nor me." followed Rhodes with pretend enthusiasm.

The trio met outside The Blackest Morn and took the road that took them past The Wyvern & The Witchfinder and The Bladud's Midriff. They stood at the foot of Ferndale Road and prepared themselves for the steep climb toward the church.

"Brace yerselves, lads, an' don't blame me if it all goes tits up."

***

"Who is it?"

"Good afternoon, I just want to ask a few questions."

The heavy old door creaked opened a few inches before it was restrained by a chain.

"Who the bloody 'ell're you?"

"My name's Jeremy, and I'm a teacher at the local secondary school. My students are doing a project about local history, and I wonder if you could give me some information regarding the old wives' tales of Larkhall?"

"And what the bleedin' hell d'ya expect me to know?"

"Well, I understand your cottage is a place of interest in the local legend?"

The door slammed shut and was followed by the sound of its chain being unlatched. The old man opened the door fully.

"I suppose you better bloody come in."

Jeremy Bennett-Brewer nodded his gratitude at the underwhelming welcome and wiped his feet on the doorstep. Although he was still feeling jittery from his nasty experience a few minutes earlier, it made him more determined to question the old man.

"You better take your shoes off and leave 'em on the mat, yer'll get 'em filthy in 'ere."

The old man re-chained the door, and Bennett-Brewer abided with the strange request before following his host toward the sparsely decorated and ornamented lounge. Two armchairs were placed in opposite corners of the room, and no television set or other entertainment device was visible. Dark brown wallpaper gave the room a claustrophobic feel, and the stench of several decades of musty tobacco hit Bennett-Brewer's nostrils and churned his stomach.

"D'ya wanna cup of tea?" offered the host as Bennett-Brewer took the chair nearest the window to the back garden.

"Yes, that'd be lovely, thank you."

"Yeah, well yer'll 'ave to get down the hill to the village; I never drink the stuff an' aven't got any tea bags."

Bennett-Brewer was so struck by the old man's lack of hospitality that he almost started laughing.

"How long have you lived here?"

"Ever since I was born here." replied the host before he casually lit a high tar cigarette.

The old man emitted a groan of effort as he took the other armchair.

"...I suppose you want to ask me about that backward bloke that ran into my gatepost?"

"Uh...yes please, if you'd be so kind."

Bennett-Brewer's kittenish reply was met with a serious stare.

"Right then, but don't point yer bloody finger at me if you get yerself in trouble for it."

The old man pointed an accusing digit at the teacher, who nodded back with nervous acceptance.

"I don't wish to appear nosy, but do you mind if I ask why you don't have a television?"

"That numbskull weirdo nicked it. First time he nicked me telly, I got it replaced straight off, but then he nicked that one, an' all, so I thought it weren't worth the trouble. Forty years I've lived without a telly or radio."

The teacher looked through the window and was reminded of the cottage's picturesque garden.

"I must say, your garden looks absolutely beautiful in the summer sun."

"Yeah I know, but you haven't come here to admire me silene bleedin' fimbriatums an' iris fuckin' sibiricas, have you?"

As if taking sides in the issue, the Sun hid itself away.

"Well, I wouldn't call myself especially green fingered, I'll admit."

"Get on with it, then, an' stop wastin' me bloody time!"

The old man banged both fists against the soft sides of his armchair several times, and clouds of dust were catapulted into the air.

Bennett-Brewer nodded obediently before taking another look around the room. He noted that thick layers of dust lay on top of the few pieces of furniture and ornaments.

The cottage owner stubbed out his cigarette and immediately lit another.

"...My younger brother was killed by Chatterton."

"How did you know it was Chatterton?" asked a freshly ruffled Bennett-Brewer.

"Because Chatterton never had his tongue out of the Witchfinder's arse. My brother was a local journalist, and he got signed up by the Larkhall Tromboner to write a piece about the legend. The Witchfinder was a right pervert, and my brother didn't hold back writing about it. Chatterton was livid, even though he was a vicious pervert himself.

***

Dick Joy and the teenagers were approaching the old cottage as the Sun returned behind the clouds. Joy told Lee and Rhodes not to stop as they passed, and they were happy to follow his advice.

After visiting the hardware store the previous Wednesday, Joy returned to meet the boys back at the Wyvern & The Witchfinder to inform them that he managed to twist the owner's arm into doing the job on their behalf.

"Just carry-on and don't look back." Joy reiterated.

The old cottage wasn't given a single glance as it was left behind, and soon they reached the flat part of the lane. The owner of the hardware store was leant against the wall opposite the tin church, and as he saw Joy and the teenagers approach, smiled and held the bolt cutters high above his head to snap the air several times.

"You must need yer bloody 'eads felt!" shouted Willie Woodman as he leant the bolt-cutters against the wall and affixed his heavy-duty gloves.

"I've needed mine felt for years...!" answered Joy light-heartedly. "I dunno about these two, though..."

"We need our heads felt, an' all!" quipped Lee.

"Well that's alright, then!"

The store owner was rather more jovial than when the trio confronted him with their provocative plan a few days earlier, and with Joy's threat hanging over him, decided that being his slave for the day was a price worth paying. He flexed his fingers inside his thick, stainless steel mesh gloves before picking-up his industrial sized weapon.

"Come on, let's get on with it. Don't wanna miss me Sunday lunch!"

With the gate heavily chained and padlocked, the store owner decided that too much energy was required to cut those as well as the ones on the church door, and that it was best to climb the gate.

Dick Joy volunteered to go first, and warned the other three about the old mantrap awaiting on the other side of the gate. He mentally prepared himself by pulling a small bottle of gin from his coat pocket and taking a moderate glug.

Joy led with his left leg and placed it well to the left of the trap. As he stood astride the gate, he informed the others that they should wait until he'd cleared the pathway as best he could. He then swung his other leg over the gate and began to swat his way through the wild greenery.

"Looks like someone's been 'ere not that long ago." Joy surmised, as he noted footsteps of flattened grass and weeds leading up the steps to the church. He continued to sweep and tug his way up to the church door, and his clumsy attempt at garden clearance was successful enough for the other three to view him clearly as he stood atop the final step.

The other three easily negotiated the gate and freshly weakened foliage, and thanked Joy for his work when they joined him at the church door.

***

"Thomas Crabbings was behind dozens of killings a few hundred years back, and he killed most of the witchcraft suspects by ducking 'em under Lam Brook. When he wasn't drowning 'em, he brought villains into the centre of Larkhall Square in front of huge crowds. When the villains got flimsily convicted, Crabbings would grab them by the collar, and run 'em about fifty yards until he smashed their faces and broke their necks against the stone wall of the wheelwright's workshop. If they were still alive, Crabbings and his mates would then stamp on their ribs to finish the job."

Jeremy Bennett-Brewer widened his eyes and went scarlet as he saw the connection with Chatterton's death.

"...The wheelwright himself was killed by Crabbings. The wheelwright owned a goat, and it went missing one day. He searched high and low for it, until he eventually discovered Crabbings beside Lam Brook giving it a good porking."

Bennett-Brewer coughed an involuntary laugh in response, but immediately returned to his worried expression.

"...The witchfinder reacted by takin' his cock out of the goat, picking up his staff, and using it to knock out the wheelwright. He then dragged him back to his workshop and tied him to one of his coach wheels. Crabbings then invited some cronies into the workshop, and after convincing them that the wheelwright was a Devil worshipper, took him outside on the wheel, and rolled him viciously for hours up and down the hills of Larkhall 'till he died of dizziness."

"Oh crikey." Bennett-Brewer whispered.

"Soon after my brother's article was published, Chatterton got one of the local kids to help him kidnap my brother and tie him to the sycamore tree by Lam Brook. That tree was planted near to where Crabbings was caught shagging the wheelwright's goat."

Bennett-Brewer involuntarily laughed for a second time, but apologised immediately for appearing to make light of the demise of his host's sibling.

The old man carried on as if Bennett-Brewer wasn't there.

"My brother was eventually released from the tree, but Chatterton caught him again a few days later. Him and that kid took him up to the tin church and chained him to the door. He was dead by the time he was discovered the next day."

Bennett-Brewer offered his spooked condolences to the old man. As he did so, light rain began to tap against the cottage windows, followed by a distant growl of thunder.

"Aye aye..." whispered the old man as he turned his head toward the window overlooking the front garden. "I reckon summat's afoot, an' don't say I didn't bloody warn yer!"

The two men stared at each other in silence as the rain became slightly heavier.

"HARK!"

The shout made Bennett-Brewer jump, and the teacher detected very fast twitches below the old man's left eye.

"Can you hear it...?"

Bennett-Brewer cocked a reluctant ear toward the front of the cottage.

"I'm afraid I can't hear anything."

The old man continued to twitch below the eye as he again requested his guest to listen.

Bennett-Brewer still couldn't hear anything other than the rain tapping against the windows, and decided it was time to make a move.

"It's been lovely meeting you..." offered the teacher, who tried to sound relaxed as he stood-up. "Thank you so much for all the information you've given me, and I'm sure it will be of huge benefit to my pupils..."

"SIT DOWN AND SHUT UP!!" the old man bellowed, before he picked up the glass ashtray beside his armchair and threw it violently. Bennett-Brewer had to sway his head quickly to avoid a direct hit, and the ashtray shattered against the wall. The brown wallpaper was darkened further by ash smears as dozens of dog ends rolled around the floor.

"...FUCKING LISTEN!!"

The teacher turned white and began to shake as he retook his seat. Finally, he heard a noise other than that made by the rain, and it gradually increased in volume as it got nearer. After a few seconds, Bennett-Brewer recognised the sound as a fast-approaching pitter patter of feet. Somebody or some-thing was sprinting straight toward the cottage. The crescendo of the nearing footsteps was suddenly replaced by a sickening crack that sounded like a rifle shot. The impact was forceful enough to momentarily wobble the cottage.

21

TROUBLE DOWNSTAIRS

After the commotion caused by Adam Abrahams during his previous sermon, Victor Carping was pleased that the latest Sunday Service had gone according to plan and without drama. Carping always found it easy to forgive his adversaries, so was happy to say a prayer on behalf of the retired vicar.

On completion of outstanding paperwork, Carping found himself with some free time, and decided on another clamber up to the church tower. The weather had become more amenable in recent days, but his spare cassock and underwear had been crisply laundered in case the elements decided to play another trick on him. Carping let out a sigh of relief as he unfastened his rollerblades and substituted his saturated socks for a fresh pair.

The Rector of St Swithin's was filled with great optimism as he began to make his way up the twisting iron steps. Upon arrival at the top of the tower, he leant against the parapet and filled his lungs with fresh air. Victor Carping rubbed his hands with glee and uttered an enthusiastic *what a gay day!* to himself on being confronted with such an agreeable early summer afternoon.

Carping spent a couple of minutes scanning the view from all angles. First, he gazed northward toward the hills of the village, and was met with a far lovelier view than during his previous visit to the tower. Shuffling to the west, the Rector viewed Bath Abbey standing proudly in the city centre. He turned in the opposite direction and noted that the stone pillar of Solsbury Hill, his church and the Abbey formed a mini ley line. Turning south, Bathampton Down was an absolute picture as its sunbathed greenery contrasted sharply with the blue sky.

Carping adjusted his posture toward the east and saw the climbing hills that bordered Wiltshire. In the middle distance, he could make out the Tin Church of Bailbrook Lane basted blood orange by the bright sun. He'd heard strange stories about the church, but felt it was local superstition gone mad.

Every now and again, a wave of unsureness about his place in the universe hit the Rector. He stroked his chin with puzzlement as he pondered whether there was a great creator, or whether his existence was the result of some gigantic and purposeless accident. Anyway, whatever the truth, peace, love and understanding was his answer. Carping found that singing helped during times when his mood was subdued, so he burst into song as he rested his elbows between a turret.

When I was just a little boy...I asked my mother what will I be?
Will I be pretty? Will I be rich? Here's what she said to me...

Victor Carping removed his elbows from their resting place and aimed his arms skyward.

...Que sera, sera, whatever will be will be, the future's not ours to see...que sera, sera..."

The sky suddenly darkened as Carping completed the chorus that explained his philosophy toward his place in the grand scheme of things. He returned his gaze to the east and again viewed the tin church.

"Oh Lordy Lord, not again!"

The Rector braced himself for more unpleasantness as a large haze developed above the church. A few seconds later, the haze developed into the form of Rupert Chatterton's pulverised face, and Carping was transfixed as the alarming image floated toward the tower of St Swithin's.

***

The old man leapt from his armchair with an agility that defied his age, and more clouds of dust rose into the air. Jeremy Bennett-Brewer simultaneously sprang up from the chair in the opposite corner, and the two men faced each other amid the dancing particles.

Eventually, Jeremy Bennett-Brewer broke the silence.

"Wh...what the hell was that?"

"Someone bein' taught a lesson in not bein' a complete bloody idiot, I'll bet."

Both men stared toward the front door.

"...Brace yerself, 'cos it's gonna be a right bleedin' mess."

Bennett-Brewer prepared himself as best he could as he followed the old man through the living room, along the narrow hallway and toward the front door.

The old man leant his back against the front door with arms outstretched as if to prevent his guest trying to open it. Such an act was unnecessary, as the teacher had no compulsion to view whatever was on the other side. Bennett-Brewer never took his eyes off his host as he reaffixed his shoes; almost losing balance in the process. The door was unchained while Bennett-Brewer half hid, and the old man stepped aside to allow his visitor a good view after the door was slowly creaked open. Both men were blitzed by heavy and gusting rain before being confronted with a pair of inanimate legs sticking out from behind the right-hand gatepost.

***

Victor Carping again held his arms above his head as the hideous spectral menace approached.

... When I grew up and fell in love, I asked my sweetheart what lies ahead? Will we have rainbows, day after day? Here's what he said to me...

Carping was determined to fight the attack on his senses and injected even more gusto when bellowing-out the song chorus for the second time.

QUE SERA, SERA, WHATEVER WILL BE WILL BE, THE FUTURE'S NOT OURS TO SEE, QUE SERA, SERA...

The final syllable of the chorus was as elongated as the Rector's breath allowed, and several years of singing with various choirs ensured that it was accompanied with impressive vibrato. Carping turned his face toward the sky on completion of the chorus, and his mouth was immediately filled with rain as the heavens burst.

Carping was thoroughly drenched well before he could retreat down the spiral staircase. He momentarily stared again in the direction of the tin church, and through rapidly blinking eyes to offset the deluge and wind, noticed that the apparition of Chatterton had vanished.

Despite the physical discomfort of another soaking, Carping felt immensely proud and rejuvenated that his singing had been enough to see off the beastly vision. This sudden infusion of wellbeing didn't transmit through to the Rector's lower body, and his legs and feet became starched with paralysis.

Priding himself on keeping his head during adverse situations, Carping decided to again burst into song, and this time strained his vocal cords to produce every last ounce of fortissimo.

HEAVEN...MUST BE MISSING AN ANGEL...MISSING ONE ANGEL CHILD, COS YOU'RE HERE WITH ME RIGHT NOW...

Carping's top half was still functioning normally, and he clapped along to every second count of the upbeat melody.

...YOUR LOVE IS HEAVEN-LY... BAB-Y-Y-Y... HEAVENLY TO ME... BAB-Y-Y-Y...

Suddenly, the drenched Rector's lower half returned to life, and he calmly began to descend the spiral staircase. *You just can't whack a good tune for keeping evil spirits at bay!* Carping thought as he rubbed his hands with proud satisfaction. As he stepped back on to the church floor, he continued his state of self-righteousness by congratulating himself on having his spare cassock neatly folded on the altar table, together with spare boxer shorts and vest.

Striding along the main aisle between the pews, Carping still felt enough agitation to glance left and right through the stained-glass windows in case the maddening apparition of Chatterton was pursuing him.

The relief in seeing nothing untoward transmitted itself into him suddenly feeling rather silly. As a clergyman who took an unusually sceptical stance regarding the supernatural, Carping put both of his alarming experiences down to hallucination. He had no doubt that that was the reason for the mass hysteria regarding both Chatterton and the local legend.

Physically, the Rector still felt decidedly uncomfortable after the warm deluge he'd just endured left his underwear and cassock glued to his skin. Steam formed a narrow aura around the outline of Carping's body as he trod the final few steps toward the altar. As the spare cassock was lifted and flapped into its full length, Carping could hear two slowly repeated notes; the same two dissonant and horrid notes that thumped inside his skull during his previous visit to the church tower.

The Rector's fear returned afresh, and he frantically thought of another uplifting disco anthem to sing and ward off either the malevolent spirit or aural hallucination. Carping slung the replacement cassock back onto the altar table and stood proud and confident in front of his pretend congregation. He then outstretched both arms to theatrically play the air piano intro to his choice of song.

AT FIRST I WAS AFRAID, I WAS PETRIFIED...

As soon as the first line of the tune was sung, the repeated dissonant notes quickly faded inside his head until everything became silent. The Rector again wore a broad smile as he effortlessly quashed his latest spooky experience. As Carping was about to launch into the second line of his favoured anthem, deafening thuds that seemed to emanate from on top of the church roof resonated at regular intervals, before the alternating and grinding notes returned to haunt the Rector's ears. Carping's lower half failed him for the second time, and after a few moments of semi petrification, he gamely gathered enough energy to free his vocal cords to use as ammunition against whatever was continuing to thrash his senses.

...KEPT THINKING I COULD NEVER LIVE WITHOUT YOU BY MY SIDE...

As if taking note of Carping's latest vocal offering, a blackened silhouette of a hideously misaligned head and neck appeared through the stained-glass window directly to the left as the Rector quickly swivelled his body. The apparition vanished almost immediately, and Carping registered the sight as self-manufactured phenomena.

There are no such things as ghosties and ghoullies! Carping resolutely reminded himself as the fresh cassock was re-flapped. He gathered it up along with his spare underwear and made his way toward the sharp gradient of steps leading below ground to the burial vault. Carping couldn't quite score an emphatic victory with his logic, and he retained enough concern to slowly turn a circle to look for visions that shouldn't be there.

The burial vault was strictly out of bounds to parishioners, and the Rector had to open its huge old oak door with a huge several decades old key. The key slid smoothly inside the lock, but failed to turn more than twenty degrees before jamming. Carping angrily swore under his breath. This wasn't the first time he'd had trouble opening the door to the vault, and he cursed himself again for failing to act upon something that should have been fixed. The irked clergyman stood with a perplexed hand on hip, while the other clutched the change of clothes to his chest.

The moment of troubled pondering was broken spectacularly as the two horrendous alternating notes returned to punch against the inside of Victor Carping's head. This time the returning phenomena was violent enough for the Rector to drop his spare clothing, fall to his knees, and clamp both hands against his ears for fear of them exploding. The reverberations soon spread through Carping's whole body, and he drooped forward from his kneeling position to lay flat on his front while keeping his hands in place as an effort to help stop the possibility of his head fragmenting. As he did so, Carping could feel his legs spasming and twitching, and the points of his shoes made clicking sounds as they momentarily contacted the floor several times each second.

The Rector began to writhe in panic and discomfort as he felt that whatever had overcome his body was trying to escape it from every part. After a few tortuous moments, Carping felt great relief as the internal invasion began to gently subside. Although still severely discomfited, he felt a big enough surge of adrenalin and positivity to clamber to his feet, stagger across to the alter table, climb on top of it, and use what he hoped would be his trump card to quell the current malevolence afflicting him.

The Rector ignored what was left of the pain, raised both arms dramatically into the air as if overseeing a sacrifice, and scraped together every last vestige of vocal capability to resolutely sing a carefully chosen line from his recently aborted anthem.

I SHOULD HAVE CHANGED THAT STUPID LOCK!!!

Carping's passionate voice resonated throughout the church for several seconds, and as the echo died away, so did the last dregs of the thumping dissonance inside his body. The Rector suddenly felt as right as rain as he skipped off the altar table and made his way assuredly back to the entrance to the vault. This time the key turned effortlessly, and Carping was relieved as the old door creaked open. He fumbled for the switch to the left of the door, and was only mildly perturbed as the light bulb expired with a gentle ping.

Ahead of the Rector were thirteen steep steps without hand rails on either side. It was a tricky enough test of balance as it was, what with many of the steps missing large chunks due to many centuries of withering. To make the journey in near darkness, and being further handicapped with one arm out of commission due to it clutching his change of clothes, Carping steeled himself for the compounded challenge by mustering one final vocal attack against further bombardments of his senses.

...BUT I'LL SURVIVE...I WILL SURVIVE!!!

***

The old man walked with a purposeful stride toward the gatepost, while his guest half followed and half cowered.

Through the heavy wind and rain, Jeremy Bennett-Brewer saw the old man reach the end of the front garden and then stoop down to reveal the identity of the latest unfortunate creature to meet his end against his property.

The teacher had to battle against the urge to look in every direction except straight ahead as he finally caught up with his host, and dry retched several times as he clapped eyes on an unrecognisable and bloodied face that was attached to a head snugly resting horizontal against its body's left shoulder.

"If I've warned the stupid bleeders once, I've warned 'em a hundred times!"

The exasperation of the old man's remark only just registered with Bennett-Brewer through his involuntary heaving, before he eventually gath-

Trouble Downstairs

ered himself to again confront the vile sight. It was enough to inspire an encore of dry retching.

"D'ya know who this is?" asked the old man, who was oblivious to the teacher's severe physical reaction.

Bennett-Brewer had to wait several seconds for his wits to come back into operation.

"No idea...do...do you...recognise him?"

The old man turned to Bennett-Brewer with eyes blinking rapidly against the sheeting rain.

"It's old Willie from the hardware shop."

Jeremy Bennett-Brewer had to fight against giving a sigh of relief on discovery of the smashed face belonging to someone he didn't know.

"...The poor bastard. He's been running the store in Larkhall for donkeys' years, and I was always worried he'd one day say yes."

"Yes to what?" asked the teacher in a manner that didn't display any great thirst to discover the answer.

"If I 'ad a pound for every time someone local went into his shop and asked him for help breakin'-in to the tin church..."

Bennett-Brewer clamped his hands to the old man's shoulders in an unashamed display of fear.

"But...but I thought everyone in the area stayed well clear of the church?"

"That all depends on whether they've got any fuckin' sense."

As the wind and rain began to ease, the old man stared at the teacher with anger and dismay.

"...Whoever twisted Willie's arm into doin' it, they better go to sleep with one eye open."

***

"Where was Moses when the lights went out?" Victor Carping whispered light-heartedly to himself. He concluded that, like himself, he was left in the dark. The Rector gingerly took the first step of his steep downward journey; right arm clutching his spare attire, and left stretched horizontal to provide his only means of balance. He took rhythmic two-second intervals between each step to show extra respect to the challenge ahead.

Carping numbered the steps aloud as he descended and was relieved as he counted the thirteenth and final one to reach the darkened vault. The lumpy stone floor was gently negotiated as the Rector made his way in the general vicinity of the table that housed the candles and box of matches. Carping had to keep the door to the vault open to see anything at all, and a sweeping arm amongst the shadows eventually located what he was looking for.

Although the Rector was known for his self-assuredness, he'd always make sure that whenever he changed clothing, it would be out of sight of any onlooker. The one chink in the armour of Carping's confidence with his body was caused by a long and thin birthmark that ran vertically from the top of his buttock separation for several inches. It was the cause of much merriment amongst class mates when changing before and after P.E. Cries of *double ass* and *two bums* would greet him every time he removed his underpants, as a seemingly unbroken foot-long ass crack greeted his delighted fellow pupils. Even as a successful and mature adult, Carping was still affected by the ridicule of long ago.

Carping snapped out of the angst inspired by his strangely comical backside, picked up the matchbox, and attempted to light one of the candles randomly spread along the table. Everything contained within the vault was dank and musty, and several matches were discarded before the candle was successfully lit.

The candle was placed inside its holder, put back on the table, and Carping began the process of switching his saturated and still-steaming clothes. He self-consciously stepped a few yards away from the table and its accompanying light to peel-off his cassock, and then bend down to remove his boxer shorts. As Carping returned to an upright position clutching his used underwear, there was enough light for him to notice that the three jars of pickled eggs he kept against the far wall of the vault had all been removed. The Rector shook his head quizzically as he was confronted with the latest titbit of strange phenomena to test his mettle.

Carping was becoming fatigued from the constant odd happenings of the day, and was determined not to give any thought to the whereabouts of the missing jars. After swapping his damp and humid items of clothing for crisp and fresh ones, the sheer comfort felt by Carping boosted his wellbeing massively as he prepared to leave the vault behind. The journey back up the steps would be a lot less taxing now that he had a candle, and even more so when the decision was made to leave his discarded clothes behind until the light bulb by the door could be replaced.

Carping made his way back up the steep steps easily with the aid of the candle, and breathed deeply with a mix of satisfaction and relief. Just before swinging the door shut, the Rector heard a repeat of the sinister alternating notes. The difference this time was that the notes were much quieter, and not emanating from inside his body. Carping stood still to try and pinpoint the sound, and discovered it was coming from the vault.

Compulsion overpowered the logical side of Carping, and he decided to make a return journey down the steps. Whatever enemy was waiting, he felt a great determination to confront it head on.

I'VE GOT ALL MY LIFE TO LIVE, I'VE GOT ALL MY LOVE TO GIVE...AND I'LL SURVIVE...I WILL SURVIVE!!

The quiet alternating notes duly vanished as Carping's latest vocal riposte again did the trick. With great self-satisfaction, Carping stood at the top of the steps and gestured a robust and playful V-sign with his right hand toward the vault as he prepared for his second descent.

The Rector felt confident enough to return down the stairs by doing away with the two-second wait between each step. Rapid progress was made until the ninth stair crumbled beneath his right foot. Carping's famed skills of co-ordination was no match for the laws of physics, and the candle flew from his grasp as he fell forward to clonk the side of his head against the vault's stone floor and knock himself out.

***

"Who do you think got him to do it?"

Jeremy Bennett-Brewer had calmed down appreciably after the old man draped a sheet over the wrecked body, and his question was free of panicked pauses.

"Dick Joy would be my guess."

"But every time I saw him in the pub, he was always telling me to keep well clear of the church."

"Why? You weren't planning to go there yerself, were ya?"

"What? You must be joking!"

Although Bennett-Brewer managed to retain fluent speech, the fearful pounding inside his chest ensured that he'd spectacularly fail a lie detector test.

"No, I'm not joking, and you better bloody not be, either!"

The old man stared intently at the teacher, who responded by looking the other way.

***

Victor Carping had no idea who or where he was when his consciousness bashfully returned in instalments. The process was speeded up indecently as the two nasty repeated notes again began to hum from somewhere in the near distance.

Carping delicately sat up in the darkness, placed a hand against the still throbbing side of his head, and immediately removed it in reaction to a violent stab of pain. He got to his feet before his senses had properly re-gathered, and he staggered across to the table to find another candle to light.

The Wyvern & The Witchfinder

The alternating notes became slightly quieter the nearer Carping was getting toward the table, which convinced him that the sound was coming from beyond the narrow annex that led from the burial vault toward the tiny room originally built to imprison the troublesome heretics of centuries ago.

The table was deep in shadow, and Carping had to find the matches and candle purely by feel. They were found easily despite the poor light, and the new candle was lit first time of asking. The blow to the head had knocked all the self-satisfaction out of the Rector, and he felt rather nervous as he made his way toward the narrow annex, accompanied by the gradually increasing volume of the two dissonant notes.

The passageway was a mere three feet wide as Carping made the journey toward the heretic room, and he was fighting both claustrophobia and the unevenness of the stone floor. He was aware that his senses were still short of full capacity, so thought his nostrils were deceiving him as they picked up the mild whiff of vinegar as he approached the source of the sounds.

After cautiously treading about ten yards along the passage, the Rector found himself outside the door of his destination. The whiff of vinegar turned into an overpowering stench, but Carping fought valiantly against the urge to spew-up. He wasn't quite as successful placating the other physical manifestation of his fear, and the candle began to click regularly in its holder as his right hand started to tremble.

The old door to the heretic room was hesitantly pushed open, and in the middle of the windowless and otherwise empty cell, the candle revealed three twisted and intertwined bodies with faces smashed beyond recognition. Fragments of broken glass protruded and twinkled from all three pulped faces, with the stone floor strewn with pickled eggs amid puddles of vinegar.

Victor Carping immediately recognised one of the victims as Dick Joy from his frizzy grey hair, though he couldn't identity the other two. He deduced from their style of clothes that they were much younger than Joy. Carping stood over the bodies as nausea caused by a mix of shock, horror and vinegar rose toward his throat. To complete the ignominy of the trio's demise, the Rector of St Swithin's garnished their bodies with copious amounts of vomit.

22

AN ALCOHOLIC'S ANGST

Graham Curnow's latest ramble was a nocturnal affair that began a little after three-am Monday morning. He left his house behind in the darkness, passed the old sycamore tree, crossed the tiny bridge over Lam Brook, turned right along the main road of Larkhall and stopped outside The Bladud's Midriff. Curnow scratched his cheek as he pondered whether he should turn left or right, or carry on straight ahead. If he turned to the right, he'd face the challenge of Ferndale Road, Bailbrook Lane, and the unforgiving ascent to Solsbury Hill. Taking a left turn would mean a two-mile climb up to the flat and lofty elevation of Lansdown. The views from Lansdown were spectacular, and as it was the highest point in the entire area, he could look down at the misshapen plateau of Solsbury Hill, and a few miles beyond, view the long escarpment that contained the Westbury White Horse.

As this was a rare night time ramble, the selling point of a journey to Lansdown was negated, and Curnow eventually decided to take the gentler climb of Dead Mill Lane straight ahead.

The ease with which Graham Curnow staved off any desire to drink himself stupid had been steadily eroded in recent days, and he struggled to banish the imagined pleasure of glugging a full bottle of whiskey down in one. It was a battle Curnow had to fight hard to win, but his victory was short lived as the thought was immediately replaced by the imagined pleasure of gulping down a bottle of cream sherry in one. The process was repeated six times with bottles of various types of alcohol.

The freshly troubled former alcoholic sat on the small wall outside Larkhall's most easterly pub and placed his head in his hands. After a few moments submerged in self-pity, he resolutely got to his feet and began his journey up Dead Mill Lane.

Curnow told himself that experiencing the peace and quiet of a dead of night ramble would be just the medicine he needed to forget about his dangerous desires, and the serenity was underlined by the stillness and clarity of the wee small hours; just an occasional cooling breeze that gave him a small lift each time it was felt against his face.

The top of Dead Mill Lane merged with the old A46, and Curnow glanced to the right and saw the large house a hundred yards distant that used to be The Bladud's Head pub. The old alehouse had been converted into a bed and breakfast, and the owners were happy to retain the name and original pub sign that caricatured Bladud's severed head. Even though visitors to Bath from the north no longer took this road, the guest house still did healthy trade as a base camp for curious visitors to Solsbury Hill. Curnow couldn't avoid reminiscing about old times, and salivatingly wished he could return to the days when the house was a pub and drink himself into nirvana in front of the roaring hearth.

It was quite an effort for Curnow to eventually wrench his gaze away from the former pub, and he finally continued along in the opposite direction. Since the building of the bypass, the old road became semi dormant, and outside of daytime, virtually extinct.

The stillness of the night continued to soothe Curnow and help quell his perilous urges. He reached the country lane that led first to Upper Swainswick, and then the hamlet of Tadwick where he suffered the Chatterton hallucination.

Curnow approached the small primary school in Upper Swainswick, and outside its entrance, saw Ally Lee and Ronan Rhodes sat cross legged next to each other and weeping quietly. Curnow leant a hand of support to the shoulder of each and promised them everything would be alright.

He left the whimpering teenagers behind as he turned right up the small hill that took him to the corner of the lane leading to Tadwick. The signpost that indicated a further mile and a half journey was tilted acutely toward the ground, with the point of the sign now aimed toward the southern hemisphere.

The first part of the lane divided the east and west graveyards of St Crispin's Church, and at the gate to the left, Dick Joy appeared, and he dangled a tasty carrot in the form of a full bottle of gin in front of Curnow's face. The reaction was a raised hand of calm abstention, and as Joy retreated to deep within the graveyard, Curnow carried-on toward Tadwick; heart pumping from his false gesture of non-temptation.

Looking east and over the horizon of the elevated Solsbury Hill, Curnow noticed the breaking light of the new morning. It was approaching the summer solstice, and Curnow's wonder at the early dawn helped take his mind off more pressing concerns. He looked down at his analogue wristwatch and saw its hands spinning anti-clockwise with ridiculous speed. Curnow put the odd phenomenon to the back of his mind and continued to marvel at just how early daybreak was this time of year.

The budding morning saw a rise in temperature and a snuffing out of the cooling breeze. The last thing Curnow needed was a raging thirst that required more than mere water or herbal concoction to fully quench. He reached inside his rucksack to pull-out his flask and pour himself some dandelion and liquorice tea. Curnow slurped greedily from the cup as an attempt to physically bombard his thirst into submission. He didn't get quite the result he was looking for as he immediately spat out the entire contents of his mouth over the hedge that separated him from St Crispin's Church. Curnow's confused state of mind transmitted itself into his taste buds experiencing the phantom kick of alcohol.

Curnow's demons were now working seamless shifts, and in a rare display of anger and resentment, he backpedalled a few steps to violently kick open the gate to the western section of the church graveyard.

As he looked around the graveyard seeking the answers to questions that he wasn't sure he was asking, he spotted Dick Joy casually led against the huge slab that was the gravestone of Rupert Chatterton. Joy returned the stare, raised a bottle of something toward Curnow in a toasting gesture, drank its entire contents, and then smashed the bottle against the gravestone.

Curnow took confused steps toward Joy, who reacted by running in the opposite direction to leap over the graveyard's southern wall.

The anger inside Curnow rose further at the incessant tweaking of his Achilles' heel, and it was all directed toward the backward and malevolent thief buried a few yards away. Curnow's confused steps turned into a purposeful stride toward the grave, and just before reaching it, turned his head to the left to notice Ally Lee and Ronan Rhodes pop their heads above the graveyard perimeter wall on the school side.

Curnow thought of the teenagers being bullied by Chatterton after seeking sanctuary inside the church on a previous occasion, and this made him determined to be confrontational on both his and their behalves.

Rupert Chatterton's grave stood directly in front of Curnow, and it became bathed in brilliant light as the Sun decided to side step the known physical laws to suddenly reach its zenith.

Graham Curnow was shaking with rage, and oblivious to the unpleasantness he could be pitting himself against as he spat with derision and fury at the headstone. Curnow was pleasantly surprised by just how much phlegm his lungs had managed to cobble together, and the top of the headstone was well and truly splattered and dripping. His resolve was further stiffened as the area around the impact began to bubble and fizz in the manner of sulphuric acid. A small hole began to appear at the epicentre of the spit, and slowly bubbled and fizzed in an outward ripple until all the lettering was destroyed; and followed shortly after by the headstone itself crumbling pathetically. As Chatterton's epitaph ceased to exist, the Sun again performed a magic trick by suddenly shifting to the western horizon and hover just above the high plateau of Lansdown. The shadows from other gravestones were cast long toward the cemetery gate, and as Curnow stared toward it, saw Dick Joy hold up a bottle of something and shake it invitingly. Curnow heard Joy shout toward him but couldn't make sense of his words. Even so, it was obvious from the pleading tone of the shouting that Joy was encouraging Curnow to give himself a top-up of Dutch courage. Curnow held up a hand of appreciation toward Joy to indicate that it was an option he was grateful to have.

As Curnow turned back to stare at Chatterton's grave, the Sun ping-ponged around the sky and gave it a strobe-light effect. After a few seconds, the Sun finally retreated below the elevated flatness of Lansdown to blanket the graveyard in sudden twilight.

The ground underneath Curnow's feet began to tremble; at first barely noticeable, but growing steadily as the seconds went by, and complimented by a further deepening of the twilight. The shaking ground became violent enough to knock Curnow off his feet. Even though he lost complete physical control, Curnow remained calm and reasoned as the waxing progress of dusk speeded up appreciably to leave the graveyard in total darkness. He stared up at the heavens from his horizontal position and noticed that despite the cloudless night, he couldn't see a single celestial twinkle.

Curnow closed his eyes for several seconds as an attempt to end his dream. When he opened them again, both his status and view of the sky hadn't altered, so he tried again. Curnow found the whole thing highly exciting, but he'd had enough for one night, and was weary enough to want to step off the ride.

As he opened his eyes for the second time, the ground became still, and Curnow noticed a darkened silhouette slowly emerge from the bottom of his vision. It rose gradually from horizontal to diagonal to vertical, and standing over Curnow was the pre-accident Rupert Chatterton staring back

An Alcoholic's Angst

vengefully.

Curnow felt curiosity rather than fear at being confronted by the six-foot-seven-inch apparition looking down disdainfully at his own flattened posture. Curnow turned his head to the left and saw Dick Joy stood by the gate and shake his bottle more vigorously and pleadingly. Another raised hand of gratitude was returned.

Turning his head to face the monstrous figure of Chatterton, Curnow saw its mouth widen slowly as if being controlled by a secret mechanism. A violent blast of hot, putrid air raped Curnow's nostrils as he battled the rising sensation of nausea, which deepened further as he felt his horizontal body rise slowly until it stood upright to directly face its spectral nemesis.

As Curnow's body reached the perpendicular, the apparition screamed into his face with demented fury, accompanied again with a disgusting bouquet from its mouth. Curnow was desperate to be sick, but he could only gulp instead of heave.

Curnow suddenly felt great fear, and the lucid quality of his dream had now disappeared. Chatterton's arm reached out toward Curnow's head to yank at its hair and pull it spitefully in all directions. Curnow's nausea was becoming unbearable, and it didn't improve when Chatterton eventually withdrew his arm and stared hatefully into his eyes.

A missile of some sort flew over Curnow's shoulder and smashed into Chatterton's left eye. The apparition reacted by stretching its long arms horizontally, turning its head toward the invisible Pole Star, and screaming in agony. Chatterton retained the pose for several seconds, and Dick Joy bounded across to Curnow unnoticed, tilted his head back, placed a funnel in his mouth, and emptied the entire contents of his bottle into it. Curnow's severe nausea was gradually being lessened the more he glugged the fiery liquid, and he could hear himself produce sounds of sensual ecstasy.

Dick Joy scurried back toward the cemetery gate as Curnow removed the funnel and wiped his mouth with the back of his hand.

The apparition was done with its screaming and returned its gaze toward Curnow from a couple of feet away.

"I'M GONNA KILL FUCKIN' EV'RYONE I CAN LAY ME FUCKIN' HANDS ON!" shouted the ghost of Chatterton as it trembled with blind rage.

Curnow's thirst was utterly satiated as he confronted the monstrous apparition, and as he replied to the lanky spectre, was surprised at the deafening decibel level of the words produced by his mouth.

"CALL YOURSELF A GHOST? HA! I'VE SEEN BETTER GHOSTS ON MY OLD TELLY!"

The apparition reacted with a look of bewilderment, and its rancid mouth closed tightly.

"...I BELIEVE THAT YOU UNDERWENT AN ASSHOLE TRANSPLANT?"

Chatterton again couldn't answer and continued to look bewildered.

"...AND I UNDERSTAND THAT THE OPERATION WAS A FAILURE BECAUSE THE ASSHOLE REJECTED YOU?"

The words were uttered in a calm and monotone way that defied their thunderous volume, while tears began to fall from the good and bad eyes of the apparition as its scabby bottom lip trembled.

"...I ALSO UNDERSTAND THAT YOU APPLIED TO JOIN THE ASSOCIATION OF PATHETIC, UNLOVED MORONS?"

Chatterton stared powerlessly back.

"...AND THAT A LARGE GROUP OF PATHETIC, UNLOVED MORONS HELD A PROTEST MARCH?"

Chatterton wailed pitifully as his monstrous head drooped toward the ground. Curnow felt enormous satisfaction from seeing the cowering state of the apparition as a result of his cutting words, and looked toward the graveyard gate, where he saw Dick Joy, Ally Lee and Ronan Rhodes cheering him on enthusiastically.

Curnow awoke from his dream without a single bead of sweat. After a few moments, he dressed himself and made his way purposefully downstairs to breakfast on rice cakes smothered in dandelion preserve, and thin strips of raw parsnip lightly brushed with cod liver oil.

The reformed alcoholic reminded himself that despite his dream producing the very real sensation of returning to the drink, he was still teetotal. However, Curnow thought deeply about giving in to his yearning, and for the rest of the morning, agonised about reinstating his alcoholism.

A loud rap at the door temporarily freed Curnow from his anguish, and after being faced with a downcast and dishevelled Victor Carping notifying him of the violent deaths of Willie Woodman and the three people featured in his dream, finally made up his mind.

23

DOUBTFUL FOLLOWERS

Trevor Expectorant wore a sombre face as he invited his disciples through the door of his shop. His second in command had done the necessary reconnaissance in the north eastern corner of Somerset and felt that he and his followers needed to show solidarity toward their near neighbours.

Expectorant looked left and right along Midsomer Norton high street as he ushered his disciples inside before quietly closing the door and pulling down the blind.

"Thank you all for attending today." Expectorant began, as his disciples shuffled through to the stockroom and sat themselves down.

"...My word, these are testing times indeed, and it must be our unwavering aim to get to the bottom of this sorry saga."

Expectorant banged his fist against a tray of sprouts, which caused a few to fall and bobble across the floor.

"Please allow me to pick-up the misplaced items as a result of your justified wrath and determination, o sacred one."

Sir Leonard Hutton followed his enthusiastic reply by getting on all fours to retrieve the stray sprouts.

"Thank you, Sir Leonard; the diligence and bloody-mindedness you currently display by picking up my fallen sprouts is exactly what we'll be requiring over the coming days."

Hutton got back to his feet, returned the sprouts to their home, and rigidly saluted his leader.

"Anointed one; what is the latest development in this sorry saga?" asked Iftikhar Ali Khan.

Expectorant faced Khan with a look of regret.

"Ifty, I'm afraid that the Tin Church of Bailbrook Lane has very recently proved that its forces are far from being dormant."

"And in what way are these forces far from being dormant, supremest one?"

"Well..." began Expectorant as he turned toward Denise Compton to answer her question. "four local men rather unwisely let curiosity get the better of themselves, and each one has now moved on to the next world under the most unsavoury and messy of circumstances."

The leader and his disciples stood silent and pondered the situation, before Expectorant shifted the focus toward his deputy.

"Under his Earthly status of Charles Ubley, we must all thank Sir Jack Hobbs for showing great resourcefulness by forcefully pleading his case to take over the route of the Number 7 omnibus that caters for Larkhall, and thereby being able to sensitively enquire with passengers about the nature of the passing of these gallant but ill-advised fellows."

The other disciples took turns to show their appreciation to Hobbs with a mix of hugs and high-fives.

Readdressing his followers after nibbling on a carrot, Trevor Expectorant proceeded to remind them of the unusual and highly significant planetary positions that were due to click into formation on the following Sunday.

"Sunday, June fifteenth will see the grand-cross of Mars, Pluto, Saturn and Uranus fully formed. The waxing moon will see a conjunct with Mars, as Saturn and Pluto begin their journeys in retrograde motion. With Mercury and Venus transiting the Sun, it makes for a veritable hot pot of upheaval."

The disciples nodded back with determined faces.

"...As you all know, I don't condone blue language, but I feel that the only way to tackle this kind of unpleasantness is by confronting it head on."

Expectorant reached across for a stick of celery to use as his conducting baton. After a count-in of four beats, the disciples burst into their favourite chant.

Thom-as Crabb-ings, is a wan-ker, is a wan-ker
Thom-as Crabb-ings, is a wan-ker, is a wan-ker

When the chant was complete, the disciples sniggered against the soundtrack of a distant rumble of thunder.

Expectorant could feel the emotion and energy rising within himself and his disciples, then began to snarl away at the other entity that focused their disdain and derision.

"And as for that thieving, backward and simple wiper of Thomas Crabbings' backside, he'll not scare and threaten us with his spectral bullying!"

The group leader again swished his stick of celery; this time counting-in a beat of three and a half, and his disciples came in on the mid beat anacrusis to launch into their anti-Chatterton verse to the melody of Jerusalem.

And did that twat, in modern times
Foul upon Larkhall's mountains green?
And was that do-zy, backward clot
On Larkhall's pleasant pastures seen?

The disciples again sniggered; this time more animatedly, and this time followed by a bright sheet of lightning that temporarily illuminated the darkened store room. One or two disciples cowered anxiously before Expectorant put them at ease.

"Worry ye not, o brave and fearless crusaders against wrongfulness!"

A markedly beefier growl of thunder answered Expectorant's jovial statement.

***

News of the demise of the four locals spread rapidly throughout Larkhall, and it was agreed that Rector Victor Carping should chair a special meeting to form a plan of action. The pews of St Swithin's Church would be the venue.

The meeting was to take place on the final Sunday evening before the Larkhall Village Festival got underway the following weekend. The long-term forecast for the festival was clear and sunny, though another deep depression could be moving in during the weekend's climax.

It was testament to the gravity of the situation that this extraordinary meeting took place instead of the scheduled Evensong. Invited along for the discussion with the Rector were Graham Curnow, Lenny Yeo, Barry Loadall, Jeremy Bennett-Brewer, Mrs Tanning and Mrs Mordent.

Rector Carping arrived well before the meeting to give the pews a good polish as he heartily sang the chorus of *You Should Be Dancing*. As Carping completed the polishing to leave the pews sparkling, he congratulated himself by spinning slowly with yellow duster and tin waved about in the manner of a Morris Dancer.

You should be dancing…YEAH!!

Carping stopped twirling as he exclaimed the final word of the song line, and when he became stationary, thrust his tin of Mr Sheen toward the church door. He was rather taken aback when his tin of polish came to rest on Barry Loadall spluttering his way toward the altar. The Rector bade him good evening.

"I'm not so sure it is a good evening, Rector. And I'm also not so sure that good evenings will be a common phenomenon over the coming days."

"Now then, now then!"

Carping wagged a playful finger at Loadall as if he was a young child caught picking his nose.

"...I would've hoped that with your logic and wisdom, you'd be rather more enthusiastic about tackling the nasty pestilence currently residing in the parish."

Loadall began his reply by suffering a coughing fit that compelled the Rector to give several hearty slaps to his back.

"Thank you, Rector...well, I'm nothing if not a realist, and realistically speaking, the odds are very much stacked against us."

Carping stroked his chin in ponderment before looking back toward the entrance of the church. This time he viewed an uncomfortable looking Jeremy Bennett-Brewer enter flanked by Mrs Mordent and Mrs Tanning; who each had an arm intertwined with the teacher's.

***

"SIR LEONARD HUTTON AND IFTIKHAR ALI KHAN – NAWAB OF PATAUDI; UNCOUPLE YOURSELVES THIS INSTANT!!"

Hutton and Khan were the two most easily scared disciples, and the markedly beefier rumble of thunder was enough for them to seek sanctuary in each other's arms. However, their leader's rare outburst of bellowed wrath scared them even more; and after uncoupling, Hutton and Khan immediately ran across to WG Grace and Denise Compton respectively to find more physical solace.

"HUTTON AND KHAN; RELEASE GRACE AND COMPTON RESPECTIVELY AT ONCE!!!"

The anger in Expectorant's voice moved up a notch, and Hutton and Khan reluctantly released their colleagues and stared bashfully at their leader.

"It's only thunder, for goodness sake..." added the group leader after returning to a level mood. "Unless you're caught out in the open during a thunderstorm and unwisely seek refuge under a tree, or, rather provocatively, stand on top of a high building holding a golf club high above your head, there's very little harm that can be done."

Trevor Expectorant rested a serious stare on each disciple in turn.

"...These are grave times, and fear and timidity should be confined to the dustbins of your emotions. Valiance and dogged determination should replace them and be at the forefront of your humble personas."

Doubtful Followers

Expectorant's disciples burst into spontaneous applause in response to their leader's stirring words. One by one, the disciples shook hands with their leader, and Expectorant nodded his head with a touch of smugness as his decisive leadership was again displayed.

The sudden crash of a very nearby thunderbolt wobbled the stockroom, and every single member within it was spooked enough to willingly participate in a tight group hug.

***

"And the warmest of Larkhallian greetings to this fine trio of specimens."

Jeremy Bennett-Brewer gave the Rector an awkward half smile as he slowly chaperoned the two old ladies up the aisle.

"The only thing missing is the organ starting up the intro to the Wedding March!" quipped Carping.

The two old ladies burst into laughter, while the man they clung to wasn't quite so tickled.

"Yes, well I'm not sure this is quite the image Mendelssohn had in mind when he composed it."

"I must say, it is rather nice to see three people so joyously intertwined." Carping enthused.

"Well...." Mrs Tanning began. "we saw this gorgeous young creature making his way toward the church behind us, so we thought we'd force our affections on him, didn't we, Else?"

"We certainly did, Mild. There's not nearly enough virile crumpet in Larkhall, and we need to get what we can at our age!"

Jeremy Bennett-Brewer had to be quite firm with the old ladies in letting go of his arms, and they wore disappointed looks as they unattached themselves to take their places along the front pew.

A few minutes later, Graham Curnow entered, and despite the fact that he as much as anyone had a right to be worried and wary about the days ahead, wore a bright smile. Just as Curnow sat himself down next to Mrs Mordent and cheerfully greet his fellow committee members, Lenny Yeo appeared to complete the line-up.

Victor Carping took his seat behind the altar table and slapped his palm on it three times to signify commencement of the meeting.

***

As part of Sir Jack Hobbs' undercover mission, he attended a recent Sunday Service at St Swithin's, and reported back with a positive review of the Rector's sermon.

The shock of the nearby thunderbolt was wearing off, and it had now been several minutes since any interruptions from the weather. Trevor Expectorant invited Hobbs to take his place in front of the tray of butternut squash to address the group.

"What I discovered recently at St Swithin's was that it is home to a modern and liberal Rector who, like ourselves, champions niceness and love."

Hobbs' leader and fellow disciples nodded with approval.

"...And what's more, the Rector and congregation made a complete dipstick out of a retired vicar who had the most horrid and outdated views about goodness and loveliness. Comrades; St Swithin's Church is no longer the breeding ground for supporters of Thomas Crabbings, and it should be our aim to make haste there to show our unswerving niceness and appreciation that any kind of love is absolutely alright!"

The stockroom exploded with wild applause and cheering, and after the celebratory noise died away, Expectorant decided that the disciples should take a vote on Hobbs' suggestion of visiting the church.

Trevor Expectorant was immensely proud of the democratic way he led his group, and a secret ballot was hastily arranged to gauge their unanimity. Each member was handed an apple and a tomato; apple for yes, tomato for no. Expectorant created the makeshift voting booth from stacking several trays of fruit and vegetables on top of one another to form a three-sided rectanguloid approximately five feet high, and just large enough for one group member at a time to fit inside and drop their favoured fruit into an old banana box. Expectorant used his potato knife to cut a rough circle into the top of the box just large enough for the apples and tomatoes to squeeze through.

Expectorant was first to vote, and one by one the disciples followed by casting theirs. Last to enter the polling booth was WG Grace, and after his item of fruit was dropped through the small hole, Expectorant raised his eyebrows excitedly as he picked up the box and ripped it open. Wild cheering again erupted as a smiling Expectorant displayed the open box containing the unanimous verdict of six green apples.

***

After slapping his palm against the altar table to signal commencement of the discussion, Victor Carping reminded the small gathering that every entrance to the church had been locked tight. Jeremy Bennett-Brewer had made the request as he was the most frightened member of the group, and Carping was happy to put the teacher's mind at rest; although the Rector also reminded him that mere locked doors was hardly a guarantee that hairy phenomena could be kept out.

Doubtful Followers

"It's more than a little clear that both Thomas Crabbings and the Larkhall Simpleton are very much pulling the strings..." Carping began. "and we need to placate this evil with our weapons of love and understanding."

Mrs Tanning got to her feet and angrily shook her fist.

"The only thing to make those two buck their ideas up is a good clout 'round the ear!"

Graham Curnow replied before the Rector had a chance.

"With all due respect, Mrs Tanning, giving apparitions a good clout 'round the ear is easier said than done, and even if we could do it, I hardly think it'd be enough to suppress centuries of bad vibes."

"I have to agree with Graham..." the Rector responded. "We need to put in place a strategy that takes these supernatural murderers completely off guard; and peace, love and understanding is something they'd regard as the beastly trinity."

Jeremy Bennett-Brewer was next to weigh in.

"We all know that the appearance of the Larkhall Simpleton is accompanied by the dreadful alternating pitch of the augmented-fourth musical interval."

Bennett-Brewer stared at the Rector, who looked back with an expression that requested he continue.

"...So how about we respond to his visitations by summoning-up the altogether more pleasing and uplifting interval of the *perfect*-fourth?"

Carping raised his eyebrows in a manner that suggested the idea was worth considering.

"And how exactly do we summon up these so-called pleasant notes to which you so glowingly refer?" asked an unimpressed Loadall.

"Simple...!" replied the teacher with an enthusiasm rarely displayed over recent weeks. "If you'd all like to accompany me up the stairs to the church organ, I'll demonstrate both the augmented-fourth, and the perfect-fourth interval."

After looking left and right, and then toward the altar table to take a visual opinion poll, Bennett-Brewer was pleased to see that none of his fellow committee members were against the idea of giving his plan a try.

"I think that sounds like an idea worth implementing...!" answered the Rector enthusiastically. "Shall we give Jeremy's idea a try?"

Carping's question was met with nods and affirmative grunts.

The organ of St Swithin's was housed on the upper tier of the church and stood directly over the central aisle. Rector Carping invited the committee members to join him as he trod three carpeted steps behind the altar and toward the staircase to the left of the quire.

Carping led the way up the gently twisting staircase and was followed diligently by the other six. Apart from the occasional splutter from Barry Loadall, the journey to the upper tier was made with a gentle buzz of anticipation.

Jeremy Bennett-Brewer was horrified to find himself behind Mrs Mordent and in front of Mrs Tanning as the staircase was ascended. Mrs Tanning occasionally grasped the teacher's buttocks to help with balance.

"I bet your long, tapering fingers could play a good tune on us old-timers, eh young man?"

Bennett-Brewer heard suggestive giggling from both behind and in front. He occasionally closed his eyes to avoid the alarming sight of Mrs Mordent's generous posterior taking up his entire forward and upward view. Thankfully for Bennett-Brewer, it was only a short climb to the upper tier, and all seven committee members strode out on the landing in front of the grand, centuries-old pipe organ.

"I shall now hand over to Jeremy and his musical expertise." uttered a smiling Carping as he allowed the teacher to take his place in front of the staggered trio of keyboards.

"As you can all see, the black notes on all keyboards alternate between groups of two and three; and if we concentrate on the groups of three, then the white notes immediately to the left and right are the notes of F and B respectively."

Bennett-Brewer pulled-out a few stops and flicked a few switches to find the sound he was after.

"...Right, here is the note of F."

The mighty volume and vibration of the pressed note echoed throughout the church, and most of the gathering put their hands to their ears in response.

Bennett-Brewer removed his thumb from the F note and followed it by playing the note of B with his fourth finger. Again, a deafening sound shrieked through the church.

"Right, I am now going to play the F note again, and after I've played it, I want you all to sing the note with a hearty laaaa."

The music teacher looked at the rest of the group and encouraged them to relax their muscles and fill their lungs with plenty of air.

After playing the note again, Bennett-Brewer was pleasantly surprised by just how well it was replicated by the rest of the group. He repeated the B note straight after, and again the group copied the sound impressively.

"Hark!"

Lenny Yeo was the first to hear what he at first thought was a lingering echo of the recently sung note. The other committee members took heed and listened closely for alien sounds.

"I can't hear a thing..." Victor Carping responded. "It's important at times like this that none of us let our imaginations run..."

"LISTEN!!"

Several of the others jumped in response to Yeo's alarmed shout, while Barry Loadall responded with a coughing fit, which was severe even by his standards. Loadall removed a hip flask from his jacket and soothed his chest with pressed parsnip.

After finally silencing his lungs, Loadall joined the rest in listening out for strange sounds. Yeo was found to have not let his imagination run amok as the others simultaneously heard the repeated notes, which grew in volume and seemed to emanate from outside the main door to the church.

***

Trevor Expectorant kept the accelerator pedal trapped to the floor of the minibus as it sped along the A367 approaching the city of Bath.

The group leader stared into the rear-view mirror.

"Are we all in fine and chirpy spirts, dearest followers?"

After a chorused reply of *we are, indeed, dearest leader*, Expectorant's left-hand man, Sir Jack Hobbs, turned his head from the passenger seat and addressed the other four in the back.

"We should make it in good time for Evensong, especially as our glorious leader is driving like the very Devil Itself on lots of drugs!"

Expectorant returned his gaze to the mirror and aimed his smile at his disciples, then turned his head to the left and smiled at Hobbs.

"Once we get to the church..." continued Hobbs. "we have to immediately make ourselves known and make the Rector and his congregation aware that we're on their side to offer our complete assistance!"

The other disciples cheered heartily, and soon the minibus entered Bath from the south westerly suburb of Odd Down. With Larkhall being on the north eastern outskirts of the city, Expectorant informed the rest that it would be a while before they reached the church. As the vehicle sped through the Red Lion Roundabout to join the Wellsway, it began the two-mile descent to the centre of the city.

Expectorant switched on the windscreen-wipers as light drizzle began to fall, which slowly became heavier the further they descended toward town. The sky followed suit by becoming darker, and as the vehicle reached the flat terrain of the city centre, the headlights were switched on to full beam.

The minibus threaded the railway arches twice to join the A36, with the road following the curve of the River Avon and toward the east of the city.

Expectorant again glanced at his rear-view mirror to check on his disciples, and this time he detected a distinct nervousness about them.

"Are we still in fine and chirpy spirits, dear disciples?"

Bar Sir Jack Hobbs, the disciples shook their heads.

"Wise one, we are all feeling the vibe that our presence will be most unwelcome when we reach the church."

"Let's not have any of that kind of talk, WG...!" responded the driver with a wide smile. "We are approximately one week away from what we all hope will be the end time!"

Expectorant was optimistic that this reminder of the common denominator of their beliefs would snap the disciples back into cheery mode, but the response was a mixture of quiet apathy and fear.

Sir Leonard Hutton finally broke the silence after several seconds.

"But wise one, we feel that our continued existence in the next world will be handicapped by the ghost of the Larkhall Simpleton!"

"Just hang on one cotton pickin' minute, Sir Leonard...!" Expectorant replied with agitation. "This is no time to be getting cold feet! Our Earthly duty is to tackle local evil before we cross the bridge into the next life, so let us not have any more wavering!"

Expectorant drummed his fingers impatiently on the steering wheel as the minibus stood on the corner of Sydney Place waiting for the lights to change.

"...Any of you who are less than one hundred percent committed better get out now!"

Iftikhar Ali Khan – Nawab of Pataudi, was first to crack. He frantically slid open the side door of the minibus, slammed it shut behind him, and ran across the road to the entrance of Sydney Gardens, causing a screech of brakes and tooted horn as he skipped between vehicles.

The steady drizzle and gloom had deteriorated markedly during the past few minutes, and about fifteen yards distant, nothing could be seen beyond the grand stone columns that marked the entrance to the old pleasure garden. As soon as Khan passed through the pillars, the dank air swallowed him completely.

"We must go after Ifty and rescue him!"

Trevor Expectorant looked at Hutton via the mirror with a serious stare before replying.

"I'm afraid Ifty has made his choice, and he must be allowed to live or die by his decision."

The lights on the corner of Sydney Place and Bathwick Street turned green, and Expectorant quashed any possible rescue attempt from his disciples by taking a ninety-degree left turn and speeding toward the Cleveland

Place junction that joined the A4 and the final half mile of the journey.

The minibus came to a stop on Cleveland Bridge, about a hundred yards before the lights. Visibility was so poor, the red light in the distance was no more than a dull fuzz that just about pierced the gloom.

"May I add my own thoughts as we battle this mini crisis of confidence, o wise one?" asked Sir Jack Hobbs.

Expectorant turned his head to the left and nodded seriously at his second in command.

"...To bring our Earthly duties to a fitting conclusion before doomsday, it is absolutely essential that none of us left inside this vehicle have any doubts whatsoever about what is required of us."

Tears welled up in Expectorant's eyes as he was again reminded of the unswerving loyalty of his left-hand man.

"I can always trust you to bring calmness and logic as weapons in the face of doubt and fear, Sir Jack."

The driver rested a thankful hand on the shoulder of Hobbs, who reacted by slowly looking across at his leader with an expression sagged with doubt. He gently removed Expectorant's hand from his shoulder.

"Please forgive me, wise leader, for I am a man consumed by both doubt and fear."

Sir Jack Hobbs calmly opened the passenger door to the stationary vehicle, closed it behind, and through the window, saluted his leader in a final display of obedience. Hobbs quickly removed his cricket whites and underwear, climbed on top of the barrier at the halfway point and stood above the display of roman numerals that revealed the age of the bridge. Hobbs faced into the gloom-filled distance before briefly turning his head back to the minibus to say farewell, then stretched both arms horizontally before allowing himself to slowly topple forward to dive head first into the murky waters of the Avon deep below.

Trevor Expectorant raised a pathetic hand and silent shriek in response to his closest ally taking his own life, and his head slumped to thud against the steering wheel. He and his remaining colleagues crossed their torsos sideways. Despite the shock and despair of losing Hobbs, Expectorant again pressed the accelerator pedal as the lights finally turned green.

As the minibus turned right and onto the final stretch of the A4 that led to the Larkhall turnoff, the driver was enthused with even more determination to reach the church and do whatever he could to tackle the evil atmosphere that had seeped into two of his disciples.

"Remaining followers, it is now only a few hundred yards until we reach our destination. If any more of you are riddled with doubt and fear, I ask you to speak now, or forever hold your peace."

The Wyvern & The Witchfinder

The three disciples nodded back unconvincingly but kept their peace.

The vehicle came to an enforced stop at a pedestrian crossing adjacent to the Snow Hill Estate, and Expectorant turned around to look closely at Hutton, Grace and Compton to see if he could detect doubt and fear on their faces. All three displayed empty expressions, and although this was preferable to obvious displays of angst, was hardly the rollicking defiance Expectorant was hoping to see.

After a few moments, the crossing lights changed, and Expectorant had to hurriedly turn around and move the vehicle toward its final part of the journey. He revealed his own anxieties by stalling the engine before eventually crawling forward at the second attempt. Visibility was becoming worse, and Expectorant struggled to see the tail lights of the vehicle a few yards in front. He almost missed the turn-off to Larkhall, but after a nervy bit of braking, swerved left and up the gentle incline to the village.

Despite the dire visibility, the tower of St Swithin's stood clear and proud on the left amongst the fuzzy blur of houses each side of St Saviour's Road. Expectorant took a final left turn and parked the minibus directly opposite the main gate of the church. The driver let out a sigh of relief as the journey was finally completed and turned to face his remaining disciples.

What Expectorant saw was Hutton cowered and whimpering in the foetal position on the seat directly behind, while Grace and Compton were sprawled lifeless and on top of one another along the aisle. The heads of both were tilted ninety degrees to rest against their shoulders.

***

The alternating augmented-fourth notes slowly grew in volume, accompanied by the almost as loud sound of sheeting rain lashing the southern windows of the church.

"Oh bloody nora." Bennett-Brewer whispered under his breath, before Lenny Yeo reminded him of his duty.

"Don't just stand there you dozy sod, play those good notes you were harping on about!"

Bennett-Brewer nodded his reply and turned back to the keyboard stack and hovered his hand above the nearest and lowest.

"Right, here is the F note again, and everybody sing it back to the best of their ability!"

This time the volume of the note struggled to compete against both the phantom echoes of the augmented-fourths and the irate weather.

"Laaaaaaaaaaah."

The entire group strained their vocal cords as an effort to drown the unholy sounds from outside the church.

Doubtful Followers

"GOOD!" Bennett-Brewer exclaimed in response to the accuracy and loudness of the chorused note.

"...Right, I'm now going to substitute the note of B for the note of B flat. Listen closely and repeat!"

The B flat note was played, and again it struggled to make itself heard against the echoes of the ever-increasing volume of the augmented-fourths and spiteful rain. Even so, the other committee members concentrated hard on replicating the recently played note.

"Laaaaaaaaaaah."

"BRILLIANT!"

"...Right, now sing the F and B flat continuously one after the other with everything you've got!"

All seven throats sung the two notes back and forth in unison, and Bennett-Brewer was delighted with both the accuracy and volume achieved by the group.

A thunderous crash was heard against the church roof directly above their heads, and the group used the sudden scare to infuse themselves with adrenalin and push the volume up another notch.

"KEEP GOING!" the teacher implored.

Several repeated notes later, the whole group noticed that the echoes of the augmented-fourths outside the church were beginning to recede, and complemented by the rain slowly easing. Finally, Bennett-Brewer instructed the exhausted group to stop singing.

The rain stopped, and after the echo of the group's final note faded to nothing, so had all other noise.

"Do you think that's the end of it?" Rector Carping asked the teacher.

"I'm not sure, but there's no doubt that the perfect-fourths we've just sung is no friend of the Larkhall Simpleton!"

The group took a while to compose themselves and regain their breath before making their way back down the stairs to the floor of the church. This time, Bennett-Brewer made sure he was last to descend to avoid any unnecessariness from the old ladies.

All seven committee members gathered around the altar table to decide on their next plan of action.

"Well, are we going to continue the discussion?" Lenny Yeo asked Victor Carping.

Carping scratched his chin as he pondered his response.

"I think we should call it a night. Due to Jeremy's foresight, it looks as though we at least know a way of discomfiting the local spectre. What we need to do now is to take stock before we plan anything further."

The rest of the group agreed with the Rector's suggestion, and they wearily plodded toward the main entrance. Victor Carping led the way as he had to unlock the door. The key turned easily, and the group had to shield its eyes against the brilliant light of the improved weather. After a few seconds of blinking to acclimatise their vision, seven pairs of eyes looked down and saw two men sat cross legged wearing saturated cricket whites and sobbing spectacularly.

24

DEMISE OF THE DISCIPLES

Graham Curnow awoke on Friday morning refreshed after a dreamless sleep and made his way down the stairs to enjoy his latest puritan breakfast. The village festival was due to kick off at seven that evening, and he thought long and hard about how the weekend would unfold; and although he had no time for Barry Loadall's planetary mumbo jumbo, realised that the assorted supernatural happenings were a lot more difficult to dismiss.

Since making up his mind that he'd sacrifice his health, and possibly his life, to counter the local trouble, Curnow had completely lost his recent urge to return to the bottle. He thought little of it and hoped that the decision wouldn't be necessary anyway.

After breakfasting, Curnow left his house to begin the Bath skyline walk, an elevated trail around the hills to the south and east of the city. The weather was agreeable by the standards of recent weeks, and the three-hour trek gave Curnow plenty of time to clear his mind and reinvigorate his being for the weekend ahead.

Shortly before six-thirty that evening, Curnow rapped Barry Loadall's front door.

"And a very good evening to you, Graham, my trusted friend!"

Loadall was full of enthusiasm as he invited Curnow inside.

Curnow sat himself down while Loadall fixed a herbal tea.

"So, how are those chaps we found outside the church?" asked Curnow as he took the steaming mug from his host.

"They're still in a state of shock, which isn't that surprising considering the other four members of the group chose to end their lives during the journey from Midsomer Norton to Larkhall."

"I find it all so hard to believe..." responded Curnow before taking his first sip of tea. "Do you still believe the world is going to end on Sunday?"

"Although that's what I believe, it doesn't necessarily mean it's going to happen."

Loadall topped-up his lethargy by having a suck on the rubber tube of his bong.

"...Though if I were a betting man, I'd bet that the world will end, even if I wouldn't be in much of a position to pick up and enjoy my winnings."

The side of Curnow's mouth curved into a half smile in response to Loadall's humourlessly intoned response.

"Did you manage to get anything out of the survivors about the deaths of their colleagues?"

The vibraphone jingle of the Westminster Quarters put Loadall's reply on hold.

The host returned from answering the door accompanied by two new arrivals.

"Why don't you ask them for yourself, Graham?" smiled Loadall.

The two men didn't say a word as Loadall invited them to take their places either end of the battered sofa.

"How are you both bearing-up?" asked Curnow sensitively.

After a pause of a few seconds, Trevor Expectorant eventually replied.

"I'd be lying if I said our faith wasn't being severely tested."

Sir Leonard Hutton nodded his head in agreement.

"You're both Devil worshippers, aren't you?"

Barry Loadall's forthright interjection was more of a statement than a question.

Hutton raised a hand and opened his mouth to reply, but Expectorant held a halting palm toward his last remaining disciple and answered instead.

"Yes we are, although we don't see the Devil in quite the same way as He's traditionally portrayed."

Loadall replied with nods of approval.

"...The fact that the Larkhall Simpleton saw the Devil as his sworn enemy, and also the fact that he saw Witchfinder Crabbings as his closest ally has left us in no doubt."

"I'm very sorry to hear about the loss of your colleagues." sympathised Curnow before he drained his mug.

Expectorant and Hutton nodded a thank you at Curnow for his concern before Barry Loadall made an explicit contribution to the conversation.

Demise Of The Disciples

"Would you care to tell us how your colleagues met their ends?"
Loadall gestured across to Curnow with an outstretched arm.
"...Only Graham here is dying to know."
Curnow was annoyed at Loadall for speaking on his behalf.
"Yes, I'd be happy to do so." replied Expectorant with a willingness that surprised the former alcoholic.
"...Let me just say before I continue that Larkhall has our unstinting support in getting rid of the meddling influence of both Crabbings and Chatterton; and let us all be in no doubt that these scheming ruffians are the ones responsible for our dear colleagues taking their lives."
Expectorant and Hutton looked at each other dolefully and sideways-crossed their torsos.
"I gather that one of your disciples fled into Sydney Gardens, laid across the railway tracks, and was sliced into three roughly equal parts?"
Curnow was again dismayed at Loadall's insensitive directness and was again surprised to look across and see that no offence was taken.
"Yes he was..." answered Expectorant. "And he was so badly mangled that he could only be identified by the name *IFTY* that was tattooed in large lettering across his chest. The top and bottom halves of his tattoo were neatly severed, and the mortician had to carefully align the split torso so I could identify him."
Expectorant stared philosophically into space.
"...Ifty always struggled with his allegiances, and that's why I named him after the only Test cricketer to have played for both England and India."
The leader of his recently decimated group then returned his gaze to Loadall and continued to describe his disciple's demise.
"...In a rather macabre postscript, as the train went over dear Ifty's body, his head and shoulders were shot across over the other line, and another train smashed into his head to leave it an unrecognizable blackened pulp."
"Well..." Loadall replied. "If a job's worth doing, it's worth doing well."
Curnow again winced at his friend and host's latest example of bad taste, while Expectorant and Hutton nodded back at Loadall with serious agreement before Expectorant continued.
"A few minutes later, as our vehicle was stood on Cleveland Bridge waiting for the lights to change, my second in command nonchalantly got out of the passenger door and threw himself to his death into the river."
"Well, at least his demise was a bit less messy than Ifty's." answered Curnow as an attempt to look for positives.
"I'm afraid it was messier than intended..." replied a regretful Expectorant. "You see, Bath's foremost river boat was passing under the bridge at the time and making its way back to Pulteney Weir to offload and pick up

dozens of tourists.

"I saw Sir Jack fall head first from the bridge and naturally assumed that he was headed straight for Davy Jones' locker, but after watching a story about an unusual death on *Points West* the following day, I tracked down the boat skipper, and he gave me some facts that were too disturbing to be aired on a regional news show.

"Dear Sir Jack must've made a perfectly straight final journey, as his head smashed through the last bit of decking right at the front of the boat. The impact was so clean that his head pierced the decking and was wedged tight while his naked body was upright with legs slightly apart, providing a posture not dissimilar to that of a human catapult. The weather was so poor at the time that all the tourists were inside the enclosed section of the boat, and they apparently could do nothing but stare in shock. According to what I heard, dear Sir Jack's parting gesture to this world was an angry erection that was pointed toward the cowering passengers."

"A very nasty event indeed..." responded Loadall with a blank expression. "and not the kind of thing one would expect to find in the promotional literature of people who offer river cruises."

While Graham Curnow again felt embarrassed at Loadall's sardonic humour, Expectorant and Hutton nodded their heads in enthusiastic agreement before Expectorant again continued.

"The skipper frantically tried to pull Sir Jack's head from the hole in the decking while trying to avoid his aroused member, but his head had pierced such a neat hole that he couldn't be budged. You can only imagine the sheer horror of passengers waiting to alight from beside the weir as the boat passed under the central arch of Pulteney Bridge and slid against its mooring, with Sir Jack's upside-down and naked body on full display; lifeless save for his defiant manhood."

"Obviously another job that wasn't worth doing unless it was done well." added Loadall.

"I couldn't agree more." replied a serious Expectorant.

"...By the time our eventful journey came to an end as I parked opposite the gates to St Swithin's, I turned around to see my friend here cowering on a seat, and the brother and sister duo of dear WG and dear Denise laying lifeless in the aisle between the seats."

"Please do continue." invited the host.

"Both had thin cords of string from potato sacks deeply enmeshed in their throats, and it was plainly apparent that this was the result of mutual strangulation."

Both Loadall and Curnow stared back at Expectorant with fascination, before Hutton made his first contribution to the conversation.

"With all due respect, glorious leader, that isn't quite right."

Expectorant looked across at his last remaining disciple with surprise.

"...I saw very clearly that it was an apparition that strangled our beloved WG and Denise."

"And I think we all know who the apparition was." added Loadall without expecting a reply.

"Rupert Chatterton?" Hutton asked.

"Oh REALLY, Sir Leonard, of course it's Mr Chatterton!" Expectorant snapped at his disciple.

Hutton reacted to his leader's raised voice by sulking, while the other three carried on the discussion.

"This is quite a development..." began a serious Loadall. "It's one thing for Chatterton to scare people, but it's quite another to also murder them."

"Well, I hope you understand why Sir Leonard and myself are determined to help Larkhall be rid of that horrible creature."

Expectorant confidently looked across to Hutton, who reacted by pointedly looking the other way and humming a tune. Expectorant took no notice and looked across to Loadall.

"Did Chatterton kill anybody while he was alive?"

"Not that I know of, though he was partly responsible for an accident that killed a young boy in Sydney Gardens."

Loadall gave Expectorant and Hutton brief details of the bizarre tragedy forty years earlier.

"...It was near the part of the track where your late friend was sliced in three."

"I see." replied a thoughtful Expectorant.

Graham Curnow looked across at Loadall.

"Didn't Chatterton also get someone to commit a murder for him?"

"Yes, he got Dick Joy to kill the journalist who mocked Crabbings."

Loadall suffered his first coughing fit for a while, then turned toward his other guests.

"Did you meet Dick Joy when you visited Larkhall recently?"

"Not that I can recall..." responded Expectorant. "How about you, Sir Leonard?"

Expectorant looked across at his disciple, who appeared to be emerging from his sulk as he shook his head and politely repeated what his leader said.

"Dick Joy spent most of his life being haunted by Chatterton..." Loadall continued. "Joy was a heavy drinker, and when he had too much, he'd sometimes push the limit of how wide he should open his mouth."

All three guests looked at Loadall, and Expectorant requested him to continue.

"...He would've been sixteen when he killed the journalist outside the tin church, and from that point until Chatterton's death, Chatterton made Joy's life a misery."

"In what way?" asked Expectorant.

"Well, Chatterton violently buggered Dick Joy on a regular basis." Loadall replied casually.

This revelation was news to Graham Curnow as well as the other two visitors, and all three widened their eyes in shock, while Expectorant and Hutton re-crossed their torsos with shaky index fingers.

"...And Chatterton told Joy not to spill the beans, otherwise he'd make it clear that Joy was responsible for the killing of the journalist. Although it was an open secret with some locals that Joy carried out the murder, he was terrified of whatever threat Chatterton chose to throw at him.

"Dick Joy was at breaking point after being continually raped and bullied by Chatterton, so he hatched a plan with a few of his friends. Everybody heard stories about how people who tried to enter the tin church were either driven mad or ended up dead soon after, and Joy was desperate to see Chatterton dead. He got his wish instantly and spectacularly.

"However, Chatterton made Dick's life even more miserable from beyond the grave. Dick continually saw Chatterton's apparition, and it continually informed Joy that he'd have to keep committing murders, otherwise he'd spend his eternity being buggered by him. As far as anybody knows, Dick didn't commit any more murders, but he was driven crazier year after year."

Curnow, Expectorant and Hutton were all startled when a loud knock on the front door interrupted Loadall's telling of Dick Joy's unpleasant life story, and the host wriggled himself free of the armchair. He returned a few seconds later accompanied by Lenny Yeo.

As Yeo sat down on Loadall's yellow and black striped deckchair, Loadall informed him of the subject currently being discussed.

"I've just been explaining to our guests how Dick Joy was continually bullied and raped by Chatterton."

"Don't I bloody know it...!" responded Yeo. "I'll never forget the time not so long ago when I found Dick unconscious at the back my shop. Flowers were strewn all over the place, and Dick was led on his front with his trousers round his ankles and a bunch of wilting roses stuck-up his arse; thorns an' all."

Hutton and Expectorant again crossed their torsos; this time with digits that were a little shakier than previously, while Graham Curnow experienced a brief flash of desire to drink himself daft. He looked across to Expectorant and Hutton.

"Before we go any further, we still haven't had actual confirmation that the apparition that strangled your two colleagues was indeed Chatterton."

Barry Loadall weighed-in before Expectorant or Hutton could answer.

"I don't think we need waste time worrying about that." the host replied emphatically. "If your colleagues were indeed strangled by an apparition, it could only be Chatterton."

Expectorant nodded back with full agreement, while Hutton wasn't convinced.

"Are you totally sure that you never saw Dick Joy when you visited The Wyvern & The Witchfinder recently?" Loadall asked both Expectorant and Hutton.

"Well, we can hardly be sure because neither of us actually knew what he looked like..." answered Expectorant. "Could you describe him for us?"

"He was only a small chap..." Loadall began. "About five-feet-five, quite scrawny and sickly from years of heavy drinking, and he had a lot of frizzy grey hair."

Loadall pointed to his *Hair Bear Bunch* clock on the wall.

"...In fact, his hair wasn't dissimilar to that of the central animated figure displayed on my clock."

"Doesn't ring any bells..." Expectorant answered before looking across to his colleague. "Are any of your bells being tinkled, Sir Leonard?"

Hutton stared into space for a few seconds with a quizzical look before suddenly jumping to his feet.

"THAT'S HIM!"

The other members of Loadall's living-room were startled by the volume and passion of Hutton's exclamation.

"...THE APPARITION I SAW THAT STRANGLED DENISE AND WG, THAT'S *DEFINITELY* HIM!!"

25

THE SHOOTING STICK

The itinerary for the latest Larkhall Village Festival was more crammed than ever, and the locals put the troubling recent phenomena to the back of their minds and were determined to fully enjoy the annual feast of fun and frolics.

Along with the perennial favourites such as the face painting, art exhibitions, trampolines and the spliff designing competition, a couple of new events were hastily tinkered with as a reaction to the strange happenings. The *Pin The Tail On The Donkey* game had the image of the donkey's behind painted over and replaced by a caricature of the reviled face of Rupert Chatterton, while the archery competition swapped the traditional ringed target for an image of Thomas Crabbings' face; with a bullseye to be scored for arrows piercing either eye.

Larkhall Square was a hive of activity with stalls being set out and props being shifted into position. Triangular black flags were decked from houses across all four roads that led to the Square; all of which were pedestrianised for the three-day event. The black flags were introduced especially for this festival as a tribute to the four men whose curiosity with the tin church had cost them their lives, and for the locals who fully believed the stories, war was now officially declared on Crabbings and Chatterton.

The Blackest Morn had hosted the opening ceremony of the festival since its inception a couple of centuries earlier, and a large crowd gathered inside it to witness the latest get underway. Each year, a deserving local resident

The Shooting Stick

was invited to make the opening speech, and this year it was decided that the recently widowed wife of Willie Woodman from the hardware store would be a fitting choice to commence proceedings.

A strong and defiant speech was made by Mrs Woodman before she was invited through the side door toward the skittle alley, and dozens of people followed to watch the widow do what she had to do to start the festival.

Each year, a life-sized moulding of Thomas Crabbings' head was placed on the spot of the back skittle pin, and the designated skittler had to knock it down with however many attempts it took. Once the target was hit, the festival was officially underway, and the word would spread to the other venues across the village simultaneously hosting opening-night events.

The biggest headache for organisers happened three years earlier when Mrs Mordent was invited to start the festival. Many people were concerned that an old lady with rheumatism and a walking stick was required to hit a small target with a bowling ball from a distance of twenty yards, but the head of the festival committee had no doubts that she'd be up for the challenge.

As it transpired, Mrs Mordent took thirty-one minutes to finally bowl a ball that knocked Crabbings' head flat into the back gutter. The old lady's aches and pains were being aggravated every time she attempted to flatten the target, and she countered this by taking several puffs on a self-crafted, eight-inch Paraguayan woodbine. Although her pain was soothed, the accompanying loss of co-ordination resulted in most of her throws ending up in the guttering each side of the alley.

Another part of the process that many people were uncomfortable with was the tradition that sticker-uppers were forbidden from returning the bowling ball back along the side chute, and groans of discomfort accompanied Mrs Mordent each time she made the slow and laborious shuffling and clacking to retrieve a failed effort. Further to the already strict ruling was that only one bowling ball could be used.

The long delay in getting that festival started caused havoc in The Bladud's Midriff, which was the venue for the more adult-themed events. The *Eating A Vindaloo With Laxatives* competition was badly hit, as all the competitors' meals were served on the dot of seven o'clock. Instead of the expected minute or two delay, by the time word got to the pub that Mrs Mordent had finally managed to get the festival officially started, all the meals were stone cold, resulting in its abandonment for that year.

After that debacle it was agreed that at the next opening ceremony, no more than six failed attempts would be permitted in knocking over the target, and if that happened, the chosen local resident would be allowed to walk down the alley toward the image of Crabbings and either kick or punch it into the gutter. Also compromised was the 'no sticker-upper' rule, and the bowler would be allowed to designate a trusted friend to return the ball after each failed effort.

At the current festival, the widow of Willie Woodman bent her knees with determination in preparation for her first bowl as the crowd around her hushed. The ball was delivered from the dead centre of the alley, travelled straight as a die, and slammed Crabbings right between the eyes and flat into the back gutter. The crowd roared with approval, and right on schedule the latest festival was underway.

***

Another tradition of the Larkhall Village Festival was that The Wyvern & The Witchfinder was exempted from hosting any of the events. According to the legend, the site of the pub was the epicentre of the weird happenings of centuries ago, and the locals were wary enough to avoid any possibility of stirring up trouble.

On the evening of the day when the deaths of the four local men was confirmed, the festival committee held an emergency meeting. Its members were enraged that evil was still demonstrably being spread around Larkhall, and that leaving the pub that spawned the legend out of the festival schedule was a sign of fear that galvanised the spirits of Crabbings and Chatterton. The main item on the agenda was whether the closing ceremony should be switched from The Blackest Morn to The Wyvern & The Witchfinder. Each committee member was in a defiant and combative mood, and by a margin of twelve votes to none, the motion was unanimously carried.

Dave Rensenbrink wasn't too fussed about his pub breaking with tradition by hosting the closing ceremony, especially with the influx of trade it would bring. After all, whatever bad things happened in the village since the time of Thomas Crabbings, not a single strange occurrence was reported from inside his pub.

Jeremy Bennett-Brewer walked through the door a little before seven. The pub was empty apart from the landlord, as most villagers were spread around the five venues hosting the opening events of the festival. Bennett-Brewer wasn't especially in the mood for festivals and was much more concerned with discussing plans about how to defeat the local menace.

"Evenin', teach, me ol' babber."

"Evening, Dave."

Bennett-Brewer asked for a lemonade shandy, then informed Rensenbrink that he'd soon be off to Barry Loadall's to discuss with him and a few others what plans could be hatched.

The Shooting Stick

"Good for you, mate. As long as all the weird stuff doesn't happen in my pub, you can all do what you bleedin'-well like."

Bennett-Brewer received his change before the landlord informed him that his pub would be hosting the closing ceremony of the festival instead of The Blackest Morn.

"Blimey, do you think that's a good idea after what's been going on recently?"

"Course it is. Ev'ryone gets wankered on the last night of the festival, and about time this place was full. Besides, would be nice to see Dick again."

Bennett-Brewer was startled by what he'd just heard, but didn't get a chance to question Rensenbrink further as his attention was diverted by a new customer unexpectedly walking through the door. He looked down at his watch and noted that he was already a few minutes late.

***

A couple of minutes later, Barry Loadall opened his door for Bennett-Brewer, who strode through to the lounge to find Trevor Expectorant, Sir Leonard Hutton, Lenny Yeo and Graham Curnow already there.

Expectorant and Hutton were sat either end of the old sofa, while Curnow occupied an armchair, and Yeo the yellow and black striped deck chair. Noticing that Bennett-Brewer had nowhere to sit, Loadall went to the small store cupboard underneath the stairs and returned with a shooting stick.

"Not exactly the most comfortable of seats one could imagine, but needs must."

Bennett-Brewer looked quizzically at the walking stick-cum-fold out chair.

"I never had you down as using one of these, Barry." uttered the teacher.

"I don't. This was bequeathed to me by my grandfather in his will."

Loadall unravelled the shooting stick.

"...It's not in mint condition, and the footplate's a bit wobblier than in its heyday, but perfectly usable."

The host turned the shooting stick upside-down and discovered two screws from the footplate were missing.

"...It'll be wobblier than I forecast because of the missing screws, but the more you relax your muscles, the easier it'll be to sit on."

Bennett-Brewer took his seat and was surprised by how comfortable it was.

"I'd gather your grandfather enjoyed the countryside?"

"He was a keen grouse-shooter, as well as being the fourteenth Marquess of Chipping Sodbury. Late in life, he became very fond of all wild animals, and it turned him into an opponent of all types of hunting. It was probably the guilt of killing so many birds that led to him sticking both barrels in his mouth and decorating the immediate vicinity of woodland with his brains."

Bennett-Brewer gawped at Loadall and began to sway on the shooting stick.

"...That's a piece of history you're sitting – or rather, swaying on."

"Yes, well it's not the type of history I relish, to be perfectly honest."

"Indeed, and no doubt the fact that my grandfather shot himself while sat on that stick will make it an even less relishable piece of history."

Bennett-Brewer turned another shade closer to white.

"...Though the violent force of my grandfather's suicide could explain the screws of the footplate being loosened."

As the teacher swirled like a gyroscope, he tried to take his mind off the unpleasant history of his seat by asking Loadall about his noble heritage.

"I find it strange that someone with aristocratic blood should, with all due respect, live in such a modest house."

Loadall showed a hint of regret on his face as he answered,

"The family found me a bit of an embarrassment, especially after I was charged with supplying the locals of Chipping Sodbury and Yate with illegal central American yields. I was told to leave the area, change my name by deed poll to make myself sound as un-aristocratic as possible, and in return I'd receive financial security. One thing's for sure; 'Barry Loadall' certainly sounds a lot less regal than my official title of The Right Honourable Hilary Thruxton-Duvall."

Bennett-Brewer, Yeo and Curnow all burst into laughter at the absurdity of Loadall's spectacular title, while Expectorant and Hutton appeared nonplussed at each end of the battered sofa. Loadall had always been guarded about his heritage, but now had no qualms about revealing the truth.

"I may as well let you all know seeing the end of the world is probably nigh."

Loadall began to splutter and cough, and Lenny Yeo slapped the host on the back several times.

"Is there anything further His Lordship requires?"

"Yes..." Loadall answered as he completely ignored Yeo to turn toward Expectorant and Hutton. "I want you two to tell Jeremy about the latest developments."

Before the Devil worshippers could respond, Yeo rose from his deckchair.

"I'm afraid I'm going to have to love you and fuck off, I've got tickets for the festival play at the theatre."

The rest of the gathering wished the departing florist an enjoyable experience, and Yeo promised to return after the show if there were any spooky happenings to report.

As Yeo left the house, the host, Graham Curnow and Jeremy Bennett-Brewer turned their attention back toward Expectorant and Hutton.

Expectorant addressed Bennett-Brewer and spoke matter of factly.

"One of my disciples was killed by a train in Sydney Gardens, another jumped off Cleveland Bridge, and the other two were strangled."

Bennett-Brewer turned a little paler as he continued his attempts to not sway on his temporary seat.

"...At first, I thought the strangulations were mutual, but according to Sir Leonard here, the double deed was perpetrated by an apparition."

The four other occupants of the room stared at Bennett-Brewer before Loadall revealed that the description of the murderous apparition matched that of Dick Joy.

Jeremy-Bennett Brewer turned even whiter before finally falling off his seat.

26

THE ANIMAL-LOATHING VET

The opening Friday evening of the festival got off to a smooth start. The Vindaloo competition in the Bladud's Midriff was won by Charlie Sparrow, the huge owner of the burger shop just off Larkhall Square. It was Sparrow's ninth consecutive victory, and such was his dominance, the local bookmaker's odds on his latest victory was 1/500. By the time Sparrow's red-hot meal was consumed, none of the other competitors were even halfway through theirs, and many had to continually pause for breath and be on constant guard against fouling themselves. Sparrow underlined his dominance by going on to eat four packets of ready-salted crisps; again without any liquid refreshment, and poked even more fun at his lesser rivals by casually and continuously breaking wind.

Over at St Swithin's Church, the simultaneous opening night event of *Slapsies!* took place, enthusiastically refereed by Victor Carping. The leathered hands of garage mechanic Rich Pleiades had seen him triumph in six of the seven previous competitions, and he was angling for his fifth straight victory. Five years earlier, Pleiades controversially lost out to the village veterinarian, Ralph Mogford, who was accused by many of numbing his hands with injections. Although the vet was subsequently cleared of any wrongdoing by the festival committee, he was never again the same force and had failed to get beyond the quarter-final stage in any of the following years. Several villagers saw this as proof that Mogford had indeed cheated to claim his solitary Slapsies! title, and that the suspicion aroused rendered him too scared to repeat the trick. Rich Pleiades was the runner-up on the single occasion he didn't win the competition, and was one of the most vocal accusers of his victorious opponent.

The current festival saw a return to form for Ralph Mogford, who surprisingly reached the final again after his recent lean years. Rich Pleiades made the final for the eighth consecutive year, and again wasn't remotely tested by any previous opponents, who were comfortably seen off with viciously bruised hands and tears of pain.

Victor Carping invited Pleiades and Mogford to shake hands in front of the altar. After they'd done so, Carping rested a hand on a shoulder of each competitor.

"I want a good clean fight. You play according to the Larkhall version of the Queensbury Rules, and whoever triumphs, I want the cherished sport of Slapsies! to also be the winner...so come out fighting!"

The final turned-out to be an embarrassingly one-sided affair, with the back of both Mogford's hands massively swollen and horribly bruised after a dozen fearsome slaps from Pleiades. The reigning champion finished the job with a beautifully timed and forceful slap to Mogford's pus-weeping right hand, which caused the vet to let out a final scream of submission before he burst into tears.

As Ralph Mogford spun around in pain with his hands clamped tightly between his thighs, Pleiades was in no mood for charity, and pointed accusingly at his destroyed opponent.

"Not so easy without the numbing injections, eh?"

Mogford responded by stomping sulkily down the aisle toward the main church door to the accompaniment of boos and jeers. Mogford turned around just before he reached the door, folded his arms to clamp his throbbing hands tightly and shouted hysterically at Pleiades through his sobbing.

"NEXT TIME YOU NEED DE-WORMING TABLETS FOR THAT MANKY, PATHETIC EXCUSE FOR A C...C...CAT OF YOURS, YOU CAN F...F...FUCKING WELL GO ELSEWHERE!"

Rich Pleiades casually removed two packets of worming tablets from his coat pocket, waved them provocatively back at his defeated opponent against the soundtrack of wild cheering, and Ralph Mogford's humiliation was complete.

Mogford angrily stropped away from the church and along St Saviour's Road toward the tiny theatre, which was hosting a re-enactment of the confrontation between Thomas Crabbings and Satan on top of Solsbury Hill.

The theatre had sold every ticket for re-enactment night, and Mogford had to offer the bribe of a lifetime's supply of premium flea collars for the

The Wyvern & The Witchfinder

Dachshund-owning manager to gain access. Once inside the cramped venue, Mogford stood behind the six rows of seats and watched the two actors in witchfinder and devil costumes engaged in heated verbal sparring.

Over the years, Ralph Mogford made no secret of his admiration for Thomas Crabbings, and occasional dirty looks were aimed his way from audience members who'd spotted him, including the recently arrived Lenny Yeo. Mogford reacted by tilting his head slightly upwards as a sign that he was ignoring them. All eyes were soon aimed back toward the small stage.

"My name is Thomas Crabbings, and I have been dutied by the villagers to rid the locale of your scheming and revolting presence!"

The audience almost unanimously booed the latest line from the actor playing the witchfinder, who in-turn looked toward the audience and let out a dirty chuckle in the manner of pantomime villain.

"GOOD ON YA, TOMMY BOY. YOU CAN DO IT!"

Mogford had several curses thrown his way from the audience in response to his impassioned endorsement of the witchfinder. He continued to show that he couldn't care less as he leant against the back wall of the theatre, and both actors momentarily stopped their performances to aim clenched fists at the aggravating vet before continuing.

"Who are you to cast me aside...?" the Devil responded. "For MY duty is to allow the people of Larkhall to indulge in all manner of erotic pleasures they find fulfilling and refreshing!"

This time Mogford maintained silence, while the rest of the audience cheered.

"Um...I have been summoned by the elders of the...er...village to rid it of your meddling presence." answered the witchfinder with a shaky and hesitant voice.

The theatre technicians had worked for several days to get the pyrotechnics and various special effects co-ordinated for the scene where the Devil brought fire upon the witchfinder. A flamethrower was mounted at the back of the stage, invisible to the audience through the blackened backdrop. The theatre manager was told that the scene would be very difficult to get right, but after three rehearsals, the effect was successfully achieved, and the manager was relieved when the special effects department gave it the green light. The plan was for a huge plume of smoke to entirely envelop the half of the stage where the witchfinder stood, and for the few moments where the audience was being deceived, the witchfinder would be lowered through the stage trap door, and quickly swapped for a five-foot high prop of the stone pillar of Solsbury Hill. Just before the pillar was returned to the stage via the trap door, a huge ball of flame would further blanket the stage and make its emergence invisible to the audience.

"So, you have been summoned by the elders of Larkhall to be rid of me, have you?"

The Devil's tone became far more threatening as it pointed a sinister and accusing finger toward the witchfinder, who began to cower defensively.

"Y...y...yes...I think so." spluttered the Witchfinder.

"If that is the task to which you are assigned, then perhaps we should ask the people of Larkhall?"

"Uh...alright then..."

The witchfinder's voice and body language continued to weaken as the Devil turned to face the theatre audience.

"WHAT SAY YOU GOOD PEOPLE OF LARKHALL VILLAGE?" the Devil screamed at the top of his voice as the witchfinder continued to cower pathetically.

"LET'S RID THIS VILLAGE INSTEAD OF THE WITCHFINDER!" chorused the audience with a manic enthusiasm.

The witchfinder turned to the audience and angrily shook his fist, while the Devil rubbed his hands with glee.

"NO, NO NOOOOOO!" shouted a lone dissenting voice from the back of the theatre.

The audience turned to stare hatefully at Ralph Mogford in response to his second unscheduled interruption. The actors playing the two characters managed to ad-lib their response successfully; the Devil stared at Mogford with disdainful hands on hips, while the witchfinder held aloft a double thumbs-up toward the meddling gate-crasher.

"DON'T JUST STAND THERE, TOMMY BOY...!" pleaded the unperturbed Mogford. "SLAY THE EVIL CUNT!!"

The audience jeered and booed angrily at the vet's latest act of provocation, while the nonplussed performers tried to ignore the latest interruption and remember their next lines.

Behind the stage, the man in charge of both the release of smoke and flamethrower was linked by walkie-talkie to the trap door operator; poised to co-ordinate the spectacular climax to the re-enactment of the legend. Both waited nervously for their cue, each knowing that should the effect misfire, the whole play would be ruined.

When the audience finally finished with their disapproval of Ralph Mogford, all eyes were turned back toward the stage.

"THE GOOD PEOPLE OF LARKHALL HAVE SPOKEN!" screamed the Devil in triumph.

"OH NO, THEY HAVEN'T!" countered the witchfinder in a game show of defiance.

"OH YES WE HAVE!" the audience responded with childlike hysteria.

The witchfinder cast his eyes around the tiny theatre and aimed scathing looks at several individuals to threaten them into allegiance. He then campily attached both hands to his hips to make a double teapot, and stood his ground with a final shriek of defiance.

"OOOOOOHHH NO YOU HAVEN'T!!!"

"OOOOOOHHH YES WE HAVE, WITCHFINDER CRABBINGS!!!"

The latest piece of audience participation was the cue for the finale, and as the lights dimmed, the special effects operators prepared to flick their switches and pull their levers.

***

An hour after hearing the alarming news that Dick Joy was apparently still at large after his death, Jeremy Bennett-Brewer had calmed down, and shared the determination of the rest of the room to defeat the current ghastliness.

"So, what exactly has the Wyvern got to do with all of this?"

"Absolutely nothing; a complete red herring." replied Barry Loadall before he took a sip of onion juice with a cocked little finger.

Bennett-Brewer was pleased to have vacated the shooting stick and its macabre history. Instead, he enjoyed the relative comfort of the yellow and black striped deckchair vacated by Lenny Yeo. He invited his host to continue answering his original question.

"...After Crabbings ran the wheelwright's head into the side of his workshop, the brother of the wheelwright swore to take revenge, and he took several painstaking weeks making a wyvern costume."

"So the Wyvern doesn't actually exist?"

"Of course it doesn't."

Barry Loadall wagged a disdainful digit at Bennett-Brewer.

"...This isn't a fairy story, you know."

The teacher shook his head in bewilderment, while Trevor Expectorant looked downcast.

"That's a shame, I was really looking forward to meeting the Wyvern."

Expectorant looked across to Hutton, who returned his master's disappointed look.

"Regarding what happened all those centuries ago..." continued Loadall. "the wheelwright's brother spent a long time sat in the apple tree that used to stand opposite the old inn, patiently waiting for Crabbings to turn up and perform his exorcism. When he eventually arrived, the wheelwright's brother dropped from the tree in what I'd assume to be an impressive costume, pelted the witchfinder with apples, and successfully made him run in terror all the way to Devizes.

The Animal-Loathing Vet

"Many people knew about the wheelwright's brother's plan to help scare Crabbings away, and no doubt plenty of those gathered outside the inn were looking forward to seeing the witchfinder receive his just desserts."

"And we all know what splendid desserts can be made from apples!" interrupted Hutton with a playful grin, before his leader cuffed him around the head as punishment for his flippancy.

Expectorant turned back toward Loadall.

"But what about those stories of the Wyvern taking up residence in the ramshackle barn halfway up Solsbury Hill?"

"Just a bit of fibbing put about shortly after Chatterton had his discussion with the cottage gatepost."

Expectorant and Hutton exchanged deflated looks.

"...All designed to keep the Crabbings-loving creeps away from the stone pillar."

The room fell silent for a few seconds before an agitated Jeremy Bennett-Brewer spoke.

"So how are we going to get rid of Crabbings, Chatterton, and now it seems, Dick Joy?"

"It doesn't really matter if the world's going to end." replied Loadall dismissively.

The host looked around at each guest in turn as he took a huge inhalation from his bong. Various degrees of apprehensive expressions were returned.

The doorbell chimed, and Loadall again glanced at each visitor before leaving his armchair.

The drug dealer returned with Lenny Yeo, who appeared a little disorientated.

"How did the play go?" asked Jeremy Bennett-Brewer nervously.

"Very interesting." answered Yeo in a deadpan voice, before he returned the vacated shooting stick to an upright position and sat on it with an assurance that was beyond its previous occupant.

Yeo went on to address Loadall exclusively.

"Ralph Mogford caused a right commotion."

"No surprise, he's a Crabbings-loving carbuncle."

"Who is Ralph Mogford?" asked Trevor Expectorant.

Graham Curnow answered before the host and Lenny Yeo had the chance.

"He's the local vet, and one of Thomas Crabbings' most hard-line supporters."

"Did anything unusual happen?" an enthusiastic Hutton asked Yeo.

"Yeah, Mogford kept interrupting by egging on the bloke playing Crabbings, and most of the audience were getting a bit pissed off with it.

"He came straight from the Slapsies! competition in the church, and I 'eard he got battered by Rich Pleiades in the final."

"Always refreshing to hear about that hot-headed irritant getting his comeuppance." answered Loadall as he re-lit his bong.

"Couldn't agree more..." answered Yeo. "and there's nobody in Larkhall as hot-headed; or at least was."

The other members of Loadall's lounge shifted further toward the edge of their seats as an invitation for the florist to continue.

"...Mogford was stood against the back wall, about ten yards from the stage. He must've interrupted half a dozen times before the end.

"There was a massive load of smoke covering the stage, and most of the crowd started cheering. Mogford kept shouting and being a right prick, and loads of people were turning round and arguing with him. I couldn't be bothered with it, so I kept looking at the stage. Nothing happened for ages apart from even more smoke coming out, so I finally turned round and saw Mogford arguing with an old woman. Hard to imagine how the bloke ever became a vet with the things he said about the animals he treated. I heard him tell that woman that her pet spaniel was a complete wanker and an embarrassment to the dog world."

"He's a vet who wears his heart on his sleeve..." interrupted a serious Loadall. "but his surgery also has the highest success rate for treating animals in the area. Mogford somehow has the Midas touch, and that's why people put up with him hurling insults at their pets."

Lenny Yeo nodded in agreement.

"Yeah, people came from miles away to have their animals treated, and none of 'em cared about Mogford's attitude. All they were concerned about was the health of their pets, and even if they were told that their dog was a right tosser or their rabbit was a long-eared twat, they were more than happy to pay their bills. I remember visiting Mogford years ago; he told me he'd seen explosions that were better looking than my cat, and that it was only when it meowed that he knew which end to stick the suppository. He did a great job though, and my cat was never much of a looker, so fair enough."

Barry Loadall noted that everyone in the room looked impatient at Yeo for not getting to the point.

"All very charming, but we want to hear about Mogford's histrionics inside the theatre tonight rather than his buccaneering approach to animal care."

Yeo held up a polite hand of apology.

"Oh sorry, didn't mean to go round the houses."

Every other person in the room stared at Yeo as he finally returned to the present.

"...The stage was covered in smoke for ages, and it seemed something was going wrong with the special effects. The whole audience knew what the ending was supposed to be, and it certainly wasn't a theatre full of smoke and bugger all else.

"Everyone was getting impatient waiting for something to happen, and Mogford started shouting even more about Crabbings being invincible. Anyway, by now it was clear that they made a right fuck-up of the ending, and after a couple more minutes of nothing but smoke, some of the audience started to leave, and I got up as well. My seat was two rows from the back, and Mogford was right behind me stood against the back wall. He was busy telling some old fella that his Jack Russell was a freeloading little cunt.

"Don't know if there's such a thing as fate, but as luck would have it, I sat down again, and for the life of me I don't know why. As soon as I took my seat again, a bright flash of light flew from the stage and burst through the smoke. I felt a whizz of boiling air fly right over me, and as I looked round, saw Mogford's head get melted into the wall by a massive ball of fire."

27

GOING UNDERGROUND

Victor Carping arranged to visit Graham Curnow at ten o'clock Saturday morning. He assumed the previous evening's violent death of the village vet would be on the agenda, together with the issue of whether or not the world would end the following day. Before setting off for Curnow's house, Carping dropped in on the theatre manager to see what information he could get. According to the manager, the operator in charge of the flamethrower had scarpered several minutes before Ralph Mogford's head was incinerated, and nobody was found anywhere near the smoking prop immediately afterward.

It was another mystery to untangle as Carping crossed the tiny stone bridge that straddled Lam Brook to enter the front garden of Curnow's house. The garden had no ornamentation whatsoever and was nothing more than two modest rectangles of overgrown grass and weeds that almost entirely encroached each side of the central stone path. As Carping approached the house, he became a little anxious as he spotted that all four windows had their dark curtains tightly drawn.

A deep breath was taken as he pressed the doorbell. Several silent seconds went by, and Carping's anxiety level duly increased. He tried to look through both downstairs windows, but only received a second opinion that he didn't have x-ray vision. Carping returned to the front door and decided to give it a few hearty fist thumps. He was startled when the door flew open after the first thump and began to feel the same dread as when he approached the tiny room next to the church burial vault.

The kitchen and lounge had no separating wall, and peering beyond the lounge, Carping saw that the dark, floor-length curtains in front of the French windows to the back garden were also tightly drawn.

The Rector took a few steps inside the house as the gloomy interior was brightened a little by daylight coming through the open door. On the kitchen table was a sealed envelope addressed with the single name VICTOR, and twice underlined.

Carping immediately picked-up the envelope and ripped it open.

Dear Victor,

It's imperative both for myself and for the village that I go into hiding for the rest of this weekend. I'm sorry that I couldn't forewarn you about my absence, but it's a decision I made very suddenly. Please respect my wish that NOBODY tries to discover my secret hiding place.

Over the past few weeks, my dreams have become more worrying. I think you know me well enough to realise that I take a rational approach to the weird happenings of recent times, but I've been sober for over a year now, and I can no longer blame a pickled brain for what I've been experiencing.

I WILL NOT RETURN TO DRINKING – AND YOU MUST LET THIS BE KNOWN!

Please try to keep your wits over the next couple of days. I am now certain that unexplainable forces are at work, and that continuing to be in denial will be more dangerous than confronting it. I hope all will be well when the weekend is over, but you and the others MUST be prepared for events to take some very nasty turns. It's going to be a very bumpy ride if we're to get through to the other side of this, so batten down the hatches and stay strong.

One final thing – keep a close eye on Barry Loadall. He's been my friend for many years, but I now have a strong sense that he isn't what he seems.

Take every care,
Graham

***

A worried but determined Graham Curnow finally managed to prise the door open. Deceit and cunning were his bywords during the drunken phase of his life, and he felt that he had to reinstate those qualities if he was to get through the weekend.

It had to be done in the wee small hours for obvious reasons, and not long before dawn broke that Saturday morning, Curnow finally made a successful break-in. He had to keep reminding himself that there was no option but to cheat and deceive a friend, and eventually his mind became free of guilt.

The dream where Curnow effortlessly saw off Chatterton had proved to be a one-off, and every night since was filled with far more sinister content. He now knew that he had to get out of the house and find a hiding place for the rest of the weekend, and the dream that finally pushed him over the edge was from about an hour earlier that featured several macabre twists to festival events. The most terrifying part of the dream was where Victor Carping stood between Rupert Chatterton and Barry Loadall in front of the church altar. Carping had a hand on the shoulder of each before inviting them to begin the fight. Both competitors were completely lifeless, and the heads of both rested backwards against their shoulders with eyes pointing heavenward. Victor Carping blew two sinister musical intervals on his whistle before he retreated into the shadows.

Standing behind Chatterton and Loadall were the murdered youngsters Ally Lee and Ronan Rhodes; who clasped their designated competitors by the side of their upper arms to shake violently as if they were life-sized puppets. Curnow was horrified as he viewed a head-butting competition between two dead people who were being controlled by two other dead people. It seemed like a pointless competition, as although tall himself, Loadall was still several inches short of Chatterton's unusual height. Instead of innocent giggling, the boys cackled manically as they fruitlessly attempted to land the knock-out blow.

During a moment of lucidity, Graham Curnow realised that Barry Loadall was still alive, and was alarmed at the dream's insistence that he wasn't.

Neither of the dead youngsters were getting anywhere with their head-butting attempts, so Victor Carping reappeared to blow his whistle to signal abandonment. Carping, Lee and Rhodes turned their gaze toward the author of the nightmare and were quickly followed by the zombified reawakening of Chatterton and Loadall; whose heads slowly snapped back into upright positions. Curnow's vision of Chatterton's face was with his pre-accident features, but together with the faces of Lee, Rhodes and Loadall, slowly morphed into shattered messes, while the smile on Victor Carping's face grew correspondingly wider. When the transformations were complete, all five faces opened their mouths wide and projectile vomited toward Curnow.

Curnow awoke suddenly with his arms covering his face. He eventually removed them to discover daybreak was just beginning to fill his bedroom with murky shadows. He looked at his bedside clock and it displayed three-am exactly. Even though it was the time of the year when the nights were at their shortest, three o'clock was too early for daybreak. Through his disorientation, Curnow became freshly troubled by the apparent tweaking

Going Underground

of the known physical laws. He turned his gaze away from the clock and toward the corner of the room, where he saw Dick Joy sat on the dressing table staring hatefully back at him. Joy's features slowly changed into its post-death catastrophe before he opened his mouth to projectile vomit.

Curnow awoke suddenly with his arms covering his face, but this time it was for real. He looked at the bedside clock and again saw exactly three-am displayed. The difference this time was that his bedroom was blanketed in darkness, and that proved to him that he really had woken up. It was at that moment that he decided to pack a few things and exit the house.

Before he left, he composed two letters, and made sure that the first was easily discoverable by Victor Carping. Each letter was very different in tone and outlook, and circumstances would dictate whether or not the second would receive a communal reading. As soon as Curnow finished the letters, he scurried from his house with the front door deliberately left unlatched.

Struggling to shake off the horrors of the dream and its encore, Curnow returned to the present. He closed the door behind and prepared to descend the steep staircase. He made sure that the practical necessities of his break-in and residence were thoroughly covered; a powerful torch and several spare batteries, together with a basic duvet, covering sheet and pillow. Many hours of fear and loneliness were ahead of him, so it was important to at least give himself a bit of physical comfort.

The torch shone brightly as Curnow turned its beam on the descending steps. He had to tread carefully due to the severe angle, and rhythmically took two-second intervals between steps. When he reached the bottom, Curnow flashed his torch all around the underground room. Everything looked exactly as it should, and Curnow remembered it well from his invited visit a few months earlier. He shone the light toward the little secret room that was going to be his abode for the rest of the weekend. He was told on that occasion that the small connecting room was never used, so was confident that he wouldn't be troubled – at least not by human visitors who were still alive. The thought of the occasional rat or cockroach paying him a visit in the pitch black was a little disturbing, but in the grand scheme of the enormous challenge ahead, was only a minor concern.

No doubt people would think of him as being incredibly brave to spend so many hours alone here, but nothing could be considered brave if it was the only available option. As Curnow prepared to bed down for the new day, he removed the few necessities he allowed himself from his rucksack. Toilet paper, air fresheners, two airtight plastic containers and a few thick bin liners were his only concession to material comforts. He would be down here a long time, and he'd have no option but to use the small room without sanitation as a lavatory. To try and make his stay more bearable in that respect, Curnow would fast the entire time. Thirst would be a far more serious problem in such a confined and airless place, and he allowed himself a one-litre flask of water, which was to be sipped from only when seriously parched. He was confident that the two plastic containers were plenty big enough for his waste.

Curnow was determined not to leave his hideout at any time apart from the middle of the night, and only then to stretch his legs with a few yards of barefoot walking around the slightly less dark outer underground room. He could also leave the door ajar at night to allow some air to circulate. When closed, the door had tiny slithers of space around it anyway, and he was confident that the chances of suffocation were minimal even if he did the unthinkable and fell asleep.

Staying awake was a major worry. Earlier in the night, Curnow remembered that it wasn't until at least two o'clock that he finally drifted off. Waking up at three-am meant that he'd had barely an hour's sleep. He had more than a day and a half of seclusion to get through, and he hoped that his alert state-of-mind would be enough to combat any physical tiredness.

As he rolled his duvet along the stone floor, Curnow steeled himself for what lay ahead. Spending many hours alone in the total darkness with nothing other than his own mind for company was hardly going to be a relaxing weekend getaway, but he hoped that the sacrifice of the means would justify the ends.

Curnow placed the uncased pillow on top of his duvet and against the back wall of the cramped room. Making up his bed was a rare occasion where he allowed himself torchlight, and together with falling asleep, unnecessary use of the torch would be regarded as a cardinal sin.

After draping the thin covering sheet over himself, he led back and tried to make himself as comfortable as possible. He wasn't enthusiastic at the prospect of the many hours of ultra-spartan living stretched before him, but as he constantly kept reminding himself, he had no option.

Curnow allowed himself a brief flash of the torch to check his watch. It was just after four-am, and it had now been an hour or so since he awoke from his latest nightmare. Within his hiding place, he was far more concerned about what would happen when asleep than awake, and that was the thought that made him confident he could stay fully conscious throughout the duration.

He turned his thoughts to the outside world and realised that it would be at about this time when the first signs of daybreak would appear behind Solsbury Hill to the east. As he contemplated the breaking Saturday, he dearly wished for the coming day of festival fun at the local park to pass without incident.

Going Underground

Thinking about the local park made Curnow nostalgic, and he turned his thoughts back a few decades. He fondly recalled his childhood best friend. Before or since, he'd never known any child or adult to have been so likeable and talented, but his fate was one that puzzled and haunted him ever since.

By the time they both reached adolescence, his friend had become a multi-talented achiever at all subjects. Captain of both the school football and cricket teams, Curnow watched his progress with great admiration and not an ounce of jealousy. Curnow himself was a modest achiever, and he knew and accepted that he was nothing special. He held nothing but sincere hope that his friend's many talents and wondrous character would one day see him become a big success.

Curnow's eyes began to moisten amongst the memories from his deep past, and from the day everything changed forever.

The two thirteen-year-olds often visited the local park together, and although his friend was far in advance of Curnow in all sports as well as academically, they often played tennis together. Out of the three pairs of tennis courts, they always chose the middle one, as it had a little wooden hut to change in, and a small ramp that connected the door of the hut to the court entrance. Both would imagine they were gracing the Centre Court at Wimbledon as they made the short journey from changing room to the arena, and both would hear the phantom cheers of the crowd as they stepped on court.

Curnow's lack of natural racquet skills meant that the pair never competed on equal terms, but both enjoyed their long knockabout sessions. It was especially hot on the day that everything changed, and after half an hour, Curnow's friend suggested they take a break so he could return to the changing room to change his shirt. Curnow didn't bother with a change of clothes and decided to use his moments alone on court to practice his service.

Curnow became concerned as the minutes went by without his friend re-appearing, so he walked toward the changing room hut in the hope that he was on the wrong end of an innocent prank. What Curnow discovered instead was his friend gently swaying lifeless with a noose around his neck.

To discover that his talented and wonderful best friend had taken his own life went way beyond his adolescent reasoning, and the sheer incredulousness Curnow felt was enough for him to raid his parents' drinks cabinet a few days later. Curnow had never even tasted alcohol before, but something inside told him that it would be the miracle therapy.

It was a vicious irony that a boy so full of promise, goodness and empathy should be responsible for Curnow making such a mess of his own life, but he never held anything other than warmth and affection toward him.

Curnow often went for a stroll around the local park to remember his friend, although he always avoided the painful associations of visiting the tennis courts.

As he lay in the blackness of his confined cell, Curnow's body and mind tossed and churned from the memory of the long-ago tragedy. The sharpened state of his emotions toward his long-lost mate was enough for Curnow to inadvertently lower his defences. His final thought on the matter was that he hoped his friend was now at peace. He then wearily closed his eyes and performed the cardinal sin of falling into a deep sleep.

28

ANYONE FOR TENNIS?

Straddling the city limits to the east and sandwiched between the old and new A46s and the A4 London Road, Chalice Park was the main venue for the Saturday of the Larkhall Village Festival. The park was home to no less than thirty exhibitions and competitions, and during the course of the morning, its perimeter was to be dotted with stalls selling everything from hot food to home-made curios. The main entrance was on the old A46, and along with the roads that branched off Larkhall Square, was also pedestrianised for the weekend.

A zebra crossing stood outside the park gates, and as the road was closed to vehicles, the council gave permission for the orange Belisha beacons atop the poles each side of the road to be exchanged with glowing blood-red orbs that mockingly depicted the faces of Crabbings and Chatterton.

Just inside the park, the façade of the park-keeper's house featured a large clock, and Barry Loadall suggested to Jeremy Bennett-Brewer and the remaining Devil worshippers that meeting underneath the clock would be a good idea. Trevor Expectorant wrote a sick note on behalf of Sir Leonard Hutton to explain his absence from work, while Expectorant himself didn't have any qualms about closing his shop for the day. If both he and Loadall were right about the world ending on Sunday, then he'd hardly bemoan the lost profit.

The clock on the park-keeper's house had been stuck on nine-thirty-seven for many years, and it was Loadall's suggestion that nine-thirty-seven should be the actual meeting time that morning, as it would guarantee nobody would be early or late.

Expectorant and Hutton arrived punctually, followed swiftly by Bennett-Brewer, then twenty minutes later by Loadall, who announced his arrival by praising the other three.

"Right on the dot of nine-thirty-seven, well done everybody."

Bennett-Brewer, Expectorant and Hutton were all first timers to the festival, and all three were keen when Loadall suggested they attend the main part of it. At that stage of the morning, most of the stalls and exhibitions were yet to be set up, with much of the park's eight acres still empty. Loadall decided that he'd be the tour guide for the other three and invited them for a stroll around the park's perimeter.

"...I do hope you're all full of positivity as the weekend continues to unravel itself?"

Expectorant and Hutton both forced a half smile, and Bennett-Brewer answered in a tone hardly brimming with zest.

"Well, I think we all know how important it is that we confront this nasty business, although I have to admit that after everything that's happened, I'm more than a little worried about what may be unleashed over the course..."

"EXCELLENT!" interrupted Loadall. "Great to see the look of bloody-minded determination on all your faces!"

The other three gazed nonplussed at each other and received confirmation of nothing more than shared apprehension.

Loadall stretched his arms forward as a signal to begin the leisurely ramble.

"Looks like it'll keep fine for the day." mentioned Loadall, as the group began to walk the slight uphill gradient of the path toward the north east of the park.

"It does indeed..." replied Expectorant. "Although it looks like another deep depression will be moving in tomorrow evening."

"One would expect nothing less for such an epoch-making occasion!"

Loadall's high spirits didn't transmit to the other three, who all struggled to respond favourably.

Bennett-Brewer looked across at Loadall.

"Barry, are Mr Expectorant and Mr Hutton aware of how sexually aware the old women are in Larkhall?"

The looks of surprise on the faces of both Devil worshippers answered the teacher's question.

"Young Jeremy here is quite the Valentino, you know..." began Loadall. "I can't remember any male specimen having quite such an effect on the pensioners of Larkhall since the Earthly existence of Rupert Chatterton."

Jeremy Bennett-Brewer came to a sudden halt just before the other three.

"WHAT??"

Barry Loadall unfurled his widest smile before answering.

"Don't let Chatterton's spiteful persona and delinquent word skills fool any of you. Dozens of local women willingly fell prey to his highly charged sexuality."

Bennett-Brewer shook his head incredulously, and Expectorant and Hutton were just as shocked by Loadall's revelation.

"How the hell could any woman possibly find such an unpleasant person desirable??"

Bennett-Brewer continued to shake his head after making his reply.

"It's a mystery to me also, Jeremy..." answered Loadall, who retained his wide smile. "If you want to know the secret of whatever it was the ladies found so desirable about Chatterton, I suggest you interrogate both Mrs Mordent and Mrs Tanning."

The four of them continued to stand still on the path, and Bennett-Brewer showed how appalled he was by covering his face with a hand.

Barry Loadall appeared to savour the anguish felt by the teacher and continued to grin.

"Mrs Mordent and Mrs Tanning were both married, middle-aged women when Chatterton was getting up to his mischief, and both regularly submitted themselves to his prowess behind their husbands' backs."

Loadall stretched his arm toward Bennett-Brewer as an invitation to shake hands, which the teacher accepted with a look of complete bewilderment.

"My warmest congratulations, Jeremy. The lothario is dead...long live the lothario!"

***

Along with five helpers, Winston Wellington was setting up his food stall just in front of the tennis courts near the south eastern corner of Chalice Park. It had been a heady and tumultuous few weeks for Wellington, whose agonised choice between his convictions and his family had cost him the latter. He knew just how big a deal it was to suddenly shun generations of family beliefs and teachings, but as he kept reminding himself, a man is only a man if he follows his convictions.

Wellington's elderly father offered him a deal through snarling teeth; in return for getting the hell out of town and officially changing his name, he'd receive a generous lump sum. Furthermore, it was required of Wellington that he'd have absolutely no communication with any of the family for the rest of his days. A contract was drawn up to make the deal legally binding, and as Wellington signed, several members of his family stood in front of him with nasty scowls and clenched fists.

After a moment of regret, Winston Wellington returned to the present, and was full of hope and optimism as he resolutely closed the door on his former life.

***

"I say, what a delightful little section of park!" exclaimed Trevor Expectorant.

His joyful reaction was duplicated by his last disciple, while Bennett-Brewer was too haunted by Loadall's recent bombshell of what he had in common with Rupert Chatterton to take any notice.

The quartet of Crabbings-Busters had reached the north eastern corner of the park, and Barry Loadall pushed open the gate to the little side garden that contained the rockery of the three varying-sized and connected ponds.

"A slice of paradise in a weary world." offered Loadall, as the four of them ambled the few yards to gaze into the nearest and middle-sized of the ponds.

"My word...!" blurted an enthusiastic Sir Leonard Hutton. "The pond is quite teeming with life!"

"Indeed it is...." answered Loadall. "Although there was a time when a certain Mr Chatterton committed aquatic genocide with the ancestors of the plentiful newts that are currently frolicking within their modest home."

"What a surprise that this idyllic place isn't what it seems." snapped Bennett-Brewer, whose constant unease had now taken on a cynical edge.

Loadall grinned yet again at Bennett-Brewer before continuing.

"Rupert Chatterton would often bring unsuspecting children up to these ponds so he could bully and terrorise them."

"A truly uplifting and nourishing piece of information." Bennett-Brewer again snappily answered, and whose newfound cynicism had now mutated into full-blown sarcasm. He was also starting to get seriously riled with Loadall.

In what appeared to Bennett-Brewer as an act of deliberate provocation, Loadall again smiled back at him.

"Chatterton would bring along a cricket bat, and he delighted in telling the children that he'd throw newts in the air one at a time for them to hit for six and kill. If they refused to do it, then Chatterton would get them

Anyone For Tennis?

into a headlock and force-feed them live newts. As he did so, he'd munch on the newts himself while making exaggerated sounds of gastronomic ecstasy."

Expectorant and Hutton shook their heads disapprovingly while Bennett-Brewer turned away from the pond in disgust and walked back toward the gate. Expectorant addressed the half grinning Loadall.

"If ever there was a time when Sir Leonard or myself had even the remotest doubt about the evil of Mr Chatterton, that time has now gone."

"Hear hear, glorious leader. This really isn't cricket!"

***

There was still some way to go before Winston Wellington and his colleagues had completed the setting up of their food stall. They were pleased that the weather was set fair for the day, and Wellington invited his helpers to take a break for a few minutes to enjoy the gentle warmth and intermittent sunshine of mid-morning.

"How're you feeling, Babe?" Wellington asked one of his helpers.

"Why, I'm just fine, sir!"

Wellington turned toward Goose Goslin and asked the same question.

"Why, I'm on top of the world and looking down on creation, sir!"

"That's terrific to hear, Goosey!" replied Wellington with enthusiastic approval.

"We've all had to make enormous sacrifices to be here today..." interjected George Sisler. "but let's be in no doubt that our convictions must be true and straight!"

"Yeah, I should say so, George!" responded the only female helper, Warrena Spahn, before an impromptu round of applause was begun by Joe DiMaggio, and immediately joined in with by the other five.

***

Loadall, Bennett-Brewer, Expectorant and Hutton were walking the eastern perimeter of the park that ran behind the three pairs of tennis courts.

Loadall came to a halt before a small wooden building that was annexed to the middle courts.

"I assume this would be the changing room used by all those with dreams of gracing the lush lawns of SW19?" asked Trevor Expectorant sunnily.

"I wouldn't say that..." replied Loadall. "Have you ever heard of a Wimbledon champion who also happened to be dead?"

The other three pondered Loadall's spoilsport reply in silence before the uneasy peace was shattered by a bellowing voice.

"HEY, Y'ALL!!"

The owner of the voice dashed the fifty or so yards toward the tennis courts, and Loadall's group immediately recognised him from his pilgrimage to Larkhall and Solsbury Hill a few weeks earlier.

"Say, it sure is good 'n wholesome to meet you great guys again!"

With the exception of Barry Loadall, the reaction of the group was one of great surprise.

The American enthusiastically shook hands with everyone before inviting them over to his stall to meet his helpers. The group accepted the invitation, and as they walked across to the half built wooden shack, Trevor Expectorant was first to seek an explanation.

"I'm very surprised to see you back in our country, as I was under the distinct impression that you heartily disapproved of the attempts to rid Mr Crabbings from the local area."

The American nodded his head rather than offering a verbal response.

Loadall was next to speak, but unnerved the other three by displaying an apparent sixth sense in sussing-out the visitors' new status.

"I must say it's very refreshing to see that you and the rest of your group have now totally rejected Thomas Crabbings in favour of becoming his sworn enemies."

"HELL, YEAH!"

As the five of them reached the food stall, Loadall and his group shook hands with the helpers, while the stall owner held out an inviting arm.

"The warmest welcome from the heart of Tennessee to *WELLINGTON'S WITCHFINDER WHOOPIN' WIENERS !!*"

Expectorant and Hutton were particularly impressed by the name of the stall, and Expectorant was first to respond.

"Well I never! So, after the mystery of not knowing your name from your previous visit, I gather that you are in fact Mister Wellington?"

"Winston Wellington to be precise, sir!"

"That doesn't sound very trans-Atlantic." responded the less impressed Loadall.

"HELL NO! When I told the family that I wanted nothin' more to do with Crabbings 'n his cronies, they told me to get the hell outta town and change ma name! Why, I thought I'd pay proper darned homage to yer beautiful country by taking ma first and last names from yer great war leader an' the great Sir Duke that smashed Napoleon's ass!"

"I must say I admire the courage of your convictions..." added Loadall with a hint of sympathy. "No doubt it's been the same for all of you."

"YESSIR! We were all told to get right outta the Volunteer State never to return!"

Anyone For Tennis?

"So, you not only left your family and neighbourhoods behind, but also your country?" asked Bennett-Brewer, whose mood was lifted by the group of Americans' about turn away from Crabbings.

"We sure did, and we all had to change our names, too!" answered Joe DiMaggio, before Winston Wellington addressed Expectorant exclusively.

"I heard about how you changed the names o' your followers to the ones of guys who were famous fer playin' that weird thing called cricket! I thought that was a mighty fine idea, so I named my guys after the butt whoopin' greats o' baseball!"

Expectorant, Hutton and Bennett-Brewer were heartened by the tribute paid to the former, before Barry Loadall chose to dip a mammoth-sized fly in the ointment.

"I'm very sorry to put a dampener on this jolly reunion, but I must warn everyone here that there's more than a sporting chance that the festivities in the park today will be cancelled at very short notice."

The rest of the gathering fell silent with shock, and the silence remained as Loadall invited the two Devil worshippers and Bennett-Brewer to walk back toward the small building attached to the middle tennis courts.

The American group continued to gawp open mouthed as the quartet ambled away, and Loadall slowly turned his head to deliver a cold and mocking postscript.

"I hope none of you are expecting to break the world record for wiener sales today."

"JUST WHAT THE HELL ARE YOU TALKING ABOUT?" Jeremy Bennett-Brewer shouted at Loadall, while Expectorant and Hutton remained in silent shock.

Barry Loadall's answer was a wide smile and knowing index finger tapping his nose. Bennett-Brewer was wound up even more, but chose not to respond. Instead, he simmered and stewed in silence.

Loadall's guests looked around the outside of the old wooden hut and saw that it was very neglected. The bottom half of the hut was made of stone, with its base about seven feet below court level, while the floor inside was raised about a foot above it. The right-hand metal banister to the steps leading up to the side door was missing, and the gentle slope of the wooden ramp that connected the front of the hut to the concrete arena met a dead end as continuous fencing and overgrown foliage had replaced the old door shaped hole. On the side of the hut that faced the main area of the park, a window about a square-yard contained twelve small, opaque and wire-meshed panes of glass; all of them damaged with spidery cracks, but none broken. The window sill was about ten feet above ground, and was dirty with varying shades of brown rather than its original white.

The four of them returned to the steps to the door on the opposite side, and Loadall dipped into a side pocket of his jacket to produce a large key.

"I'm about to open this door for the first time in forty years."

Loadall displayed the key with another wide smile.

Expectorant and Hutton were full of worry and apprehension, as was Bennett-Brewer, whose anger continued to rise.

"I'M GETTING SICK AND TIRED WITH ALL THIS! JUST WHAT EXACTLY IS GOING ON??"

Jeremy Bennett-Brewer was about to snap in reaction to Loadall's constant and creepy evasiveness and demanded an answer.

Loadall was on the top step of the six in front of the door, and responded to the bellowed question with another smile, and again using a finger to tap the side of his nose.

Bennett-Brewer finally blew his gasket and attempted to physically attack Barry Loadall. Expectorant and Hutton managed to restrain the teacher before he could get to Loadall, who watched calmly from the top of the steps as the flailing and struggling slowly subsided.

Loadall's expression turned suddenly from cold and distant into one filled with compassion and understanding. It was the first time any of the other three had seen Loadall display such humanity, and although it was welcome, they also found it a bit odd.

An obviously regretful Loadall returned down the steps as Expectorant and Hutton finally released Bennett-Brewer.

"Jeremy, I really must apologise. I now fully realise how difficult this is for you, and from now on I'll make every effort to be helpful. I do tend to be a little cryptic, and I truly am sorry if I've been giving the impression that I'm enjoying your unease. I can assure you that I have my worries also, and being a bit frivolous about it all is merely my defence against being overcome with fear and despondency."

Loadall placed a hand of comradeship on the shoulder of Bennett-Brewer, who was now fully placated and satisfied.

"Thank you, Barry, I appreciate both your explanation and apology very much indeed."

Expectorant and Hutton also felt a lot better after Loadall's welcome change of tone, and they smiled approvingly.

"There really is no need to be alarmed. Nothing untoward will happen when we get inside, but it is necessary so I can give you all a better insight into the daunting challenge we face."

Loadall followed his words with another sincere expression, before attempting to lift spirits further with a gentle battle cry.

"All for one?" Loadall softly coaxed as he raised an arm in the air.

Anyone For Tennis?

"AND ONE FOR ALL!" the other three resolutely chorused, before all four happily high-fived each other.

Loadall gave another genuine smile before re-climbing the steps and turning the key in the lock.

The door swung open to reveal nothing more than an empty and musty room of six-by-five yards, with wooden benches affixed along two sides of its yellowy brown walls.

"Looks just like an ordinary changing-room to me." uttered Bennett-Brewer as he stepped inside. Expectorant and Hutton followed, and the three of them were slightly underwhelmed.

"Careful of the gaps in the middle of the floor." Loadall advised.

Trevor Expectorant looked down at the centre plank of the wooden floor and noticed the faded outline of a small pair of feet.

"I was wondering who'd be first to spot that; well done, Expectorant!" responded Loadall with good humour.

The central plank of the room was separated from its neighbours by a gap of about four inches each side, and the adjacent plank furthest from them was strengthened by sharply studded metal casing along its edge.

Jeremy Bennett-Brewer looked down and noticed that the central plank sagged a little.

Loadall placed his right foot delicately on the right foot outline.

"Well, would you adam and eve it? A perfect fit!"

Barry Loadall removed his right foot from the plank, fumbled through a pocket, and addressed Bennett-Brewer in a business-like manner.

"Jeremy, I want you to take this sealed letter to The Wyvern & The Witchfinder tomorrow night. It should be opened and read at eight o'clock."

Bennett-Brewer took the letter from Loadall, and as with Expectorant and Hutton, was too mystified to respond.

"Anyway...until tomorrow night!" added a buoyant Loadall, as he calmly removed his glasses and jacket before slowly bending his knees to go into a squatting posture.

The other three immediately became unsettled, and were further spooked as Loadall again tapped a knowing finger against the side of his nose. This time the supplementary smile was rather more sinister, and topped off with a ghoulish wink.

For a man of sixty who spent most of his life abusing his body and doing little exercise, Loadall showed remarkable agility by suddenly springing high and erect into the air from his squatting position. At the apex of his leap, he pulled his arms to his body before his unusually small feet landed precisely within the faded outlines. The plank snapped like a twig beneath Loadall's gravity-fuelled weight, and his smooth and vertical descent through the floor was violently interrupted by the underside of his unusually long chin scoring a direct hit on the sharply studded metal cased edge of the neighbouring plank.

As he disappeared from view with his face pointing skyward, the three unfortunate witnesses heard the piercing crack and snap of Barry Loadall's jaw and neck.

29

TEARS OF THE CLOWNS

Graham Curnow awoke with a start, although on this occasion it had nothing to do with the scary night time doings usually served up by his subconscious. He was first slowly stirred toward waking by his own snoring, and then jolted fully awake by remembering that under no account should he fall asleep. In a panic, he scrabbled about in the pitch black for the torch next to his primal bed and shone it on his watch. It told him that he must have been asleep for a whopping seventeen hours or more, and he realised that his sleep spanned an entire midsummer dawn to dusk.

The last thing he remembered was checking his watch at four-am, and then reminiscing about his childhood best friend. Curnow became livid with himself for allowing emotion to cloud his mind and weaken his defences.

After a few moments, Curnow realised that he was being a bit harsh on himself for failing in his attempt to stay awake for almost two days, and it was a big plus that his outrageously long sleep had left him with a much-reduced target of hours to get through. Not only that, but his sleep being completely free of the usual horrors was an even bigger bonus.

Curnow suddenly felt energised. Being asleep for such a long period had left his body and mind utterly refreshed, and the remaining hours he had to see out would surely be straightforward.

He allowed himself a little smile as he pictured himself within the pitch-black confines of his room. He was led on a moderately padded duvet and covered by a basic bedsheet, with his head supported by an uncased pillow with its best days long gone. In the opposite corner of his tiny room were the air-tight containers that contained his waste. He had produced very little because of the severe austerity he imposed on his body's intake, and he hadn't even needed to use his air fresheners.

Curnow's living quarters wasn't exactly a room with a view at The Ritz, but it was luxurious enough for his purposes.

***

In the two-century history of the Larkhall Village Festival, not a single annual event had ever been cancelled. Not even the Spanish Flu pandemic or Baedeker blitzing of Bath managed to force those years' abandonments, but history was made as the current festival was completely shut down midway through the middle day of the weekend.

Every effort had been made to avoid the sudden ending of festivities, but hushing up the violent suicide of such a key Larkhall resident within the local park was a challenge too far.

At the time of the tragedy, the head of the festival committee was on an ambassadorial tour around Chalice Park with representatives from the four European cities that were twinned with Bath. As they were navigating the path behind the tennis courts, three hysterical men ran toward them and described in detail the appalling incident that occurred moments earlier.

Before calling for the ambulance, the head of the festival diplomatically requested that his international guests keep the dreadful news a secret, and was very grateful when they all displayed total understanding of the situation he was faced with.

An ambulance entering the park with its sirens blazing away wouldn't be the best start to keeping the tragedy a secret, so the festival head asked the emergency services operator to ensure that the ambulance would arrive without any noise or flashing lights. It was hardly a race against time to save a life, so he also told the operator that there was no hurry to get to the park. To avoid unnecessary attention, he suggested the paramedics should be disguised, and that he'd provide clown costumes for them to change in to. The operator was understanding and helpful by promising to pass on the message, and would also ensure that the ambulance would be parked well away from the crowds.

Everything went smoothly regarding the ambulance arrival, and the paramedics were just as co-operative as the operator by willingly agreeing to become temporary clowns. There were three paramedics in all; two to act as both body removers and stretcher bearers, and a reserve to keep lookout.

The real task they faced was to remove Barry Loadall's body from eight feet below the wooden floorboards of the hut. Getting to the scene across the far end of the park wasn't a problem, and not a single eyebrow was raised from the small gatherings of people as the three clowns plodded with their stretcher toward the tennis courts.

Once they reached the annexed wooden hut, the reserve paramedic stood at the base of the steps to the door, and any passers-by were helped on their way with a friendly parp of his comedy horn.

It took almost an hour to navigate the practical difficulties of getting to and removing Loadall from the scene, and it required a huge physical effort from both paramedics inside the hut to finally shift the body. The challenge was made even tougher with each paramedic hugely inconvenienced by wearing inflatable trousers. Finally, Loadall's body was removed, placed on the stretcher, and covered.

There was a nervous moment when a young boy wandered close to the scene with his remote-controlled model aircraft. He came to within thirty yards of the paramedics when Loadall was being put on the stretcher, and the boy kept glancing curiously between them and his airborne plane.

The lookout made a snap decision that he had to chase the boy away. If he saw the body, he could quickly pass on the news and draw a crowd.

The paramedic glowered at the boy with all the menace he could muster, then raised his arms high above his head with fingers curved downwards to form the shape of claws. He let out a huge roar before lumbering ungainly after the terrified boy, who fled in panic toward the main roadside wall. The boy's model plane preceded him to sail over the wall, and its fading buzz halted abruptly as it crashed into a rooftop across the road.

The paramedic felt sorry for the frightened and tearful lad, but told himself that sentiment had no place when big decisions had to be made. The blubbering boy scampered back to the main crowd in the distance, and the paramedic coldly reminded himself that he did the right thing as he turned and plodded back toward the hut. The other two paramedics were ready to go when the lookout returned, and they prepared themselves for the final part of the challenge. They looked toward the gate about three-hundred yards distant, and realised that there was no way of making it through without attracting attention. In the main festival area, the crowd had swelled appreciably since they arrived at the scene, and the park's perimeter paths were also busy. All they could do was grit their teeth and hope they could avoid being quizzed about their secret cargo.

With the exceptions of the flashing bow ties and arrows through the neck, the head of the festival insisted that the complete clown costumes should be worn. It would make for a slow and uncomfortable journey, but just so long as everybody believed that they were clowns instead of paramedics, then no attention would be given to what was on the stretcher. If they were asked by anybody what was under the covering sheet, they half-heartedly agreed to say that it was a lot of books being taken back to the library.

The lookout parped his horn nervously as the signal to start the return journey, and he led the stretcher bearers as they began to plod along in their outsized boots. The main gates to the park were a long way off, and with their costumes being very heavy and cumbersome, they soon began to perspire heavily. It was now midday, and the midsummer sun had completely burnt away the morning cloud to beat down on them. All three paramedics felt their make-up begin to run, and it added massively to the discomfort they already felt. Each of them secretly cursed the festival head for inviting the festival face painter into the ambulance beforehand.

The lookout and head of the trio of clowns looked behind and tried to keep spirits up by telling the other two that their memoirs could be a winner. They gamely continued to plod forward caked in sweat and runny make-up, and in the case of the two stretcher bearers, battling against exhaustion after their huge effort retrieving the body.

They eventually got to the heavily populated section of the park, and all three were pleasantly surprised when little notice was taken of them. There was the odd curious glance, but that was dealt with easily by the lookout who just smiled and gave the occasional understated parp.

The main gates to the car park were just a few yards away, and that provided enough adrenalin for the stretcher bearers to raise themselves for one final effort. By now, the unrelenting heat had made their faces an utter shambles of smeared greasepaint, and all of them were struggling with red eyes and blurred sight.

"I WANT A WORD WITH YOU THREE!"

Through their obstructed vision, the paramedics were suddenly confronted by an irate mother holding the hand of her inconsolable child.

"...WHICH ONE OF YOU CHASED MY BOY AWAY AND MADE HIM CRASH HIS PLANE??"

All three clowns feigned ignorance of the incident, and the lead paramedic gingerly pleaded that it was a case of mistaken identity.

The mother was further angered by the sheer nerve of the reply.

"...HOW MANY PEOPLE CAN YOU SEE DRESSED LIKE YOU??"

"What about these two stood behind me?"

The unsatisfactory answer was followed by the lead clown panicking, and he inexplicably lifted his horn to give a jolly double honk right in front of the woman's face.

With complete outrage, the mother flew at the paramedic and thumped wildly away at his head and chest. The stretcher bearers' eyes were now almost closed because of the stinging make-up, and their arms were cramping up with the endlessly increasing weight of their load. They fought against the urge to cry with self-pity as they stood impotent and drenched in sweat. They could hear that their colleague was taking a right royal hiding, but they could do nothing apart from wonder how long their arms would be by the end of the day.

The lead clown was now on his back and desperately squirming against the wild attack, which only grew in intensity. One of the woman's thumps hit just below the sunflower head on his jacket lapel, and she received a powerful squirt of water in the face.

In a volcanic rage, the wronged boy's mother went to pick up her folded lounge chair to continue battering the cowering paramedic. He attempted to curl into the foetal position to lessen the painful blows from the metal-framed chair, but instead became the last of the three to curse his inflatable trousers.

Virtually the entire population of the park was now congregated around the enraged woman and thrashed clown, with most of them finding the incident hilarious. The boy looked on proudly as his mother continued to bash the living daylights out of his aggressor.

Finally, the woman relented after being satisfied that the clown had learned his lesson, and she calmly walked away holding the hand of her beaming lad. It was a welcome relief to the stretcher bearers that they could finally continue the journey, especially for the one further inconvenienced by a maddening itch beneath his attached red nose.

A big crowd was still gathered around the clowns and still laughing at the treatment dealt out to one of them. The dazed convoy leader slowly and painfully got back to a standing position, but only to spin a dizzy circle and again crash to the ground. Through the humiliation of the hysterical crowd laughter, the lead paramedic ignored the many physical discomforts to resolutely get back to his feet. He stood straight and determined to do his duty, before he turned to slurrily whisper to the others that their memoirs were now *even more* likely to be winners.

They set off again, massively galvanised by knowing they were a stone's throw away from leaving the park and getting to the ambulance parked in the leafy cul-de-sac just around the corner.

The ferocious onslaught had left the lead paramedic noticeably concussed, but he steeled himself for the final effort of leading his colleagues and the mangled body out and away from the park. Through his confused and handicapped vision, he could see the head of the festival willing them on from beyond the main gates with a big smile and two thumbs-up each side of his face.

However, concussion mixed with already blurred vision and stinging eyes was no cocktail for walking in a straight line, and the lead paramedic kept stumbling and veering to the right, closely followed by his concerned and sweat-blinded colleagues.

The huge green right boot of the lead paramedic became tangled in a wire and peg that helped support the tent next to the main gates, and he took a heavy and clumsy tumble. The stretcher bearers were following too closely behind to avoid toppling over themselves, and as they crashed to the ground, so did the stretcher. The covering sheet flew away, and the badly traumatised corpse of Barry Loadall rolled over twice with its twisted head lolloping slightly behind the body. The head finally came to rest facing the sky, and displayed a jaw fracture so catastrophic that the tip of the chin almost touched the tip of the nose.

Right in the epicentre of the most congregated area of the park, the several dozen witnesses swapped their amused incredulity of a few moments earlier for horror and hysterical screaming. The head of the festival watched from beyond the gates every bit as horrified as the crowd. He put a hand of defeat over his face as he realised that as far as the rest of this year's festival was concerned, that was well and truly that.

30

THE NIGHT BEFORE THE STORM

The shock of Barry Loadall's body being discovered by throngs of people during the busiest time of the festival was a hammer blow for most of the village. As news of the tragedy spread, various events and exhibitions around Larkhall were hastily wound up and abandoned, with many residents opting to impose immediate curfews on themselves that would last until the weekend was over.

Even to those in the village who didn't know Loadall personally, they were well aware that he was one of the figureheads in the fight against Crabbings and Chatterton. The majority of locals who desperately wanted to be rid of those two had now given up the fight, and the only appearances they planned to make before Monday would be from behind nervously twitching curtains.

A handful of die-hard Crabbings supporters roamed the otherwise deserted roads and streets in drunken celebration. They saw Loadall's death as Crabbings' inspired revenge for the violent end met by Ralph Mogford the previous night, and they shouted with derision at the lily livered do-gooders who were terrified into barricading themselves away.

When news of the tragedy reached Victor Carping in the church, he immediately volunteered to take care of the traumatised trio who witnessed the suicide. He was to pick them up from the ambulance that was waiting for the body.

All three witnesses were under sedation, and just before Carping arrived,

The Wyvern & The Witchfinder

Trevor Expectorant groggily awoke to view the alarming sight of Barry Loadall's wrecked and uncovered body enter the ambulance being carried by two dishevelled and mournful looking clowns; their tears of defeat providing the final touch to their make-up horror show.

***

One of the few village residents who wasn't fazed either way by the unsavoury events at Chalice Park was Dave Rensenbrink, who kept his virtually empty pub open all day.

Just before nine on Saturday night, Jeremy Bennett-Brewer, Trevor Expectorant and Sir Leonard Hutton entered, closely followed by Victor Carping. When they arrived, they were the only customers.

"Well, that didn't go quite as planned, did it?"

Rensenbrink's jovial levity was welcomed by the incoming group, and the three witnesses to the tragedy were starting to get to grips in dealing with their earlier trauma.

All four took a barstool, and all looked forward to some alcohol-based medicine.

"It's put a bit of a spanner in the works, that's for sure..." Carping finally answered. "And I'm sorry there'll be no celebrations in this pub tomorrow night for the festival closing ceremony."

Dave Rensenbrink gave a philosophical smile.

"Well, at the end of the day, it's only money."

Everyone was again relaxed by the landlord's down to earth manner as he began to pour the drinks.

"Did you know Mr Loadall very well, Mr Rensenbrink?" asked Trevor Expectorant.

"Well for a start, you don't have to bloody well call me mister; I'm not the bleedin' taxman, y'know!"

All four customers smiled back.

"...I didn't really know him. Bumped into him now and again in the Square, but I always found him a bit of an oddbod who kept himself to himself."

At that moment, a young man wearing a white t-shirt with THOMAS CRABBINGS IS GREAT! emblazoned across it briefly stood at the door to congratulate Rensenbrink on keeping the pub open, and therefore not being one of the scaredy cats who were hiding themselves away.

Rensenbrink responded diplomatically by raising his glass, before the drunken reveller continued on down the road to shout more abuse at those taking refuge behind tightly drawn curtains.

The Night Before The Storm

"Bloody loony..." the landlord whispered to the other four. "Looks like Loadall topping himself has really got the Crabbings lot going."

The customers nodded gravely in agreement.

"...Although if anyone was gonna do a job on themselves, you'd expect it to be a bit of a weirdo like Loadall."

"I must say, that does sound a little disrespectful, Dave." protested Victor Carping.

"Yeah, yer right, sorry for makin' light of it. I'm sure he was a decent enough bloke who meant well."

Jeremy Bennett-Brewer made his first contribution of the evening by asking if anybody knew where Graham Curnow was.

Victor Carping gave Bennett-Brewer a sympathetic smile before answering.

"Bad news, Jeremy, I'm afraid. I was going to tell you earlier, but thought I'd leave it for a while after what you went through earlier."

"Oh Christ..." interrupted the landlord. "Don't tell me he's handed in his P45 as well!"

Carping smiled and shook his head, though his expression soon adjusted to display worry.

"I went to his house earlier while these three were at Chalice Park. When I got there, he'd packed his bags and cleared right out."

The Rector reached inside his trouser pocket and produced the letter he picked up from Curnow's kitchen table that morning.

One by one, the letter was passed around, and Bennett-Brewer, Expectorant and Hutton were especially worried about the latest turn of events.

"Now that is a turn-up for the books." replied a genuinely surprised Rensenbrink, who showed more concern at Curnow suddenly jumping ship than he did with Loadall's suicide.

"Has anyone got any idea where he could be hiding?" asked Expectorant.

Nobody could shed any light on the matter apart from Dave Rensenbrink.

"I saw him a couple of days ago walking around the outside of your church, Vic. Maybe he was planning to go there?"

The Rector shook his head.

"The only place to hide in there is the burial vault below ground, and can't imagine anyone would be daft enough to go down there after what happened to Dick and the youngsters."

"Well, by the sound of that letter, he was in a bit of a state..." the landlord responded. "He's obviously not thinkin' straight, so might be worth checking-out?"

Bennett-Brewer answered this time, and on behalf of the fugitive.

"It's obviously Graham's wish to be left alone, and we should respect that. He's made his decision, and we shouldn't waste time by looking for him."

Victor Carping nodded his head in agreement.

"Absolutely right, Jeremy. We've got enough on our plate as it is without being diverted by trying to find someone who doesn't want to be found."

The rest of the gathering joined Carping in showing their approval.

"...Besides, I'd be perfectly happy never to go down that vault ever again."

31

NASTY CORRESPONDENCE

Sunday finally arrived, and according to what the late Barry Loadall reckoned, today was going to be the end of the world. Trevor Expectorant and Sir Leonard Hutton had thought the same thing, but had diluted their views to it being a day where they made the journey from their old life to the new. Whether that meant their own physical deaths or a massive change to their Earthly lives remained for them to be seen.

When Jeremy Bennett-Brewer awoke Sunday morning, he was surprised by how fresh he felt and how uncluttered his mind was. Yesterday was a nightmare, but his long, dreamless and refreshing night's sleep had done a good job of lessening his worry. Although still frightened, he managed to keep the negative thoughts away by becoming strongly determined to defeat the horrible thing that was making local lives a misery. He also wasn't too bothered about Barry Loadall's apocalyptic belief. Loadall clearly stated on previous occasions that he was looking forward to witnessing the end of the world, so killing himself the day before didn't make sense.

Also, for him to back up his doomsday predictions by the positions of the planets seemed just as senseless.

Since coming round in the ambulance the previous day, he'd completely forgotten about the letter handed to him by Loadall immediately before his suicide, but remembered as soon as he awoke minutes earlier, as he did also with the instructions to when and where it should be opened and read. Neither Expectorant or Hutton mentioned the letter at last night's gathering in the pub, and he wondered whether they had also forgotten about it.

When the group left together at closing time, they had been the only customers of the entire evening, and Dave Rensenbrink invited them all back for what was originally intended to be the festival's closing ceremony piss up. Rensenbrink also mentioned that he was grateful for their custom over recent weeks and would reward them with an entire evening of drinks on the house. All four customers enthusiastically thanked the jolly publican, and they all reasoned that if the world *was* going to end that night, then having a few drinks wouldn't do any harm.

***

Situated midway between The Blackest Morn on the corner of Larkhall Square and The Bladud's Midriff right at the end of St Saviour's Road, The Wyvern & The Witchfinder was the smallest of the three village pubs.

The main entrance was a thin door on the right corner of the pub façade and situated no more than three yards from the bar. The narrow area in front of the bar widened at the other end, allowing for a few tables and chairs on the pub's left side.

Immediately to the right of the entrance stood a decades-old solid mahogany bench with high and thin arm rails; once the favourite seating location of the elderly patrons, but now little more than a decorative nod to the pub's former glories.

To the right of the bar and straight ahead of the door was a walkway and a couple of steps that led to another room with more space for customers. Just after the two steps and to the right was a side entrance that would be opened whenever the pub was particularly busy.

The landlord looked up to see the invited quartet of Carping, Bennett-Brewer, Expectorant and Hutton shuffle through the narrow front door one after the other at seven-pm.

"Prepare to meet thy doom, thy sinning piss pots!"

All four newcomers smiled at Rensenbrink's greeting, although they were all a little jittery.

Most of Larkhall village had been under self-imposed lockdown throughout Sunday, and the roads and streets were eerily quiet. The pockets of Crabbings-supporting revellers from the previous night were absent as they nursed their delicate post-celebration states.

"Do you think Mr Chatterton will turn up, Dave?" asked Victor Carping.

"Oh, he'll be turning up alright." the landlord responded matter of factly.

Nasty Correspondence

Carping and the rest became a touch more jittery.

"...Oh, don't look so worried, yer bunch of blouses! He'll be about somewhere in Larkhall, but he never came in this pub when he was alive, and he hasn't been in since he fucked his face up."

"Will your good lady wife be joining us?" asked Bennett-Brewer to keep the conversation light.

"No, I'm afraid Rose has been gettin' a bit nervous about the whole thing, and so has the dog. I told 'er everything would be fine, but she insisted that 'er and Clive were going to stay with a friend tonight."

The landlord's answer returned the teacher to being nervous, and his pulse quickened a little as he prepared his next question.

"What do you think Barry's letter is going to say, Dave?"

"It'll be a step-by-step guide on how to get rid of Crabbings and Chatterton."

All the customers secretly wished that they shared the confidence of the landlord, but together with Graham Curnow's absence and his written concerns about Barry Loadall not being what he seemed, all were fearful of what was going to be revealed.

"...Well, let's hope it is, anyway."

Rensenbrink's less forthright addition to his original answer failed to make the others any less fearful.

***

Graham Curnow shone the torch on his watch. It was coming up to eight-pm Sunday evening, and the twelve hours or so since he woke after his long sleep had passed quickly. He'd been wide awake throughout the final few hours of his marathon, and now he could finally start counting down the time until he could leave his hiding place.

Curnow's positive frame of mind was rudely shaken by hearing the door at ground level open, followed by slow, descending footsteps. He desperately hoped that it was a routine visit, and that it would quickly be over and followed by ascending footsteps and closed door.

Shuffling feet were heard by Curnow just outside his tiny hideaway, and he suddenly became terrified that the door was going to swing open to be revealed in all his pathetic dis-glory. In what seemed like an eternity, several seconds of silence followed the shuffling, and Curnow was on the verge of panicking and giving himself up to whoever or whatever was on the other side of the door. As more silent seconds went by, it became a tortuous fifty-fifty decision for Curnow to make.

The torture ended as the footsteps finally retreated to plod back up the steps, before Curnow heard the even more delightful sound of the ground-level door being closed.

***

"Okay chaps, are we all ready?"

Rensenbrink and the other three customers at the bar all signalled in the affirmative, and Jeremy Bennett-Brewer suddenly felt a lot more ill at ease when the moment finally came.

The teacher cleared his throat as he prepared to read the letter aloud.

"Hang on a minute."

Dave Rensenbrink lifted the bar hatch and walked to the main door, which he locked and bolted.

"...Doubt if we'll get any more customers anyway, and don't want to be interrupted while Mr Loadall's last will and testament is read out!"

Bennett-Brewer felt a bit more relaxed after the landlord's light-hearted comment, and he tore open the envelope.

Dear all,

Firstly, I think I owe some apologies, especially to Mr Bennett-Brewer, Mr Expectorant and Mr Hutton. Probably not your idea of fun witnessing my theatrical and messy suicide, but that's life, I'm afraid.

"What a bloody nutter!" exclaimed Rensenbrink.

Instead of yesterday's criticism of the landlord for casually knocking Loadall's mental health, a wary silence was returned.

Please send Mr Rensenbrink my best wishes. I hope he's taking care of you all on a night that's going to get a bit tense as it progresses.

The landlord raised his eyebrows in bewilderment to the dead man's tribute, before Bennett-Brewer continued reading aloud.

No doubt you all remember that I predicted today as being the end of the world, but I wouldn't take much notice of that. I needed something that resembled evidence into making that claim, so thought I'd provide it with the positions of the planets. I never believed in any of that nonsense, but I don't mind in the least if you thought I did.

Both Expectorant and Hutton were surprised to hear Loadall's dismissing of the planetary positions, as they themselves had also seen a doom-laden celestial pattern due to click into place today.

If I may address you all one by one.

All four invited guests had their anxiety levels pushed up a notch at the thought of having the spotlight shone on them from beyond the grave. Being the letter's narrator made Bennett-Brewer especially worried.

Firstly, Jeremy Bennett-Brewer; I know very well that I've frightened the wits out of you over the past few weeks, and I'd doubt that having a bird's-eye view of my rope-less hanging put you at ease. Some things just have to be done, I'm afraid. Don't expect your worries to do anything other than grow over the course of the evening.

Bennett-Brewer looked up from the page with an equal split of fright and anger.

Jeremy; I must say also that your idea of us singing and repeating two notes continuously to keep Chatterton away is and was utterly ludicrous. Do you think someone as nasty as Mr Chatterton would be terrified by two 'pleasant' notes being sung back and forth????? Do you remember singing those notes in the church and all the strange phenomena stopped? Chatterton might be very stupid and backward, but not stupid enough not to pretend it was doing the trick in being rid of him.

The teacher again looked up from the page, and this time his fright completely overrode his anger. To have his plan trashed by Loadall gave him the feeling of being doomed.

"I've got to be honest, mate..." answered Rensenbrink. "that plan of yours did sound a bit daft."

Bennett-Brewer didn't respond in any way to the landlord before continuing to read the letter.

To the duo of Trevor Expectorant and Sir Leonard Hutton; If your intention is to rid Larkhall of Crabbings and Chatterton, you could have at least not given yourselves such stupid names! I'll not waste any more precious ink on you two.

The Devil worshippers followed the teacher in being majorly spooked by Loadall's curt dismissiveness.

Dave Rensenbrink decided to lighten the mood.

"Christ, if Loadall's on your side, you'd better all have doubles!"

This time nobody found any consolation in the landlord's frivolity, and Bennett-Brewer continued to read on with barely a pause.

A few words for the revolutionary Rector of St Swithin's; Victor Carping.

Carping at least managed an ironic smile as he awaited Loadall's opinion, and wasn't getting his hopes up that he'd get any more sympathy than the other three. He thought it best to expect the worst so that he wouldn't be too perturbed if that was what he received. Unfortunately for Carping, the worst he expected fell short of what he was about to get.

Before he continued with the letter, Bennett-Brewer glanced at Victor Carping with an expression of both sympathy and face reddening terror.

You are without doubt the most contemptible piece of shit that has ever entered this village, and my soul won't rest until your face is smashed against the wall!!!!!!!"

Not even Dave Rensenbrink could see any cause for jocularity from such undiluted hatred, and all witnesses to the letter reading were united in shock and horror.

Bennett-Brewer was further terrified by the crazed anger inferred by so many exclamation marks, and even more so by the dots underneath each one being forceful enough to stab right through the paper.

"Jesus fucking Christ!"

It wasn't the reply expected from a man of the cloth, but this wasn't a normal situation, and Victor Carping followed the frightened and whispered cuss by sinking his head into his hands.

All the occupants of the bar jumped with alarm as the interior lights of the pub flickered for a few seconds. Moments later, a distant grumble of thunder was heard.

Dave Rensenbrink broke the icy silence.

"That'll be the depression movin' in. Reckon it's over the Severn Estuary now and should get here inside the hour."

"That is good news!"

Bennett-Brewer's sarcastic response was made as light-heartedly as his worried frame of mind allowed, and failed to lift the mood of the pub.

"Shall I carry on with this enthralling read?"

Everybody knew there was no option, and Bennett-Brewer's latest attempt at jollying things up a little was answered with worried and resigned nods.

***

During his entire stay of close to two days, Graham Curnow used his torch for just the sixth time to check his watch. He acknowledged that his ultra-strict rationing bordered on the ridiculous, but self-imposed hardship was something he didn't find difficult. What he did find difficult was being the hero, and he'd probably have to endure more severe unpleasantness if that were to be the case. If his own mortality was in the hands of Chatterton, then that would be that.

It wouldn't be long now until it'd all be over one way or another, and Curnow closed his eyes to do a spot of meditating in an attempt to blanket his anxiety. He spent several minutes with his eyes closed, and the longer they were closed, the more relaxed and comfortable he felt about the possibility of both himself and the village having the desired outcome.

After about ten minutes, Curnow opened his eyes. Slowly emerging from the pitch-blackness was a hazy and formless light, and the haze slowly grew until it took on the shape of a very tall man.

Curnow jumped with a massive start when a blinding flash overwhelmed his vision, and he closed his eyes tightly for a couple of seconds in the hope that it was another dream that he could awake from relatively unscathed. When he opened his eyes again, his vision was perfect, and it viewed the illuminated form of Rupert Chatterton in all its hideousness stare hatefully back at him.

This time Curnow absolutely knew that he wasn't dreaming as he gawped pathetically at the revolting spectacle in a state of petrification. The apparition opened its mouth very slowly, making its smashed facial features even more horrifyingly abstract.

A blast of incredibly strong and rancid air shot out of Chatterton's mouth and over Curnow. The paralysed recipient felt the sheer strength of the blast and was worried that his head and body would disintegrate. Curnow felt his eyes and ears being squeezed by the pressure until he was on the verge of passing out. He desperately stretched out a shaking arm toward his rucksack but was resigned to defeat. He let out a final and hard fought scream of terror as he prepared for the catastrophic consequences of being killed by Chatterton.

***

Now that I've dealt with four unimpressive specimens, it's time I said a few words about that absent waster, Graham Curnow. No doubt you're all wondering why Graham couldn't be with you tonight?

The unease inside the pub grew stronger as Loadall's words plucked the thoughts right out of their heads.

If you knew that pitiful creature as well as I do, then you'd be aware that he'd do a runner like the spineless and cowardly little cunt he is.

Everybody listening to the letter was now fully aware that Barry Loadall wasn't as he seemed, and the horror grew with every snippet read aloud by Bennett-Brewer, who reluctantly carried on with his narration.

Wherever he's hiding, rest assured Chatterton will find and terrorise him until he's dead.

The time was now eight-fifteen, and although sunset was still about an hour away, it became noticeably darker outside the pub. Another grumble of thunder was heard, but slightly louder and nearer sounding than its predecessor.

"I reckon the storm is now creepin' over the Mendips. Won't be long now."

In direct contrast to his customers, Dave Rensenbrink appeared to relish the thought of the storm arriving.

Bennett-Brewer looked down to complete his reading of the letter.

I guess I've now said enough, but this isn't goodbye...it's merely au revoir. I shall return in just over an hour's time at nine-thirty-seven to commem-

orate the moment that the wonderful Rupert Chatterton ended his life, and also leave you to ponder how I knew the identities of the four people invited along for this very special evening.

If any of you are getting cold feet, you could always take a leaf out of my book and kill yourselves; although if you knew what was in store for the lot of you after your Earthly deaths, then sadly it would be a spectacular case of robbing Peter to pay Paul.

My sincerest and most heartfelt condolences,
The late Barry Loadall.
PS. I hope the weather is nice.

As soon as Bennett-Brewer completed reading the letter, everybody jumped as the lights inside the pub again flickered for several seconds before heavy rain suddenly began to hammer against the windows.

The pub was gripped with fear before Dave Rensenbrink was eventually confronted by a probing and unsettled Victor Carping.

"You knew about this all along, otherwise how did Loadall know exactly who you were going to invite tonight?"

Rensenbrink appeared unusually bashful before making his reply.

"It looks like you've finally found me out, me ol' babber!"

The landlord reached down behind the bar and returned with a double-barrelled shotgun that he aimed at each customer in turn.

"...It's real...it works...and it's loaded."

The shock and fear of the invited customers suddenly having a firearm aimed at them was further deepened by the hateful look displayed by Rensenbrink. The four guests were united with open mouthed responses, while the rest of their bodies were paralysed.

"...Barry popped by yesterday morning to give me what his grandfather left him."

Victor Carping was the first to break free of his paralysis as the shotgun was aimed right between his eyes.

"We've been done up like kippers, haven't we?"

"You certainly have." came the cold response.

Rensenbrink's hateful expression was immovable as he again pointed the gun at each customer in turn.

"...This is only a last resort though. I'd hate to be forced into using it so you miss out on all the fun that's planned for nine-thirty-seven!"

"THIS REALLY ISN'T CRICKET!"

Sir Leonard Hutton's bellowing was completely out of character, and Rensenbrink turned the gun on him.

"Would it be cricket if I splattered the windows with your brain?"

The landlord's reply was delivered with a relaxed and monotone iciness

Nasty Correspondence

more associated with Barry Loadall.

A bright flash of lightning was quickly followed by a booming thunderclap before the heavy rain alone provided an incessant soundtrack.

"I HOPE YOU SPEND YOUR ETERNITY IN MISERY!" shouted Trevor Expectorant in response to Rensenbrink aiming the gun at his disciple.

The landlord's face contorted into psychopathic coldness as he turned his aim toward Expectorant.

"You really should watch what you say. It'd be a big shame if you weren't around at nine-thirty-seven, but just for that, I'm going to redecorate the windows now!"

Rensenbrink immediately followed his promise by sliding the catch into firing position.

Trevor Expectorant and the others were terrified, and all were absolutely certain that he wasn't joking.

"...Anything else you'd like to say before I kill you, you Devil worshipping scum?"

"YES!!!"

The loud shout came from behind the landlord, and before anyone in the pub could react, the shotgun was karate chopped downward by a stiff arm and followed immediately by an empty bottle of vodka smashed over Rensenbrink's skull.

"AND FOR MY NEXT TRICK!"

Graham Curnow stood over the unconscious body with a wide smile and his arms spread wide.

32

SAVE OUR SOULS

Despite the sheeting rain, Winston Wellington was determined to get to The Wyvern & The Witchfinder. It wasn't part of his original plan, but instinct told him he had to get there before nightfall. Everything was thrown out of the window after yesterday's sudden cancellation of the festival, and he'd seen enough to know that it'd need all hands to the pump to put an end to the wickedness inspired by the subject of his former worship. He decided to make the journey alone and told his five disciples to barricade themselves in their rooms until daybreak.

He and his colleagues were the only people in the park close enough to have heard the shouts and screams from inside the hut next to the tennis courts, and all of them were perturbed enough to sideways-cross their torsos. All six viewed three of the group running in panic from the hut and along the path on the far side of the courts.

Wellington had told the rest to carry on with building the wooden shack while he trotted across to investigate. He noted the one member of the group who didn't run away from the hut was Barry Loadall, and because of his startling prediction of the festival being suddenly cancelled, feared the worst.

What Wellington discovered as he entered the hut was a huge gap that ran along the middle of the floor. As he stared through the gap, there was enough light coming through the door to display the shadowy outline of a body. The presence of small blood spatters around the metal cased plank told Wellington that foul play was afoot. He raced away from the hut and told the others to dismantle their shack and get the hell out of the park.

As he defiantly ploughed his way through the rain, Wellington now knew that the dead Barry Loadall was the new bad guy. Soon after he passed the Bladud's Midriff, and in spite of the filthy weather, the illuminated sign outside his planned destination shone brightly on the horizon.

***

As Dave Rensenbrink was splayed unconscious, Graham Curnow lifted the shotgun off the floor and handed it to Victor Carping, who unloaded it and leant it against the bar.

"Graham Curnow, you are the pride of Larkhall!"

Trevor Expectorant had to raise his voice to be heard above the rain, and such was his hero-worship, he grabbed Curnow's hand with both of his, and the hand sandwich was augmented by Hutton.

"So you've been hiding in the pub cellar all this time?" asked Victor Carping.

"Yup..." replied Curnow enthusiastically. "To be honest, I didn't think I'd make it, and when Chatterton visited me just now, I thought that was going to be it."

Expectorant and Hutton both crossed their torsos while the eyebrows of both Carping and Bennett-Brewer were raised.

"I think that's the last we'll see of that charmless so and so..." added Curnow. "His apparition was shouting and screaming at me, so I just about managed to reach my secret bottle of vodka, drank the lot in one, and gave him a piece of my mind!"

"Was that a wise thing to do?" questioned Carping.

"It may not be wise for me, but I don't mind losing my battle if it means winning the war."

"But you said in that letter to Victor that you weren't going back to drink." half questioned Bennett-Brewer.

Curnow reacted by merely resting his arms on the bar and shrugging his shoulders.

The rain was still lashing against the pub windows, and again the lights flickered for several seconds. Several wary eyes looked up and around, while Curnow remained unmoved. When the latest unnerving moment passed, Sir Leonard Hutton was next to question the man of the hour.

"How can you drink a whole bottle of vodka without sounding drunk?"

Curnow again shrugged his shoulders.

"I really don't know; one of my special tricks, I suppose?"

Dave Rensenbrink was beginning to stir, and he let out the occasional dazed grunt as he sat up and held both hands to his head.

"Give me the gun."

The order was made calmly but forcefully, and Victor Carping handed it across the bar without hesitation.

"Now then, Mr Rensenbrink..." began Curnow as he looked down at the dishevelled landlord from behind the bar. "You really are a fat, scheming, pus, puke and shit-filled monstrosity of a wobble-bottomed cunt."

Curnow's condemnation of the landlord shocked all onlookers. His aggressive and vicious words were totally opposed to the calm and rational way they were delivered.

"Sorry about the unpleasantness..." Curnow remarked as he clasped the unloaded shotgun against his body. "It's the major side effect of my drinking, and the only way of knowing that I'm drunk. If my language turns a bit blue and insulting, it really isn't me talking, so please don't be offended."

Curnow spoke with an unbroken rhythm and didn't slur or hesitate once. He flipped the shotgun around and used the butt to viciously strike the landlord around the side of the head. For the second time in a few minutes, Rensenbrink was whacked fully unconscious. Several seconds of incredulous silence was returned from the other side of the bar as Curnow stood over the landlord. The silence was shattered as the main door of the pub was rattled by several loud thumps.

While Curnow never took his eyes away from the unconscious body, Expectorant and Hutton again crossed their upper bodies, as they, together with Carping and Bennett-Brewer turned their gazes warily toward the door.

"Who the hell could that be?" blurted Bennett-Brewer, who didn't expect to receive a satisfactory answer.

"There's only one way to find out." replied the unfazed Curnow, before he crouched down to rummage through the pockets of the motionless Rensenbrink.

Curnow quickly located the key, lifted the bar hatch, and casually strode across to unlock and unbolt the door.

Along with some gusting rain, Winston Wellington stumbled through the narrow door. As soon as he was inside, Curnow slammed the door shut and relocked and bolted it.

"WHOA, IT SURE IS A DIRTY NIGHT OUT THERE!"

All four sat at the bar were lifted by Winston Wellington's loud and smiling assessment of conditions.

"Lovely to see you again, Mr Wellington!" gushed Hutton, before he turned to address Curnow.

"...Great news, this splendid American chap who used to be a follower of Mr Crabbings is now on our side!"

Curnow didn't show much surprise or interest in the revelation but congratulated the new arrival on his conversion.

"The more the merrier, mister...sorry, how do you like to be called, you loud and obtrusive trans-Atlantic square-head?"

"I BEG YOUR PARDON, SIR??!!"

Curnow held up an apologetic palm and explained to Wellington that he wasn't in control of what he was saying.

"I really don't mean any offence. Please bear in mind also that my caustic words were responsible for getting rid of Chatterton. It's very much a double-edged sword that I'm totally unable to do anything about, you half-witted orangutan."

"I SURE AS HELL HAVEN'T COME HERE TO BE INSULTED!!"

"Well, I thought the place you normally get insulted might be closed."

"OOOOOOOH!"

Wellington did a worthy impersonation of Yosemite Sam with his steaming reaction to Curnow's latest barb.

Graham Curnow put his head in his hands through sheer embarrassment, before being even more apologetic to the man he was continually offending. Curnow used as few words as possible, and the regret on his face was enough for Wellington to finally calm down. The newcomer peered over the bar to notice the dismal state of the landlord.

"SAY, IS THE BARTENDER ONE OF THE BAD GUYS, TOO?"

Curnow decided to keep his mouth shut and let the others do the explaining. Wellington shook his head, and the next couple of minutes passed with little being said. Eventually, another groan emanated from behind the bar.

"I think mine host requires a nightcap..." noted Graham Curnow casually. "Pardon me for not paying much attention to the Weights and Measures Act, but this is no time for red tape!"

Curnow turned the virtually unconscious landlord onto his back before springing to his feet and wrenching the one-and-a-half litre bottle of whiskey from its wall mount. He turned the bottle upright, unscrewed the optic, and amongst a lot of unaware spluttering, poured the fiery liquid down Rensenbrink's throat.

"Well, I reckon three quarters of a magnum of forty percent blended malt should keep Fatso quiet for the duration, and may even keep him quiet forever."

The rest of the pub became a little anxious at the tactics used by Curnow to keep the landlord out of action. Amongst the uncomfortable reactions, Sir Leonard Hutton turned around to be the first to notice the change in the weather. He excitedly went over to press his face against the window and look upward.

"Hey everyone, the rain has stopped and there isn't a cloud in the sky!"

Every other head turned toward the windows, and everybody felt energised as they verified it for themselves.

Behind the bar, Victor Carping helped Graham Curnow tie the hands and feet of Rensenbrink, and the final touch was made as Curnow forcefully attached masking tape to the landlord's mouth. After Carping had finished his part of the operation, he returned to the other side of the bar to retake his stool, and Curnow looked down at their handiwork with pride.

"Well, unless Fatso suddenly discovers an unknown talent for being an outsized Houdini, I'd like to see him try and get up to any mischief with that lot!"

Curnow followed his triumphant musing by brushing his hands as a physical metaphor to it being a job well done. He then crouched down to lift both eyelids of Rensenbrink, which revealed the complete whites of his eyes.

"...Yes, I think it's safe to say that mine host wouldn't be any less of a danger to us if he were dead!"

Curnow followed his assessment by cruelly and forcefully kicking the landlord in the side of his rib cage.

This time, the rest of the pub were in no doubt that Curnow had crossed the line in keeping Rensenbrink quiet, and Trevor Expectorant stood-up to shout across the bar.

"JUST MAKE SURE YOU DON'T KILL HIM!"

Curnow reacted by flippantly saluting Expectorant, before again crouching toward Rensenbrink; this time to check his pulse.

"I'm afraid it's too late...Fatso has now officially waddled off this mortal coil."

Curnow got back to his feet and removed an imaginary hat to rest against his chest in a mocking display of respect.

The pub went silent for several seconds as the occupants pondered the wisdom of killing their host, and all were ruffled by Curnow's nonchalant approach to taking his life. The soon-to-be former alcoholic's expression briefly became serious before he cracked a more characteristic smile.

"...Anyway, I have a prior engagement, you shoddy shower of slithering shitehawks. So...CHEERS!"

Graham Curnow ripped the almost full magnum bottle of vodka away from its wall mount, impatiently unscrewed the optic, and drank the lot in one. He turned to face his open-mouthed audience across the bar, and he again performed a theatrical salute. Curnow stood still for several moments holding the pose while his eyes slowly narrowed. The salute was maintained as Curnow toppled sideways to crash upon the body of Dave Rensenbrink.

Amongst all the panicked responses, Jeremy Bennett-Brewer vaulted the bar to check on Curnow's condition. He stood over the two motionless bodies and aimed a worried look back across the bar.

"FOR CHRIST'S SAKE, CHECK HIS PULSE!!" screamed Victor Carping.

Bennett-Brewer snapped out of his dithering to squat down and lift Curnow's left sleeve.

After a few moments of foreboding, Bennett-Brewer got back to his feet to deliver a shattering shake of the head. Total silence was returned, and everybody knew that two deaths within a minute wasn't cause for optimism.

***

Mrs Mordent and Mrs Tanning were also making their way toward The Wyvern & The Witchfinder. They met outside the retirement bungalows that backed onto the local playing field, and they began to shuffle along the narrow alleyway that connected their starting point to the pub.

"What a relief that the blessed rain has stopped!"

Mrs Tanning nodded her head in agreement as the twilight sky displayed every colour between pale yellow and deep red.

"It's just before nine, so plenty of time to give that reprobate a flea in his ear!"

This time it was Mrs Mordent's turn to agree with a nod of the head. She then reached inside her handbag for a monster funny fag, which she smoked entirely in the time it took to navigate the alleyway.

As the elderly pair turned left to see the illuminated pub sign, Mrs Tanning asked her friend if she was confident that everything would be fine by the end of the night.

"Just relax, man. If it gets a bit heavy 'n hairy with that crazy cat, just zone out and tune in to the vibes of peace and love."

"What that ruffian needs is a sound thrashing to knock some sense between his ears!"

Mrs Mordent smiled back at her friend's more conservative approach.

"Hey, chill out, Mrs T! Love is the most powerful force in the universe, and its pulse has been constantly beating since the time our galaxy was in its nebulous cradle."

***

"Well..." began Victor Carping, "let's hope our chances of winning the war won't be hindered by Graham's lost battle."

The Rector of St Swithin's tried to utter the words calmly, but Curnow's demise was hardly an indication that things were going to plan.

"...And what a dreadful irony that he should come to rest upon the man who catered for his needs for so many years."

Everybody inside the pub wore mournful expressions and paid Curnow the extra tribute of remaining silent for a few moments.

A light and formal tapping was heard against the main door, and all eyes turned toward it.

"If that's the Invisible Man, tell him I can't see him."

The only reaction to Victor Carping's light-hearted gag was Expectorant and Hutton again crossing their torsos. Everybody kept quiet as Carping rose from his barstool to make the short journey toward the door. In his haste, Carping forgot that the door was locked as well as bolted, and he turned to lift the bar hatch before rummaging through the pockets of the lifeless Graham Curnow.

The key was quickly found, and Carping did the necessary. Standing in front of him was Lenny Yeo, who wore a blank expression and remained silent. His right arm and hand was raised high above his head holding a piece of paper, and his statuesque pose was kept for several seconds.

"Don't just stand there like Neville bloody Chamberlain!" Carping sunnily addressed the florist.

Yeo's reaction was to remain still and mute for a moment longer before he slowly toppled forward. Carping was too startled to attempt stopping Yeo's fall, and he gawped uselessly as the passing body almost reached the horizontal.

Against the right-hand wall close to the door stood the old mahogany bench with high and slim side arms. The nearest side arm proved to be the perfect distance for a toppling man of Yeo's height to do serious damage to himself, as the first part of his body to contact the one-inch wide and sharply right-angled surface was his Adam's apple. Yeo's head was snapped back by about thirty degrees, and he came to rest flat on his front with the head positioned at a peculiar angle. A punctured and inverted throat completed the wreckage.

Still clutched in the hand of the still outstretched right arm of Yeo was the piece of paper. Every witness watched open-mouthed and frog-eyed before Carping eventually crouched down to remove it and read it aloud to his unenthusiastic audience.

"DO YOU THINK THAT KILLING MR RENSENBRINK WAS A WISE THING TO DO?"

Carping looked up from the piece of paper as the hairs on everybody's necks tugged at the skin.

Finally, Winston Wellington broke the electric silence.

"IS THAT ALL IT SAYS, SIR?"

"Yes, that's it..." answered a flush faced Carping. "Apart from it being signed with the initials B.L."

The witnesses to the latest nasty incident reacted with a mixture of downward stares, heads placed in hands, and crossed torsos. After several more moments of shocked silence, Jeremy Bennett-Brewer rose from his stool to lift the bar hatch and help Victor Carping drag the newest body behind the bar.

After witnessing the aftermath of Willie Woodman's cottage gatepost death, plus Barry Loadall's spectacular suicide, Bennett-Brewer was developing a high threshold for revolting sights, and he had little problem in dealing with the latest ruined corpse.

As Yeo was unceremoniously laid to temporary rest next to the bodies of Rensenbrink and Curnow, a loud pounding was heard against the main door. The whole pub was becoming wearied by the endless unpleasant shocks, so Victor Carping again tried to lighten the mood.

"With three dead bodies behind the bar, I do hope that's not the health inspector!"

Carping's latest attempt to tickle the funny bones of the rest again fell flat. He got up to again unlock and unbolt the door, this time to be confronted by Mrs Tanning and a gently swaying Mrs Mordent.

"Come on in, ladies. Things haven't quite gone to plan tonight, and certainly not one of the more successful evenings with regard to people not dying. Still, no such thing as problems – only challenges!"

"Well, it's good to see our rector in such high spirits!" answered a similarly resolute Mrs Tanning.

Sat on barstools left to right were Expectorant, Hutton and Bennett-Brewer, plus Carping's empty stool. Winston Wellington was sat on the long ledge immediately to the left of the main door, so to keep all the occupants close together, Carping suggested that Mrs Mordent and Mrs Tanning sit on the old mahogany bench against the right wall.

Before the old ladies sat down, Carping gravely informed them of the three deaths that had already taken place, together with the colourful recent history of the bench they were to sit on. Carping then lifted the bar hatch to provide confirmation of the deaths.

"I'm surprised Dave turned out to be a wrong 'un."

Mrs Tanning showed her disappointment by tutting and shaking her head.

The single person in the room whose mood was lifted was Bennett-Brewer, who was surprised and relieved that neither of the old women were paying him any attention.

"...Doesn't surprise me at all about Loadall, though. He was the strangest bugger in the whole village, and it wasn't big or clever of him to hang himself without a rope!"

"I wish I could say we were free of him for good..." Carping answered. "but from the letter he left us before he took his leap of destiny, I've got a feeling we haven't seen the last of him."

"Oh well, no use crying over spilt milk..." replied Mrs Tanning, "but at least the plan seems to be working with Mr Curnow now dead."

All eyes turned with surprise toward the old widow, with Trevor Expectorant first to respond.

"How can poor Mr Curnow being dead be part of the plan?"

"He knocked on my door in the early hours of yesterday and told me what he was going to do."

More surprised looks were given by the rest of the pub before Mrs Tanning searched through her handbag.

"...Graham asked me to give you this, and he said I should only hand it over if he died in front of you."

A blank, sealed envelope was handed to Victor Carping.

"Thank you, Mrs Tanning. I hope it's a rather more uplifting read than what was left by Mr Loadall!"

The atmosphere inside the pub became noticeably less fraught as Carping tore open the letter.

"*Hello Everyone,*

I hope you're all in good spirits. I'll be dead by the time this letter is read, and the mere fact that this letter IS being read is good news. It means that I'll have been the author of my own demise, which is very much part of the plan..."

The mood of the pub was further bolstered by the apparent method in Curnow's apparent madness.

"*...If you all remember the letter I left for Victor to discover on my kitchen table, you'll know of my severe reservations about Barry Loadall. I'm absolutely certain that he'll have died in some way before this letter is read, but please be reassured that this is exactly what I'm hoping for...*"

Yet again, the dead Graham Curnow had successfully lifted optimism levels.

"My word, I wish I could buy that man a good drink!" enthused Jeremy Bennett-Brewer, who was now in no doubt that Curnow was to be their saviour.

"Well..." responded Victor Carping as he took a break from his narration. "We've got a free bar, so please do the honours, mine substitute host!"

Bennett-Brewer lifted the bar hatch and fulfilled the many orders while delicately side stepping the three recently deceased bodies. After everybody's favourite tipple was catered for, Victor Carping concluded his reading of Curnow's letter.

"...If, when I revealed myself to you all, I mentioned that I survived a visit from Chatterton, then it means that he won't be troubling you again."

"...The only problem on the horizon is that he'll have passed the baton on, and the man to have received it will be Barry Loadall."

The lights again flickered, but for a shorter time and less spectacularly than the previous occasions.

"...One thing I know Chatterton and Loadall shared in common; both were insanely jealous people. Arousing Loadall's jealousy will be the key to defeating him. If that can be done, then Larkhall will finally be free of the dreadful influence of Thomas Crabbings.

Everybody stay determined and strong, and one day I'm sure we'll meet again and sip tea together on the afterlife lawn!

As always,
Graham"

Such was the galvanising quality of Curnow's letter, all clinked glasses to show their determined mood. The sheer optimism everybody felt overrode all other considerations, and the jocular atmosphere continued for the next few minutes before the lights again flickered for several seconds. Instead of returning to normal, this time the lights went out with a loud fizz and crackle.

The weather outside was still clear, and there was enough twilight to bathe the pub in murky shadow. Everybody became statues the moment the lights went off, with a few glasses freeze-framed while half raised.

Sir Leonard Hutton was first to break free of his paralysis, and he again went to press his face against the window. He noticed that the lights from the three lampposts visible from his viewpoint were also out of action, as were every light in every house he could see across the road. Hutton attempted to get the attention of the others, but their glazed expressions were focused to the setting of infinity.

Hutton panicked and feverishly rummaged through the pockets of the reactionless Victor Carping. He knew the time had now come, and he had to get out. The key was found in the rector's trouser pocket, and Hutton dashed toward the door. It took him several seconds to keep his hand still enough to insert the key. After quickly unbolting the top and bottom of the door, he finally pulled it open and slammed it shut behind him.

The slamming of the door woke the other residents of the pub from their mass slumber, and none were aware of their missing moments of hypnosis. Trevor Expectorant was first to notice his absent disciple.

"SIR LEONARD IS MISSING! WHERE IS HE?"

Expectorant didn't expect anything other than ignorance from the rest, so was pleasantly surprised to see the man himself suddenly burst back through the door. All eyes turned toward Hutton as he re-bolted the door. Straight after, the key that was still in the lock was turned forcefully. Hutton pushed his back against the door while panting heavily and unevenly.

"OH MY GOODNESS, OH MY LORD ALMIGHTY!!"

The rest were startled by the passion and volume of Hutton's desperate cry, and before anybody had the chance to question him, he detailed the alarming sight he'd just witnessed outside the pub.

"THERE'S DOZENS OF MEN, WOMEN AND CHILDREN STANDING LIKE ZOMBIES RIGHT OUTSIDE AND ALL ALONG THE ROAD!"

Hutton paused to catch-up with his panting.

"...THEY'RE DRESSED AS MEDIEVAL PEASANTS, AND THE MEN ARE HOLDING PITCHFORKS! THE WITCHFINDER IS OUT THERE TOO, AND HE LOOKED STRAIGHT AT ME!!!"

Hutton's hysterical shouting was wasted on the others, as they'd again turned into vacant-eyed statues. Hutton was further terrified by the apparent ease that the unseen force was controlling the rest of the pub, and his feeling of utter helplessness now shared top billing with his terror. He spent the next minute contemplating his predicament with his back still pushed against the door.

Hutton almost passed out with relief as the others snapped out of their latest round of hypnosis. As if still being controlled en masse, several arms were raised with perfect synchronicity to check their wristwatches. Hutton looked on as the others took a sharp and unified intake of breath.

The pre-hypnosis mood of the pub was buoyant after Curnow's encouraging and upbeat letter, and it overrode everything. All were too brimmed with optimism to notice that the time had crept unnoticed to the critical minute of nine-thirty-seven.

Everybody glanced worriedly at each other in the gloom as they realised the moment had arrived. Despite full consciousness and awareness, all occupants of the pub, including Hutton, were unable to move their bodies. Every individual was unable to talk as well as move, though all were capable of producing whimpers of fright as they were simultaneously gripped at the shoulders by huge and invisible hands to be turned toward the far wall on the pub's western side.

The wall was blank apart from a large mirror, which, in the murky light of the pub, took on the appearance of a television screen waiting to be turned on. Nobody could do any more than just sit and stare at the mirror, and the more anybody tried to turn their head away, the closer they came to being invisibly strangled.

After a few moments, the grips were released, but all necks and bodies remained paralysed. Only the eyes of the pub occupants were granted permission to move, and all attempted to shift them away from the far wall.

An amplified and blisteringly loud fit of coughing circuited the pub interior several times. This was the unwelcome cue for the witnesses' vocal cords to break free of the paralysis that still locked the rest of their bodies.

"GOD, IT'S LOADALL!" shouted Jeremy Bennett-Brewer, as he was rooted to his stool with gaze fixed straight ahead.

"Nice one, Einstein." whispered Victor Carping without a hint of sarcasm.

Another round of amplified coughing swirled around the pub, followed by several amplified dry retches that in turn made the occupants want to heave, though none had the physical capability of doing so.

Sir Leonard Hutton was again the first to break free of his paralysis, and he stood in the middle of the floor facing the far wall. He outstretched an arm together with an accusing and shaking finger.

"BARRY LOADALL, YOU ARE A FILTHY, DISGUSTING PAWN OF THOMAS CRABBINGS!!"

The rest as one broke free of their rigidity, although all were too transfixed to take their gaze away from the mirror, which was beginning to display a blurred outline of a human head.

"NOW YOU'VE GONE AND DONE IT!" Carping shouted at Hutton.

The image on the mirror quickly gathered to clearly display a profile of a head, and if anybody still had doubts about the owner of the cough and dry retching, they were dispelled as the blackened profile silhouette displayed an upward jaw fracture of almost ninety degrees.

A rasping and amplified voice let the occupants of the pub know exactly what they were pitting themselves against.

"THE HAUNTER IS DEAD...LONG LIVE THE HAUNTER!"

The sinister opening salvo from the ghost of Loadall was accompanied by the outrageous sight of his destroyed jaw moving up and down, together with the horrifying and amplified sound of its clicking and cracking.

Through the fear and nausea, everybody was fully aware that Curnow's prediction of the baton swap between Chatterton and Loadall had now been made.

***

The Wyvern & The Witchfinder

The three women walked along slowly. One of them was elderly, and the other two displayed a patience that wasn't in their nature. The younger women were holding two full carrier bags each, and all four of the bags contained the items that they'd hope would break through any spectral barriers. Their journey toward The Wyvern & The Witchfinder was made in near darkness, as every street and house light they passed were off. The time was approaching ten o'clock, and the twilight had now been almost completely extinguished. The only ally they had was the waxing moon that hovered low above the horizon in the easterly direction of Sally in the Wood, and that provided just enough watery light to illuminate their route. Because of the old woman's creaking joints, progress was painfully slow, but again the other two showed commendable patience.

A swirling mist suddenly descended on the flattest part of Larkhall, and the slight visual benefit from the weak moonlight was lost. Nothing could be seen ahead of them, and progress became even slower as every step had to be careful and considered.

After several minutes of clumsy shuffling, the illuminated sign of the pub about a hundred yards away just about registered in their vision. From the moment the sign was spotted, the mist began to lift and clear their vision as the almost-full moon returned to take over lighting duties.

The three women spotted the ghostly figures of dozens of people stood outside the pub. The women looked at each another to receive mutual confirmation of what they saw, and as they looked back toward the pub, the figures of men, women and children turned toward them. Many of the men were holding pitchforks, and right in the centre of the crowd was a figure of short posture stood with legs astride and with hands on hips. The poor light could reveal nothing about the figure other than it was wearing a high crowned hat.

***

The terrifying sight of Loadall's post-death profile silhouette was joined on the other side of the large mirror by another quickly assembling human head.

The bodies and vocal cords of all the pub occupants again became paralysed, and they could only gawp silently at the unnerving spectacle. The head of the new apparition was almost spherical, and to those who knew him, it was immediately recognised as belonging to Dick Joy.

All eyes opened wider as the apparitions broke free of the mirror confines, and both developed bodies to go with the head.

The shadows against most of the west wall of the pub showed the violent and horrifying outline of Barry Loadall raping Dick Joy. Joy's whimpers could only be heard when Loadall occasionally paused his coughing and mad cackling. Loadall's jaw continued to move up and down accompanied by more nauseating clicks and cracks.

Another shape began to develop on the wall behind Loadall, and it quickly took on the form of an overweight man. The large silhouette became co-joined with Barry Loadall, and Loadall's head began to spectacularly lollop about on the base of its snapped and useless neck.

Everybody inside the pub knew that the latest monstrosity was the spirit of Dave Rensenbrink, and whoever tried to move their head away from the dreadful spectacle again felt their necks savagely compressed. The assorted whimpering and grunts of ecstasy completely swamped the ears of the audience.

Over the noise of the sickening sounds, an almighty crash was heard as the thick, narrow and opaque left-side window of the pub door was shattered. A lower arm and hand poked through the small opening and twisted the key in the lock. The door was still bolted at the top and bottom, and every couple of seconds, violent thumps tried to break the door down.

Eventually, and on the sixth time of asking, the door burst open, followed by the undignified sight of Jemima Joy sprawling along the floor of the pub.

Finally, all the occupants of the pub were free of paralysis. Instead of being transfixed by the ghostly and horrid spectacle against the far wall, they now couldn't take their eyes away from the widow of Dick Joy. She stamped across to within a few feet of the far wall and bellowed at it with utter rage.

"BARRY LOADALL, YOU MAY BE THE NEW CHATTERTON, BUT HERE'S SOMEBODY WHO NEEDS TO TELL YOU A FEW HOME TRUTHS!"

Suddenly, all the shadows from the wall froze, as did the hideous soundtrack.

An elderly woman with two walking sticks slowly entered the pub and clacked her way over to stand alongside Jemima Joy. Jeremy Bennett-Brewer immediately recognised her as the old woman who sensually accosted him along the street close to Barry Loadall's house.

"Barry Loadall; this is your Aunt Minerva speaking..."

Suddenly the pub knew that this was the moment, and Minerva was silently being egged on to do her thing.

"I know you see me as your kindly, childless and virginal aunt, BUT I HAD MY CARD STAMPED BY EVERY AMERICAN PILOT AND NAVIGATOR AROUND HERE DURING THE WAR!!"

The shadows on the wall were still frozen, but the whole pub was delighted to hear amplified and convulsing sobs, and even more thrilled to hear the sobbing occasionally interrupted by coughing and dry retching.

"...DURING THE WAR, MY LEGS WERE SPREAD WIDER THAN TOWER BRIDGE WHEN IT LET THE CUTTY SARK THROUGH!"

Suddenly, the shadowy central figure on the wall disappeared, followed by a blinding light and almighty crash.

Next to walk through the open pub door was Rose Rensenbrink, accompanied by the waggy-tailed Clive.

"Dave Rensenbrink; I know you see me as the faithful and never complaining wife, BUT I WAS THE WEEKLY SEX DRUG THAT REPLACED THE BOOZE TO BRING SOLACE TO GRAHAM CURNOW!"

The momentary shock of the revelation was soon replaced by an almighty cheer from all onlookers. All raised their glasses to toast the landlady, and also the dead Curnow, who had yet again come up trumps.

This time, the large left-hand shadow of Dave Rensenbrink disappeared; again accompanied by loud sobbing, and again accompanied by a blinding light and massive crash.

The only apparitional figure left freeze-framed on the wall was Dick Joy, and his wife addressed it.

"DICK JOY; I KNOW YOU SEE ME AS THE BULLYING WIFE WHO ADDED TO YOUR MISERY, BUT EVEN THOUGH YOU WERE A USELESS DRUNKEN PRICK, YOU WERE *MY* USELESS DRUNKEN PRICK! NOW THAT WE'VE GOT RID OF THOSE TWO, YOU'VE GOT NOTHING TO WORRY ABOUT 'TIL THE DAY I JOIN YOU ON THE OTHER SIDE!"

Mrs Mordent shuffled over to join the heroic trio of women, and she raised two victory signs gleefully in the air.

"PEACE, LOVE AND WOODSTOCK, PEOPLE!"

The shadow of Dick Joy gently faded without a sound, and was immediately followed by the pub lights returning.

Everything and everyone inside the pub were back to normal, and Jeremy Bennett-Brewer was first to show his appreciation.

"Three cheers for these wonderful women...HIP HIP...!"

The invitation was responded to heartily by everybody before Winston Wellington walked across to congratulate Barry Loadall's elderly auntie.

"WOW, LIL OL' LADY! YOU SURE KNEW HOW TO DEAL WITH THAT HORRIBLE 'N UNWHOLESOME PUTZ!"

The old lady's eyes lightened with surprise and delight as she saw the unmistakeable resemblance between the man and the wartime American pilot who became her sweetheart.

"Young man, you are the absolute double of dear old Raymond!"

"HEY! IT SURE IS GOOD TO FINALLY MEET THE LADY MY

PAW WAS A-HUMPIN' DURIN' THE WAR!!"

Barry Loadall's elderly aunt then joined Mrs Mordent and Mrs Tanning in apologising to Jeremy Bennett-Brewer.

"Sorry we had to make you the object of our desires...!" began Minerva Thruxton-Duvall. "We were all magnetised somehow by the Larkhall Simpleton all those years ago, and we had to display our fruitiness toward you so we could make him jealous."

Bennett-Brewer smiled with relief and toasted Minerva with a raised glass.

"...And the same goes for that double crossing nephew of mine!"

"The harmonic nuances of the universe are back to their full groovyness!" added Mrs Mordent.

Everybody clinked glasses in the joyous knowledge that Witchfinder Thomas Crabbings and his hideous, centuries-old grip on Larkhall had finally been released.

Just one thing bothered Hutton, and he hoped Jemima Joy could throw some light on the subject.

"When you arrived, did you see the Witchfinder stood outside?"

"YES I DID, AND ME AND ROSE THREW ALL OUR APPLES AT THE MISERABLE OLD TWAT."

"And that did the trick?" asked a smiling Victor Carping.

"TOO RIGHT; THAT AND ME THREATENING TO BEAT THE SHIT OUT OF HIM FOR ETERNITY IF I EVER CAUGHT UP WITH HIM IN THE AFTERLIFE. HE'LL BE HALFWAY TO DEVIZES BY NOW!"

"And you don't have to worry about the Larkhall Simpleton anymore, either...!" enthused Rose Rensenbrink. "When Crabbings scarpered, a crowd of cheering apparitions were rolling the pervert up and down on a huge, ghostly coach wheel!"

Amongst all the merriment, an amplified voice of great enthusiasm resonated.

"PLEASED YOU ENJOYED THE SPECIAL TRICKS, AND GLAD TO TELL YOU THE KIDS ARE ALRIGHT. I DON'T KNOW WHERE OR WHEN WE'LL MEET AGAIN, BUT SUFFICE TO SAY, MAKE MINE A LARGE ONE!"

THE END

Printed in Great Britain
by Amazon